OLIVIA HART

Embers and Ash

A Fantasy Romance

First edition

This book was professionally typeset on Reedsy.
Find out more at reedsy.com

Contents

Prologue	1
Chapter 1	5
Chapter 2	13
Chapter 3	18
Chapter 4	26
Chapter 5	32
Chapter 6	45
Chapter 7	49
Chapter 8	62
Chapter 9	72
Chapter 10	80
Chapter 11	84
Chapter 12	89
Chapter 13	96
Chapter 14	103
Chapter 15	110
Chapter 16	117
Chapter 17	129
Chapter 18	133
Chapter 19	137
Chapter 20	141
Chapter 21	147
Chapter 22	156
Chapter 23	161

Chapter 24 171

Chapter 25 179

Chapter 26 187

Chapter 27 192

Chapter 28 199

Chapter 29 208

Chapter 30 212

Chapter 31 220

Chapter 32 227

Chapter 33 234

Chapter 34 238

Chapter 35 242

Chapter 36 246

Chapter 37 257

Chapter 38 270

Chapter 39 275

Chapter 40 279

Chapter 41 283

Chapter 42 288

Chapter 43 298

Chapter 44 313

Chapter 45 323

About the Author 331

Prologue

Queen Sorchna

800 Years Ago

Battle raged around me when I realized I would die. My enemy hadn't beaten me with his sword. Instead, the sharp sting of shadow magic had crept under my armor and pierced my spine. Something only one man could have done.

A sense of failure tore through me as I hit the ground, my legs no longer functioning. Agony rushed through me, yet it was nothing compared to the pain of knowing that I'd lost. That my life was over, and I'd failed my people. Arturus the Hunter stood over me, the achingly familiar golden eyes glowing brightly even in the sunlight.

The dying screams of my people filled the air, but I focused on Arturus. The man who would kill me. I'd known him for so long, and I'd seen sides of him so few others had. I'd seen the broken man for who he was.

1

Sunbeams ended when they fell upon him as his darkness pulled the very light of the world into the shadows of his wings. Unarmored and without a hint of exhaustion, Arturus was a dark god surrounded by mortals, yet I knew the pain that hid under his skin. He stood as my enemy today, but he'd been a friend for far longer.

That changed nothing. Orlana would grow up without a mother. He would still be the reason that my beloved Finneon would be a widower. So many lives would end because one man had followed his father rather than what was right.

"I'm sorry that it has to be like this, Sorchna," he said. The truth of that statement bled through me, staining my thoughts, but ultimately leaving me. It didn't matter if he was sorry.

I felt the cold creeping in as I stared into Arturus's eyes. Blood pooled around me, and the last bit of my fire flared through my veins, begging to be used as my life faded. I knew it was useless, and only one thing mattered when I was moments from death.

I closed my eyes and saw the spirit that was trapped within my sword, my constant companion. Shadow Soul. He would survive this as he would survive everything.

I thought to him, "Take care of Orlana. Guide her. Teach her strength regardless of the odds and to smile against the harshness of the world. Teach her that there is always a reason to laugh and what it is to live."

A vision of my daughter flashed through my mind. A beautiful girl with gray and crimson scales on her cheeks that flashed with fire when she smiled. Bright red hair that I loved to braid. She brought a light to the darkness of the caves, and the thought of her pain broke me.

The mental image shattered as I pictured her tears, and I

continued, "Be the person she can turn to when the rest of the world turns against her. Tell her I love her and that I'll never forget her."

"Yes, Lady," he whispered back to me, unheard by the rest of the world. "When you look from the darkness upon your daughter, you'll be proud of her. I won't let her turn cold or lose the flame of life."

"Rest well, Queen Sorchna. You will find peace while you sleep. You have meant something to this world, to your husband, and to your daughter. Your memory will be the fuel for her fire, and I will never forget to stoke the flames."

I felt his touch in my mind for the first time since I'd bound his soul to the sword. Like a parent comforting their sick child, his touch soothed the pain away, and the sadness fled as I accepted my death.

"Thank you for bringing me into this world. Thank you for giving me a chance to fulfill my soul's desires. I love you, and I will never forget the light you brought to the world."

I took a breath and looked up at Arturus. He seemed to hesitate for just a moment. I was a Firebrand, and I could accept death, but dying quietly was impossible. The flames that still blistered inside me wouldn't allow it.

"Damn you, Arturus," I said. "You know your father is evil. You know that you're decimating an entire race of fae, and for what?"

The physical pain faded as my body realized that there was nothing it could do. The cold filled me completely, and a single tear ran down my cheek.

Not for the end of my life or even the fall of the arden race. I wept for my daughter, who would have to go through life motherless. It was for my husband who would have to rule without me.

I reminded myself that Shadow Soul would be there for Orlana. He would help her, and I trusted him more than anyone in the world to guide her.

Arturus answered, "For loyalty, Sorchna. For family. There is nothing greater than those." He brought his sword over my breast, and I saw his hands quiver.

I brought my hand up, knowing that it was futile to fight him, but the flames begged to have one last release. I was too slow, and Arturus drove his blade through my breast.

As I took my last breath, Shadow Soul said, "I love you, Queen Sorchna, and I will remind Princess Orlana of you so that she never forgets the love you held for her."

And then it was over. All the pain. All the struggle. All the worry. This was no longer my fight to wage, and the darkness pulled me under.

Chapter 1

I panted as Daphon walked across the practice field. He was sweating as though he'd been the one fighting, his scales sparkling in the tsero sphere lights. Like all arden fae, scales covered bits and pieces of his body that were reminiscent of the dragons of stories, our supposed ancestors. Daphon's were a swirling pattern of red and black and ran up his arms and under his tunic.

"That's what a man should look like," Shadow whispered to me. "All hot and sweaty. Nobody else has scales that are that bright."

I didn't respond to Shadow when he talked about men as a general rule. He'd started doing his best to convince me to get married when I'd only been a hundred years old, barely an adult. He hadn't stopped since then, and I'd found it best to ignore him. Anything else only encouraged him.

"The best lovers start out as friends, Orlana. Listen to me. I know these things. I bet he's a man whose idea of foreplay is giving you a massage. This is a highly desirable trait in a mate. Trust me on this."

"I bet the best lovers aren't forced to get married in a cage," I whispered back.

I wasn't ever going to marry Daphon. He was a good friend, but I was almost positive that my trousers didn't hold the parts that he was looking for. More importantly, I didn't have time to think about men right now. War was coming, and I had to be prepared to help my people escape our cage once and for all.

"Do you think you can get them to move faster?" I asked as I looked at the stone men who'd been attacking me only moments before. Long slices crisscrossed them where my sword had cut them apart. "They say that solen fae move like the wind, and these are barely faster than me."

"I'll try, but stone doesn't like to move quickly. Maybe you should have a Firewaker working with you instead of a Stonewaker."

I shook my head. The thought of fighting men made of flames made me a little sick. I'd burned myself enough times training with my own flames to know just how miserable full-body burns could be. "No. I'm sorry, Daphon. I know you're doing the best you can. I've just been hearing the rumors from the elves about a possible rebellion. We could go to war at any moment, and I need to be prepared."

Everyone had heard the rumors, and Daphon nodded. "You're right. I'll try to push them more tomorrow, but I'm spent today."

"I bet you are," I said. Daphon was a good friend, and the

best Stonewaker I'd ever met, but he didn't understand the weight I felt because of those rumors. It meant that hundreds of years of training would be tested for the first time. It would finally be time for us to fight for our freedom. And for me to avenge my mother.

The caves under the Aedenian Mountains held twenty thousand ardens, and only a handful of them took training with sword and magic seriously. They felt safe, so why worry about the art of war when you'd been safe for eight hundred years. The problem was that safe wasn't good enough. We needed to be free as well.

"Thanks for the training," I said as I put out my hand. Daphon stepped closer and pressed his thumbnail against a spot directly under my collarbone, and I did the same to him. Our sharpened thumbnails pressed against the only spot on every arden fae that had no scales. The Disciplines named it the Gesture of Faith.

Once, thousands of years ago, the arden fae had been dragons, according to the old stories. On each dragon, there was a single space on their breast that had no scales. It was the one place that was left unprotected to the world, a sacrifice made to give them dominion over stone.

Now, we showed our trust in our fellow ardens by allowing them access to that same spot. Even now, after we'd become so much closer to the shape of mortals, our nails were sharp enough to pierce the flesh, muscle, and even to reach the heart.

"If this war really happens, it will change everything," Daphon said.

I grinned. "You'll be allowed to go back to Creating instead of Stonewaking. I'm sure that will make you a lot happier."

"Gods, it would be wonderful to do something I love instead of guard duty. No offense, but I never dreamed of battle."

That was one of the worst things about living in hiding. There was no space for the Creators to work. The Producers were forced to grow only the specific crops they were told. Every Discipline had been limited in some way, and it was soul-breaking to be forced into a path that you weren't drawn to.

"It'll happen, Daphon. I'm sure it will. If not because of the elves and these rumors, then we'll find a way."

He nodded and turned to the broken stones at our feet. "I know it will. I wish other people were trying as hard as we were though."

I put my hand on his shoulder. "We just have to show them what's possible."

When I pulled my hand back, I smiled at him and said, "I'll see you tomorrow for some more training."

He nodded to me and began to put the pieces of the stone men back together for tomorrow.

Talking to Daphon had reminded me just how different I was compared to the rest of the arden fae. I had to remember that they didn't bear the burden that I did. They weren't oath-bound to seek revenge for their mother's death.

Part of me leaped for joy at the thought of leaving the Emerald Caverns, to see the sun and stars again. The rest of me worried I hadn't worked hard enough, that I hadn't become strong enough to follow through with my task.

I left my training chamber, one of hundreds of alcoves within the Emerald Caverns, and breathed in the slightly stale air of the caves. My parents and the other royal houses had decided that this would be where they fell back if Azulus won the war. We'd survived because of these caves, but that's all we'd done.

These were the glorious caves of the ardens. A hidden wonderland full of riches. From the gemstones we grew to the gold and silver that we could sense, we were the wealthiest people in all the world.

And we were trapped in a cage. No matter how beautiful the bars were, they were still bars.

Thousands of ardens lived here, but they all seemed so content to go through their lives without working towards their freedom. Why was I the only one who saw the caves as the prison they were? Why didn't more people prepare for the day when we could fight back against Azulus and his sons?

"Do you really think that there will be war?" Shadow asked.

I shrugged. "I hope so. It's not right that we're forced to live in this cage while the rest of the world lives under the sun and stars."

"But war is terrible, Orlana. You've never seen it. Is it worth all the death so that the survivors *might* see the sky again?"

I gritted my teeth. Shadow was ever on the side of peace. "Strange set of morals you have for a sword," I said.

"Who would be more intimately familiar with the tragedies of war than a sword?" he replied.

"I know the horror of war, Shadow. Remember that Arturus killed my mother in the last one. It's time that we sought revenge for the ones we'd lost in that war. We can't hide away and hope that someone else will deal with Azulus. We're living in a prison, and we can't hope that someone else will save us."

I could feel Shadow sigh. He still mourned the loss of my mother and worried about what would happen to me if we went to war.

I'd only been seven when she died, and we'd never sought revenge or freedom. I'd been born in the caves during that war, and except for the few times I'd been to Steras, I'd never left. I'd seen the sun and stars only five days in my entire life.

If there was any chance of escaping this cage, I would take it, even if that meant going to war with the most powerful men in the world. This wasn't a life I wanted to live forever. It was a stasis, a stagnation. We couldn't live until we could grow, and growth had stopped. Not only were we forced into the darkness, but no more children were allowed to be born because we couldn't feed anyone else.

The main room of the Emerald Caverns was massive, miles wide and miles long, and filled with stone buildings grown by Creators. Simplicity had been necessary for these homes, shops, and workshops because they'd been grown in haste right before the war with Azulus.

Despite their original simplicity, they were beautiful now. Daphon had helped me to decorate the orphanage in crystals before he'd turned away from the Creation discipline and become a Stonewaker.

That was before I'd realized that we should be focusing on escaping our cage rather than making it more comfortable.

As soon as I walked inside, Rania handed me a cup of ignas tea. Red and spicy, it was brewed from a special mushroom from the Ruby Plateau kingdom.

"This is what I needed," I said as I sipped the cup, enjoying the way the steam warmed my face.

"Anyone who trains as hard as you do could use a cup of ignas from time to time. I hope their crops don't fail as the Sapphire Deeps' have."

"What would we do without ignas tea?" I said, as I took another sip. The warmth flowed through me and fought off the physical exhaustion that I felt after training.

"Well, we'd better get you to the fireplace. I've already set up the flux since I know you don't have a lot of time today."

My orphans had been miserable children before we'd started supporting them. Surviving on scraps of food and the barest of clothing, they'd been barely better off than the homeless. Now they ate better than many of the merchants.

The Emerald Caverns supported many orphanages with our riches. The children grew up knowing their benefactors and some of them were given the chance to work with us. No one would have suspected that hundreds of orphans held the keys to the arden kingdoms.

They'd become invaluable as our source of news and trade with the surface. Fruits and vegetables were impossible to grow here, and there was little in the way of meat.

And this building had become the hub of communication for all of it.

I sat down in front of the hearth. "You know you could find another Firebrand to work the hearth," Shadow whispered to me. "Then you could spend more time with Daphon, and maybe you could even convince him it was too hot to wear a tunic all the time."

I sighed. Sometimes, it was hard not to cringe at what Shadow said.

He quieted down as I picked up a handful of the gray salt ash called flux. I focused on Mrs. Talbot's hearth, visualizing the details of the stone base. Inscriptions in the ancient arden language had been made along the bottom where no one could have seen. Mrs. Talbot knew to keep it covered in ash.

I'd done my training for the day. Now I'd spend the rest of it helping to receive updates and send instructions to our contacts throughout the world. It could be boring, but it was important. This was the only connection we had with the world outside our cage.

I set my mind on that specific inscription, and I threw the flux into the hearth. "Mrs. Talbot?" I said.

From the fire, a voice whispered, "Yes, Princess Orlana. I'm here."

Chapter 2

Tonight was supposed to be an important event for my father. I thought it was a waste of time and energy, but he assured me it was important enough that he'd required to attend and wear a dress.

We'd see how many more of these dinners he'd require me to attend after tonight. I patted the satchel hanging at my side as I walked down the corridor of the palace.

Wearing my typical training uniform, I didn't look like the only princess of the last thriving arden kingdom. I'd grown my short, crimson hair just long enough and styled in a way that I could clean up pretty if I had to. I may be expected to play the part of the princess, but my soul walked a different path.

I was a warrior. I was a doer, not a talker. I felt at home on a training ground or making plans over a map. Places where things were decided and acted on. Nothing was ever decided at a dinner. Its only purpose was to differentiate between royalty and the normal people. I'd rather that everyone had a bit of the feast's food than save it for only the royalty. My best friends were normal people.

Dinners were for the rich, and I didn't fit there. Maybe tonight my father would realize that I wanted nothing to do with them. Maybe he'd learn his lesson.

I stepped into the dining hall and saw that the banquet table was already prepared. Place settings were out. Chairs had been arranged. The kitchen staff would be prepping the dinner. I'd heard that one of my orphans had smuggled a whole pig into the Emerald Caverns, and these dignitaries would eat meat for the first time in months.

I wouldn't ruin that, of course. Food was too precious to ruin, and life was too precious to waste.

But chairs were easy to fix.

Each of the wooden chairs was identical and similar enough to the chair in my bedroom that I could test the devices hidden in my satchel. No one would come sit at the table until dinner now that it was ready, so it was safe to begin my plan.

Twenty-six devices for twenty-six chairs. One for each, including mine and Father's. I grinned as I took the small disk in my hand and pressed it firmly against the bottom of the first chair. I had placed a thin resin coating on the top of the disk on the opposite side of the inscription.

"*Bogthe*," I whispered, arming the device with the command. Quickly, I walked around the table, placing a device at the bottom of each and arming it. Then it was done.

I'd spent two days planning and preparing for tonight. I'd made friends with a Binder when I was still young and much

14

more mischievous. He'd become my source of devices for nights such as this. Most of the time, my tricks were pure mischief and entertainment, but tonight was about making a statement.

I'd never embarrassed Father in front of dignitaries, and I was sure that the backlash would be more severe. At the same time, what could Father do to punish me? I was already confined to the Emerald Caverns. I already spent almost all day working. The rare hours that I had to simply enjoy myself were often spent in dining halls with people I hated.

Now that the preparations were set, I walked down the halls towards the kitchen. I thought about what the orphans saw when they came to the castle for the first time.

Emeralds covered the walls with bits of sapphire grown into the spaces between. The patterns were woven into a mural of blue and green displaying the Emerald Caverns here. In other halls, they displayed ancient cities from the surface in golds and ruby.

"This is going to be your best prank yet," Shadow said.

I grinned. Even Shadow thought I should do more useful things than entertaining lazy aristocrats. "I only wonder if it will accomplish what you hope. What will happen if your father takes away the orphanage's funding as a punishment?"

"He wouldn't do that. Maybe once upon a time he would have, but not now. Not when he prospers from the trade with the surface dwellers. He may not care all that much for the children, but he cares about being powerful in the eyes of the other kings."

Shadow began humming, and everyone would have been able to hear the soft rattling in the sheath. "Do you ever wonder if he is just as eager to return to the surface as you

15

are? Maybe his political agenda is to gain control of the other kingdoms. Maybe this is your father's approach at making unified strike against Azulus. He's heard the whispers of rebellion just as much as you have."

"My father has lost sight of our purpose, Shadow. He's grown old, and his vision has become focused on the Emerald Caverns. I don't blame him. This is easy, and old men prefer easy."

The humming began again, and I knew Shadow was thinking. He did this regularly. Although some people questioned how a sword could think, I didn't. He was no different from any of my other friends except that he never left my side.

"I was not always yours, Orlana," he said slowly, being careful with his word choice. He did this when he thought I needed to listen, and it was almost always an argument of some sort. "Your mother had a very different view of your father. She thought he was exceptionally brave and the greatest leader the ardens had ever had. She never would have believed that he'd done something purely because it was easier."

"That was a long time ago. I know that time is not the same for you, but even for ardens, eight hundred years is a very long time. He hasn't had Mother there to push him to remember our true goal."

I stepped down the stairs towards the kitchen and said, "But we can talk about this again soon."

As I turned the corner and looked into the kitchen, the sound of running came from the stairwell behind me. A servant stepped into view. Nerana was the girl's name, but I didn't know her well. "I'm so glad you're here. I heard you were walking towards the kitchen, but I wasn't sure if you were still around."

"What do you need, Nerana?" I asked.

"Oh, right. King Finneon sent me to get you. There's a guest." There was a reason I hadn't ever spent very much time with Nerana. She rarely got to the point in a conversation.

"Yes, there's a feast tonight. There's going to be many guests." I took another bite of the pudding. Why would Father have sent someone to get me just because the guests had started showing up?

"No, Princess Orlana, he's not a guest for the feast. Darius the Silent is here."

Chapter 3

"Darius the Silent?" I whispered.

She nodded, and I moved towards her. I unclasped Shadow Soul, readying him for use. "Has my father brought him to a cell for interrogating?" I asked.

"No, Princess," she said, with more than a little confusion. "He's bringing him to the dining room. As you said, there's going to be a feast."

I ran up the stairs, taking them two at a time. I wouldn't be eating dinner with the enemy. Father wouldn't either if I had anything to say about it. He should be locked in a cell and tortured until he had given us every bit of information he had.

And then we should execute him. Publicly.

What kind of madness was it that made my father think he should dine with us like an ally? Like an arden.

"Don't be hasty, Orlana," Shadow whispered to me. "Your father may be many things, but he isn't an idiot. You know this. There's a reason that Darius isn't in a cell as you'd like. Listen first. Then strike if you must."

I gritted my teeth. I couldn't fathom why we should embrace a visit from one of King Azulus's sons. But Shadow had a point. I was missing something. Father wasn't an idiot.

I closed my eyes as I walked, letting the Flames of Preparation meditation wash through me. A warmth grew in my stomach as my body prepared itself to move in an instant.

I opened my eyes as I came to the doors to the dining room. I could hear my father speaking on the other side of the door, and I tried to remain calm. I pulled open the door and saw Darius the Silent standing beside my father with a smile on his face. He held no weapons, but I knew what a solen fae could do without weapons.

I stepped into the room and Father turned to me. "My daughter, Princess Orlana of the Emerald Caverns," he said as he introduced me.

"Orlana, this is…" he said before I interrupted him, my hand going to Shadow's hilt.

"I know who he is, Father. Darius the Silent. Third son of Azulus. Master of infiltration and sworn enemy of the arden fae."

"I know exactly who he is," I said, staring up at the man who was at least two heads taller than me. "My question isn't who he is. It's why isn't he in a cell being tortured for information on his father?"

Darius smiled at me. "It's nice to meet you, Princess."

I'd dreamed of the day that I'd meet the Princes of Kharn. The three winged sons of King Azulus. One at a time, I would

19

cut them down with my mother's sword, finally avenging her.

I'd been told every story of those three. I knew their weapons. I knew their skills. I knew their personalities.

I'd known that Darius was the only brother that had black-feathered wings. I'd known he had hair the color of sandstone. I'd known that he looked like the rest of the solen fae, but I hadn't known that his lips curled up in a smile like that.

I hadn't known that he smiled when facing an enemy, and that even though he was bare-chested, he looked like he belonged in the royal palace. I knew nothing about the man. Only the enemy.

Father looked over at me and stepped in front of Darius. "The elves sent him. Marcellus and he have rebelled against their father. King Sundryl sent a letter with him to prove it. He knew where the door to the caverns was, and he knew the passcode."

I didn't relax, and I slowly slid Shadow from his sheath. "Lies. All of it. There's never been a plan to convince Darius to change sides." I held Shadow in front of me as I looked behind Father at the solen fae behind him.

"I trust him. Sheath your sword. That's a command from your king." My father's words did nothing but inflame the anger inside me.

He stared me down, and I knew I was supposed to do what he said, but everything inside me urged me to just cut him down and be done with it. Slowly, I sheathed Shadow, and my father seemed to breathe a little easier.

"I apologize for that, Prince Darius," my father said to our sworn enemy. "You've been our enemy for a long time."

Darius cocked his head, and his smile turned upward even more. "I understand hating someone for their entire life. It's not as though she understands why I'm here."

He turned to my father and said, "On that note, why don't we sit down and discuss my purpose here. Though I'm sure that the hospitality of the arden fae would be wonderful, we are *very* pressed for time." He turned toward the table, and Father mouthed, "He's on our side," before following Darius to the chairs.

I'd begged the gods for hundreds of years to give me the chance to kill this man, but Father wanted me to trust him?

I sat down next to Father at the head of the table while Darius sat to the side. "Prince Darius is here at the request of King Sundryl and Princess Mianara, Orlana. Prince Marcellus and he have rebelled, and the elves are backing them. He's come to request our aid for the war against his father."

I glared at Darius. "How can you possibly believe that? I know that the elves have hoped to convince Marcellus to turn away from his father, but he was never part of that plan. Why should we believe the words of the enemy?"

"I sent a message through the flames to King Sundryl, and he has verified the information. He is to be trusted, Orlana."

"Well, I don't trust him."

Then Shadow whispered, "Calm down and listen. This is what you've been hoping for. This could be what the whispers have been about."

"You're not wrong, Princess," Darius said. "I'm sure that I could have come up with some way to trick you all into letting me in, but I didn't. I'm here for your help, and my words are honest."

He smiled again, and I wanted nothing more than to rid the world of one of the enemy. Shadow's words stayed with me, though.

Father turned to me and said, "Why would he come alone, Orlana? Why wouldn't Azulus bring his entire might against us if he knew where we were?"

I cocked my head as Darius leaned in his chair. That actually made sense. I couldn't imagine a scenario where Azulus would have sent one of his sons here, alone and unarmed. If he were acting as an emissary for Marcellus, it would almost make sense. Maybe Father was right.

I took a breath and nodded. "Then what do you need? Why are you here?" I asked. I was overstepping my place, but Father wanted me here for a reason.

"I'm here to convince the kingdoms of the arden fae to join mortal kings, my brother and I, and the elves in defeating my father. And as quickly as possible. My father will be outside the elven kingdoms within the next two months. We will have one chance to stop him."

"If I know my brother, he will have convinced the elves to open the gate to the elven kingdoms, and Inoras will be where we make our stand against my father." He turned to my father and said, "You were at the battle of Indigo Falls, correct?"

My father nodded, and Darius continued. That was the battle where Mother had fallen. The last battle of the arden fae. "You remember the might that he brought to that battle. You remember how my father crushed the arden fae."

"The same will happen to the elves and the men of the world. It will be the last chance that the world has to end my father's life. There will be no second chances. Not this time. If he wins that fight, he'll control the elven kingdoms and become immortal."

My father drummed his fingers on the table as he chewed

his lip. "The arden fae were not prepared to go to war as the elves were. It will take time." He glanced at me. "Your father will have to march his armies around the Windswept Sea. That's a five-week march to the elven gate. He won't be ready to march yet, so there will be a few weeks of preparation."

He shook his head. "That's not enough time."

"Then I will make time. How much do you need?" Darius asked.

"At least another week. Maybe two if you can manage it."

Darius took a deep breath. I could see his mind working behind the golden eyes. "You ask for a lot. I'm only one man, but I'll do what I can to stall. But we will need as many of the arden kingdoms as possible. And as much of your weaponry as you can manage."

My father nodded. He continued to drum his fingers on the table, and then he turned to me. "Orlana, you will accompany Prince Darius. Of all the arden warriors, you're the only one whom I'd trust with a mission of this much importance."

I blinked. "You want me to go with *him*?" I said the words slowly. I couldn't believe that Father wanted me to work with one of the men that I'd wanted to kill my entire life.

"I do not *want* you to do anything, Orlana. I am commanding you to go with him. Help him stall King Azulus. Prince Darius will know best how to hinder his father."

I snarled, and Shadow whispered to me once again, "This is what you wanted. Exactly what you wanted. Stop being a child and be the warrior you believe yourself to be. What would your mother have done?"

I looked at Prince Darius then. I saw the childish look in his eyes. I saw the relaxed posture. The way every piece of his body looked as though he were talking about what bottle of wine to open next rather than the fate of the world.

And I saw the muscles that ran up from his trousers tensed, ready to move. The way his eyes never settled on either of us, always scanning the room. He wasn't comfortable. It was an act.

That was good. He shouldn't be comfortable in a place where his family was hated more than anyone in the entire world. At the same time, I had to respect him for the act. I couldn't have managed that air of confidence in his home.

"Are you sure that you're willing to fight your own family?" I asked.

He nodded. "My father knows that I'm in rebellion, and that means that my life is just as much at stake as yours. More, in fact, because he doesn't know where to find you."

I glanced at Father, whose face was as serious as I'd ever seen it.

And then the room filled with the sound of tiny explosions, and I knew what it was before the chair had even begun to topple. The warmth of my body had seeped through the wood of the chair and finally reached the disks that I'd placed under each.

Their tiny explosions would break the back legs, and we would fall backward.

And I didn't have time to adjust as my stomach twisted. The room turned, and I saw the ceiling of the dining hall for just a moment before I felt the back of my chair slam into the solid stone ground.

I couldn't help but laugh as I rolled off the chair. Prince Darius was already standing, looking as though he'd stood up before the chair had fallen over, and Father was still on his back.

"What is the meaning of this?" Darius exclaimed, his hands held in front of him in preparation to use his power over the air to defend himself.

"There was supposed to be a feast tonight," I said with a grin. "I was objecting to being forced to go. Dramatically."

Darius cocked his head and asked, "This wasn't meant for me?"

I shook my head as Father finally stood up and brushed himself off. "No. There's a device under each chair that will activate as soon as it warms up. Nothing dangerous. Just enough to cause a scene."

"Tonight is an important event," Father said through clenched teeth. "You could have ruined months of planning."

I shrugged, and Darius's lips curled in a grin. "Well, I'm glad that you can be tricky. We'll need that soon enough. How long do you need to prepare for a journey? We won't be coming back here, so gather everything you'd need for war."

"How long do I have?" I asked.

If we were going to be sabotaging things, I would need to have things Bound, and that would take some time.

"I'd like to leave by tomorrow."

I glanced at Father and said, "I will need several Binders. Do I have permission to have them create what I need?"

"Yes. Do whatever you need to prepare. I assume you will have a better idea of what will be useful than I do, but before you run off, will you please disarm the chairs?"

Chapter 4

"These are explosives," I said as I loaded the largest bag I could find with Binders' creations. I'd considered not telling him about the Binding tools I'd scrounged up, but after a long talk with Shadow I'd finally given in. I had to trust him to some degree, or I would hamstring myself.

Darius nodded. "How large of an explosion?" he asked in complete seriousness. Gone was the arrogance replaced by intense study. It was hard to keep from snapping at him purely because of who he was, but the fact that he'd let the arrogance go for a moment helped.

"Large enough to blow a hole in a wooden wall. Not strong enough to break a stone wall."

He nodded. "They'll break bridges?"

"If they're wooden. Explosives strong enough to break solid stone would take too long to make. No one has made anything that strong in a very long time."

"What else do you have?" he asked as he stared at the rest of the spheres, disks, and boxes covered in inscriptions.

"These will draw in heat," I said, pointing at several large boxes. "And these will create heat. These others will begin a fire after a certain amount of time. These over here will begin screaming."

I picked them up and placed them in the bag. "There are others, but they're more complicated." Finally, I picked up two small pendants that hung from fibrous cords. "But these are probably the most important. They're called nullifiers. They will draw your magical scent into them, and hunters won't be able to sense you. They must touch the skin to work, but they will draw the scent into them even while you're currently using your skills."

I handed one to Darius and hung the other around my neck. "So this is how you've kept hidden for all these centuries," he muttered.

"No. We've kept hidden because we don't leave except for very specific reasons. These will only last about three months, and then they'll be spent. They're difficult to make as they require ingredients that aren't found in the caves. We're lucky that we still had a few."

"Lucky indeed," he said as he put his on.

"Take the bag to the entrance of the caves and wait for me. I'll be there shortly," I said.

Then I turned to Father, who had stood silently beside us, watching as I'd loaded the bag.

"Gods, don't you have anything to lighten this thing? You know we have to fly, right?"

"He sure is whiny," Shadow said to me.

I grinned. It wasn't often that Shadow complained about someone else whining.

"No. I expected that a solen fae could handle carrying a little weight. That's what you're known for, isn't it? Being big and strong? If it's too much for a big strong solen fae, I guess I can carry it."

I could see Father's teeth clench as Darius ignored my comment and began walking towards the entrance. "You know that you have to work together, don't you?" he asked.

I knew that we'd have to work together. I also knew that I wouldn't let him think he was in charge. I knew I was prepared for this. I'd spent my entire life preparing for it. I had no idea whether or not Darius was.

"Yes, Father. I'll work with him. Until he turns on us. I don't trust him, and I doubt that anything other than his father's and brother's deaths will change that. He's not any more important than I am, and truthfully, I doubt that he's as valuable as I am."

"He's the forgotten brother. If Marcellus the Black or Arturus the Hunter were here, I'd know that I could count on them for strength, but what has Darius ever done? Yes, he has power, but what has he *done* with it?"

I could see Father struggling to keep his anger in check, but we both knew that it didn't matter if he was angry. I was the correct person to send on this mission, even if I wanted to run Shadow through Darius's gut.

"He knows more about his father and brother than we do, Orlana," Father said. "He may not be known for his deeds, but you aren't either. No one knows what he's capable of. As you said, he's the Master of Infiltration. Who would be better at hiding what they'd done than him?"

I shook my head. No, he wasn't that kind of man. You could take one look at that arrogant smile and know that he'd take credit for anything he'd done of value.

"Father, I will do what I have to do. I will do what is best for the arden fae. If I have to work with Darius the Silent, then I will. If he turns on us, I'll kill him. None of that matters, though. What matters is that I stall Azulus and his army long enough for you to rally the ardens, and I swear to you I will do that."

Father nodded and some of the anger washed away, and his jaw unclenched. "I love you Orlana. We've argued with each other for a very long time, but I've always loved you. Stay safe. If there was anyone else that I trusted to do this, I'd send them instead because it's the most dangerous thing an arden has done since your mother died."

He put out his hand, and I stepped forward, letting his hand rest on my shoulder. I returned the gesture, and both of our nails pressed against the soft skin under the other's collar bone. The Gesture of Faith. It was the proper farewell, but that wasn't enough.

Even though I'd been full of anger only seconds before, in this moment, I realized that this might be the last time that I saw my father. I pulled my hand away from his shoulder and wrapped my arms around him. "I love you, Father," I whispered in his ear. "I've always loved you, and I'm sorry that I've fought you as much as I have."

When he pulled away, he was smiling. "That's just your mother inside you. You're strong like her. Keep being strong."

For the first time since Darius had arrived, I realized I wasn't just going on an adventure. I wasn't just doing the thing I'd trained for my entire life. I was also leaving the life that I'd always had behind forever. When this was over, my world in the Emerald Caverns wouldn't be there anymore.

And something different would be waiting for me. If I survived. I'd done everything I could to be ready for this day, but that didn't mean that I would win. My mother hadn't.

"You stay strong too, Father. Your part in this game is just as important as mine. Convince the rest of the ardens. Drag them kicking and screaming to battle if you have to."

He grinned at me. "What do you think I've been working on all these hundreds of years?"

I nodded to him, and he said, "May your spark ever find tinder."

"And may your flame forever burn," I replied in the traditional way, and as I turned, I saw a glimmer of a tear form in Father's eye.

I didn't know what to say. I'd been ready to go, ready to act instead of train, but now that it was time, I was realizing what I was going to lose. Both my father and I knew that this was the end of our relationship as it'd been for my entire life.

Even if everything went perfectly. Even if I left home and killed Azulus myself and ended the war before another life was lost, he would not control my life any longer. He may be my king, but his role as parent would be over. This was my trial by fire, and if I survived, I would be an adult who would make her own choices.

Part of me was excited about that, but most of me was heartbroken. I'd loved my life, and though I wanted more, I'd been happy. I'd enjoyed the work I'd done. I'd enjoyed my friends and my home. And my father. Even if we fought, I knew he would always have answers if I didn't.

I was leaving it all behind now, and that was hard.

Chapter 4

But it was harder for him. I was sure of it. I knew that when I made it to Inoras, he'd still be alive, but he wasn't sure if I'd ever make it there. This was as dangerous a mission as I could imagine, but it had to be done, and it had to be done by me.

And so we said nothing. I didn't comfort him, and he didn't comfort me. We'd said our goodbyes, and now all we could do was hope that we'd see each other again.

Chapter 5

The wall slid back up behind us as Darius and I stepped into sunlight. I had to shield my eyes against the brightness of it. "Gods, it's bright out here."

Rocky ground extended a short distance from the wall that held the entrance of the arden kingdoms. Trees and grass grew only a few hundred feet away. The slightly stale scent of the caves was gone and had been replaced by a thousand different scents from the forest.

"I know. Glorious isn't it, little cave princess?" he said with a grin.

I needed Darius to stop thinking of me as a princess, or he'd think that I was as helpless as the rest of the royalty that I'd met.

"I'd rather you call me Orlana," I said as I began to walk towards the trees.

"Where are you going?" he asked as he jogged to catch up.

"To Steras. The mining town just southwest of here. Where else would we be headed to?"

"No, I mean, why are you walking? We're going to fly."

I turned and looked at Darius then. I saw the hard muscles of his body. I saw the massive wings. "Can you actually carry me and our supplies the whole way?"

"Of course I can carry you and the supplies. We'll have to stop every few hours to give my arms a rest, and I'm not going to fly as fast as I normally would, but I'll manage." He seemed annoyed at the mere question of his ability.

"I don't like the idea of flying," I said. It was unnatural. An arden's feet should be on the ground.

"Well, we're never going to catch my father if we don't, so get over it, Princess. We're flying or you can go back to your people."

I didn't want to fly. And I especially didn't like the idea of being carried by Darius. I didn't have much of a choice, though.

"Look on the bright side. At least you don't have to walk now. He has to do all the work. And I know you don't want to hear this, but I've never seen a man with that many muscles. I bet he could do some very interesting things with them." Shadow's words didn't help much in this instance.

"Fine. What do you need me to do?"

That obnoxious smile crossed Darius's face again as he said, "Nothing, Princess. Just stand still, and don't wiggle too much."

My heart was racing as he put his arms around me. One ran across my ribs and gripped my side. The other held my hips, right below the top of my trousers. He lifted me into the air and pulled me to him.

I could feel every rippling muscle in his chest, and I felt more than a little uncomfortable. I accepted that I would need to trust Darius, but having him this close to me made me want to pull away. Everything in me still wanted to slide Shadow across his soft skin and hard muscles, and it was only through sheer willpower that I didn't succumb to the desire. His wings were the only way that we were going to get in front of Azulus, and so I would let him carry me.

He didn't even bother to ask if I was ready before his wings lifted us into the air. At first, we rose slowly, and I gasped as I looked around at the land below us. I'd only seen it a handful of times, but I'd never imagined it could look like this.

I saw the mountain that we lived under, rising all the way into the clouds above us. I saw the streams that ran from its peak down to the valley below, one of which supplied Steras with water. I saw everything in a way that no arden fae had.

"Gods," I whispered.

"Glad we didn't walk now?" Darius asked from behind me.

Then his wings shifted, and we were no longer going upward. He pulled me tighter to him as we flattened out, and I looked down at the ground hundreds of feet below us.

Now my heart began to race as true terror set in. One slip of his fingers, and I'd tumble out of his arms and end up on the ground. Crushed to death or speared by one of the many trees I would land in.

My hands tightened against his arms, my deadly sharp nails digging into him, and he shouted, "Stop that!"

But I couldn't. As I stared down at the world, I was lost to fear in a way that I'd never thought possible. My mind had no control, and my claws dug into his arm even harder.

"Let go of my arm this instant!" Darius shouted, but I didn't stop. I couldn't let him drop me on accident.

His wings shifted again, and we plummeted to the ground. Faster than anything in the world, he dove from the sky. I began screaming, and I heard Darius scream from behind me.

Hundreds of feet passed in seconds, but they were the longest seconds of my life. At the very last moment, he turned, and I felt him strain against the weight as he slowed down and landed.

He let go of me, and I fell to the ground, my entire body shaking in fear. "Gods damn you," he muttered.

I turned around and saw rivers of blood pouring from his forearms, and I looked down at my hands. They were covered in crimson. I'd dug my claws in, and his body wasn't covered in scales. He was soft.

"I'm sorry," I whispered. That was the correct response, and I was more than a little ashamed of myself for losing control like that, but there was still a part of me that enjoyed the sight of his blood flowing.

"You'd damn well better be more than sorry, Princess," he said, anger coming out for the first time since I'd met him. "You're lucky that I heal quickly, but I'm not taking you anywhere if you're going to try to claw me to death every time."

"That's not going to happen again, do you understand?" He stared at me with fury in his eyes. He said the words and then he waited for me to answer. I was still in shock. My body had locked up, and his yelling wasn't helping. My life had flashed before my eyes. I'd faced fire and stone, and I'd faced blades and magic. I'd never faced the terror that was flying, though.

"You're on the ground, Orlana. You're safe." Shadow's

words whispered in my mind. "You flew. It was wonderous. You did something no other arden has done in more than a thousand years. He didn't drop you even when you hurt him."

I closed my eyes and let the Flames of Peace wash over me. The meditation that would help my mind function through fear. I should have embraced it earlier. As the calming sound of a crackling fire filled my mind, I felt myself calm down.

When I opened my eyes, my heart didn't feel like it was trying to beat its way out of my chest, and Darius was staring at me. "I apologize for wounding you," I said formally.

"How'd you do that? You were terrified seconds ago, and now you're not. Fear doesn't leave a person that quickly. At least not naturally. You should still be shaking."

I smiled up at him and looked into his eyes. Golden flames burned continuously in them. They seemed to glow on their own. I was sure that if all the lights were extinguished in the world, those eyes would still be visible.

"It's arden magic. Don't worry about it," I said softly as the crackling fire still sounded in the back of my mind keeping my breathing even.

He crossed his arms and cocked an eyebrow at me. His wounds had already closed up, but the trails of blood were still there, marking the places where my claws had dug into his soft flesh.

"Well, are you ready to try again, Princess?" he asked.

I nodded. "I will compose myself better this time." I wanted to remind him not to call me Princess, but after trying to shred his flesh, I didn't think it was an appropriate time. The flames still crackled in my mind, and I reminded myself that if I started to get scared again, I would just go back to the meditation.

36

"Be strong, Orlana," Shadow whispered to me. "You were terrified the first time that someone fought you with a live blade. You were terrified the first time that you were cut. This is no different. Be strong."

Darius wrapped his arms around me again, and when his wings carried us into the air, I focused on the fire in the back of my mind. When he flattened out again, I looked down at the ground and felt the little tremor of terror run through me, but those flames licking the back of my mind kept me sane and in control of my body.

Though my fingertips gripped just a little more roughly, I didn't use my claws. Darius stopped moving his wings, and we began to glide through the air, the only sound in the world was the breeze that kept us aloft.

And the world seemed peaceful. Unlike the Emerald Caverns, this was freedom and silence. There was always sound at home. The noises that people made reverberated through the caverns. They were sounds that I'd grown up learning to ignore, but here, there was nothing except that gentle breeze that tasted so fresh. I'd spent my life in a world that had become stagnant, like an algae-covered pond. Now I was in a world that was alive and flowing like the rapids.

I felt like a weight fell from my shoulders as I held my body straight under Darius. Even as my muscles strained to hold myself up, I felt alive in a way I hadn't before. This was freedom.

Not flying. I didn't think I'd ever completely feel comfortable in the air, but the silence and lack of pressure. I didn't have to rush. I didn't have to hide. It wasn't like the times that I'd gone to Steras.

I'd rushed to town in the dark of night. I'd met with my

contact and hid in their home through the daylight hours, and then I'd run home the next night. There was no such urgency to this flight.

My legs began to droop, and Darius used his legs to pull them upward, straightening me out. As he did, the calmness I'd found vanished for just a moment, and I began to panic again.

I didn't claw him, but I squirmed just a bit before the calmness settled over me again. And as I did, his hand brushed against my breast. He didn't move his hand, and I felt myself becoming annoyed. I knew he'd done nothing wrong, and truthfully, I didn't want him to move it. I didn't like the idea of him shifting while he was holding me.

But it wasn't right. One of the men that I had dreamed of killing for hundreds of years was touching me in a way that few men ever had.

"Well, Princess, if we're going to be spending the next few weeks together, we might as well get to know each other. Why don't you tell me about yourself?"

I didn't want to get to know Darius the Silent. I didn't want him to get to know me. But if what I'd seen so far was any estimate for what the rest of our time together was going to be like, I wasn't going to be able to get away from talking to him.

"Your brother killed my mother, and I've dreamed of killing all three of you since I was seven years old."

My words hung in the air for only a moment before he said, "Glad that's out in the open. Not every day I meet a woman who's dreamt of me for eight hundred years."

Shadow began to laugh. "You have to admit that was a clever one. Now you know that he's got the biggest muscles you've ever seen, and he's funny. Sounds like a good reason to see what he's got hiding in his trousers."

I clenched my jaw and had to work hard at not digging my nails into him even though I wasn't sure if I was more annoyed at Darius or Shadow. He wasn't done. "How'd you imagine me in all those dreams? Was I a hideous monster or insufferably handsome? Was I clothed? I need to know what my admirers dream about, Princess."

I didn't say anything. But, of course, Shadow had to chime in. "Tell him that your sword dreams of being inside him. That's a really good one."

I couldn't keep from smiling at that. "This is going to be a very long trip if you're not going to relax a little bit. It's fine if you hate me and hope I die. There are plenty of people that do, but at least be a little entertaining about it."

"Fine. I'll relax," I said. "I imagined you like the reports described. A typical solen fae without any of the skills of a warrior. The one outcast of the race who never wielded a blade. I imagined you as a scrawny man-child who snuck around like a thief in the night."

"That's just rude," Darius said. "No one wrote anything down about how charming I was? Or what about the fact that I'm obviously the most handsome of my brothers? What kind of scribes do you have? Old men with shriveled balls?"

"Why don't you wield a blade?" I asked. "That's important if we're going to work together."

"I don't need one. The historians were correct that I'm not the warrior that Marcellus is or the duelist that Arturus is. My skills lie in far more functional places."

What was more functional than being able to kill your enemy quickly? Especially in a family that ruled through force of arm rather than prosperity and loyalty.

"Like what?"

"As you said, I'm the Master of Infiltration which happens to be exactly what we need on this mission. There are other skills I have, but that's the one that matters most."

"So you *are* a man-child who sneaks around like a thief in the night."

Darius chuckled as we neared Steras. "If you'd like to call it that, but I'm certain that you'll be requesting those same skills soon enough."

Darius the Silent. The one skill that he held over all others was stealth according to the written reports from the last war. Silent movement. Nearly invisible. Excellent perception. Difficult to surprise.

"Why are you rebelling?" I asked, changing the subject. I hadn't needed to know the why, but at least this would be more entertaining.

"I love my brother more than I love my father. When the line in the sand was drawn, I chose Marcellus over my father. It's as simple as that."

"Why was a line in the sand ever drawn? Didn't your family have everything you wanted? Wasn't life as perfect as it could be in the sandy wastes of Kharn?"

Darius chuckled even louder this time. "A woman, believe it or not. She held the key to the elven kingdoms, and both my father and brother want her. My brother wants to marry her, and my father wants to torture her."

"Your brother doesn't sound like the man that I've heard about," I said.

"From the same reports that described me as a scrawny man-child? No, I'm sure that the arden scholars from a thousand years ago probably missed a few personality traits when they talked about my brother."

Steras was drawing near, and Darius headed to ground just outside of town. Steras was a mining town just outside of the Aedenian Mountain Range where we made our home. Not large enough to be called a city, it was mostly a supply depot. But mining is a dangerous business, and there were more than a few orphans there.

It had been the first place that I'd begun supporting an orphanage, and that was where we were going to go. I knew that we wouldn't be disturbed while we were there.

I breathed a sigh of relief as Darius set me down. I glanced at him and said, "Are you going to do something about the fact that we both are obviously fae?"

He nodded. "Stand still. I have to touch you to create the illusion."

"That's not what the report said," I muttered as he stepped in front of me.

"Any requests?"

"On what?"

"Do you want to look a certain way?"

I shook my head. Why would I care what my illusion looked like?

He put his hand on mine, his fingers grazing my claws, and as he slowly moved his hand up my arm, all trace of the fae in me disappeared. I wanted nothing more than to pull away, but I didn't because I needed his illusions. The dark red of the hardened nails that ran over the top of my fingertips became smaller and clear like a human's. The gray and red scales that ran over the back of my arms disappeared and became flesh.

His other hand mimicked the movement on my other arm.

His touch was strange, almost a caress as he brushed against my body. He'd held me the entire time that we'd been in the air, but that had been different. Where I'd been at least slightly afraid the entire time we were flying, I was calm now, and I was completely focused on the way his hands felt.

He paused and smirked as he said, "I assume you don't want an illusion for the parts of you under the clothes?"

"You can keep dreaming, *Prince*," I said, but I felt a smile cross my lips. It sounded like something Shadow would have said.

He shrugged and moved to my neck. His fingers brushed just inside the hem of my tunic, erasing the scales that covered my body, and I felt a warmth rather than revulsion. How could my lifelong enemy make my body warm to his touch?

As his fingers moved to my face, I stared into those golden eyes of his and saw that he was enjoying this. I grit my teeth as his thumbs brushed across my cheek. Darius grinned as he held my chin in his hands for just a moment longer than he needed to.

Then his hand moved to my hair, and I almost pulled away. He ran his hands through my short, fiery red hair, and his fingers pulled just a little, and then it was done.

He stepped back, and with just the snap of his fingers, his wings were gone, and he was wearing a tunic. His golden eyes no longer glowed and were a honeyed brown instead.

All of his edges were softer, and he even seemed shorter. He still had that ridiculous long sandy blonde hair. The kind that no self-respecting warrior would have. His lips still curled up in that mischievous grin, but I was sure there was no possibility of getting rid of that even with illusions.

"All done?" I asked.

He nodded and said, "I think I like the shorter hair on you. Though long and brown looks more like a princess."

I huffed and began walking. "We're going to stay in an orphanage tonight. They'll make sure that we have a bed and food, and we can make a plan."

"Why an orphanage instead of an inn?" Darius asked. "I'm not arguing. Just curious."

"I support the orphanage financially. There won't be any prying ears or eyes, and if someone hears something unusual, there won't be any gossip spread elsewhere. Plus, it will be good to see the people that I support."

Darius nodded and followed me into town. It was alive. Unlike every other time I'd been to Steras, there were people all over. Some were talking to each other and laughing. Others were walking down the dirty paths that were as close to streets as Steras had.

All of them were busy living their lives. A rebellion was coming, and they had no idea. They didn't know that only a few hours away, the entire arden world lived under the mountains that they mined. They didn't know anything except what was happening in their tiny little piece of the world.

And they were happy about it. I wondered how anyone could live like this, so ignorant of everything. They may not live in a cave where the sun never reached, but they were just as caged as I had been. They would live and die in this tiny village where the only things that mattered were the price of iron and when the next merchant would be coming to town.

It surprised me that they mostly ignored Darius and me. I was sure that there were enough miners living in the mountains that they didn't know them all, but even with

Darius's illusions, we didn't look like them.

We weren't miners, and there was no way that they would have mistaken us for miners. Our backs weren't bowed. We walked with purpose instead of exhaustion. We were royalty, and even though we weren't dressed in velvet and furs, it was impossible to miss the difference between us and them.

Yet, they still ignored us.

I pointed out the orphanage and caught sight of the sun hanging low on the horizon. It would be dark soon enough.

"This is it," I said.

"Fantastic," Darius said and then paused. "I'm not going to have to sleep in a child-sized bed, am I?"

"Better than sleeping on the ground, isn't it?" I asked.

"Barely."

Chapter 6

"Take whate'er you need," Ms. Pearce said. She was a stately woman who could have passed for royalty if you'd given her slightly less of a village accent. Her graying hair hung loosely around her shoulders, and though her eyes were serious, there was a softness to her voice.

"Thank you," I said. "Is there a room somewhere with two beds that we can use?"

"Preferably adult-sized beds," Darius interjected.

She raised an eyebrow at my request. "Yes, we have a visitor's room." She turned around to lead us there, but then she stopped. "But it does no' have a hearth. Will that be a problem?"

I shook my head. She was making it known that I wouldn't be able to communicate through the flames from this room, but I had no need tonight. We would speak with my father again when we had a plan worked out.

"No, Ms. Pearce. We don't need a hearth tonight."

She nodded to me and turned to lead us up the stairs. "Look at that," Shadow whispered to me, and I turned to see Darius ignoring us and watching the children in the room play. He was smiling widely as the children laughed in a circle. They were playing Knock.

Each child had to mimic the previous one's knocking rhythm on the wooden floor. It was a game as old as I was, and I remembered playing it when I wasn't much older than them.

"Who'd have thought he'd like children? I pictured him as someone who would run from children."

"Me too," I whispered back to Shadow.

He realized that he'd been staring at the children and noticed me watching him. "We don't have a lot of children running around the palace. It's nice to see people who haven't been broken by the world yet."

That was a strange thing to say from a man who had done so much of the breaking. "Come on," I said. "Ms. Pearce is going to leave us if we don't catch up."

I walked up the stairs to where Ms. Pearce was looking down at us impatiently. She led us down a hall that was quieter and opened the door to an undecorated, simple room.

"Dinner will be in an hour, Lady," she said. "It's not much as we can't let on that we have more than we need, but it'll fill your bellies."

"Thank you, Ms. Pearce. I'm sure that it will be fine. We appreciate the hospitality."

"It's not hospitality to feed and house your patron. It's just good sense. Let me know if you need anything."

She closed the door, and Darius immediately set the bag of tools on the floor. I pulled out a chair from the table and unrolled the map of our section of the world. I traced the Windswept Sea with my finger as Darius sat down in the other chair. Ignoring him, I said, "Your father won't be able to cross the Windswept Sea, so he'll travel around it. We can catch him at specific points and cause havoc."

Darius nodded. "We have probably four days to a week left before he leaves Kharn. He'll be angry, and he'll push the troops to mobilize faster than expected, but he won't leave without being prepared."

"We shouldn't wait too long before we begin harrying him. I'm not familiar with anywhere close to Kharn. Are there any good places we can begin?"

Darius looked over the map and said, "He'll stop outside of Assama." He pointed to a small town still well within the desert region. It was probably a two-day march from Kharn.

"Assama is the largest nearby city, and he'll stop there to claim supplies. Feeding an army that size even for two months will take more food than Kharn can spare right now. He'll probably stop at each major city along the way and take anything he needs."

I nodded. "We'll wait in Assama until we hear that he's nearby, and then we'll attack."

"That makes as much sense as anything. I have a few contacts there that can keep us safe, but it's a three-day flight from here, so we'll need to take some supplies."

"Ms. Pearce has plenty of supplies, and if she doesn't, we can buy them in town."

Darius gave me a half-smile. "Are you sure that you're ready for this, Princess?" he asked.

"Ready to finally begin fighting the arden fae's enemies? Yes. Ready to be off the ground for three days? No, definitely not."

With a chuckle, he rolled up the map and put it in the baggage. "I hope you're right."

Chapter 7

Three days of flying had exhausted my emotions. Fighting off my natural fear of being off the ground was not something I'd planned on in all my training, and it was showing.

By the time that I looked at the white sand city of Assama, I was nearly ready to convince Darius to change the plan. This was the opposite of everything I was used to. As much as I had wanted to see the sun and be in the open world, this was too much.

Too open. Too much light. Too much wind. Too much heat.

I'd grown up in a cave that I now realized was far dimmer than the natural sun. My eyes ached from staring at the blinding white expanse of sand underneath us.

I'd rarely felt more than the slightest breeze as a door was opened, and here, the wind gusted constantly. Darius had to adjust repeatedly, and each time, his hands shifted, moving over my body as though I were nothing but another bag.

It was hot enough that even high in the air with the constant wind, I was pouring sweat.

But more than anything, the lack of any kind of wall was what bothered me. There were no trees and no houses. It was a vast expanse of nothing but never-ending sand.

Except Assama. There, the city's walls were made of stone. Green plants rose up from the ground that surrounded the oasis which was located in the very center of the city. A massive lake, it turned the city into a spot of green in an otherwise white world.

Goats and sheep wandered the streets, eating the plants that sprung up. Birds of prey circled the city, preying on rodents and livestock. And people were everywhere.

Darius set us down far away from Assama, putting our illusions on once again. As we walked through the shifting sands, for just a moment, I considered asking if he could fly us. The sand got everywhere. In my boots. In my trousers. In my mouth and nose and eyes.

But Darius didn't seem to mind. This was home for him. Just as the Emerald Caverns under the mountains would always be home to me. I wondered if he'd felt the same way I did now when he'd come into my home.

As we slogged through the sand, I struggled to keep up with him. By the time that we reached the walls of Assama, I was out of breath. Darius didn't seem to be bothered. Even though he'd flown for hours previously, he seemed as unbothered as ever.

It was still strange to see him without wings. They were still there, but they were invisible, hidden under the same illusion that hid my claws, scales, and short red hair.

"Where are we going?" I asked.

"We're going to get a hot meal and a hot bath. Then we're going to find out what the news is from Kharn. We need an update."

That made sense. A hot meal and a bath sounded wonderful, though I wasn't sure how people bathed here where there were no arden Binders to create heating pipes.

I'd thought that I was well informed of how the world worked, but I'd taken so many things for granted in my life. How did people function without Binders? Did people really spend days and days making candles? Or did they all have hearths in all their rooms? How did they keep bridges from becoming too slick to walk on?

And the idea of building from stone without the Disciplines to help seemed incredibly difficult. Looking at the walls, I wondered how many men it had taken to move all this stone by hand. How long had it taken to make even this small of a wall?

Darius turned down a street, and he grinned at me before he entered a large sandstone building with a red scarf over the doorway.

I walked inside and saw an empty tavern. The ardens didn't have taverns since we rarely traveled under the mountain other than for trade, and traders were always welcome in the castle of each kingdom.

I'd read about them. Places of drunken debauchery. That was typical of Darius.

He walked through the tavern and knocked on a wooden door. "What do you want?" a woman's voice called out.

"Thought I'd stop by and see a friend," he said through the door.

I heard a commotion inside the room, and the door swung open. A woman wearing barely any clothes at all stood inside the room. "Darius?"

He smirked and nodded his head. "This is Orlana." Turning to me, he said, "This is Kina, my contact in Assama."

Kina wore an emerald green piece of fabric that wrapped around her neck and across her breasts before finally wrapping around her waist. Two strips of the cloth hung from the front and back to cover just enough. I had to assume that this was a sela, and I questioned how anyone could consider this appropriate clothing.

She was a pretty woman with long black hair and darkly tanned skin. Slightly shorter than me, she seemed enamored with Darius, and her eyes barely left his.

"Nice to meet you," she said and turned back to Darius. "What are you doing here? I heard you and your brother were rebelling. Your father has called in all his soldiers."

Darius nodded. "That's why we're here. We need a place to stay for a few days, and preferably one with a good bed, a bath, and a bit of hot food. Any way you could help us out with that?"

"You're always welcome at my brothel," she said. "But you can't bring your troubles here. I don't want to be tortured for the rest of my life by helping you."

A brothel? I was going to stay in a brothel for a week? My heart began to race. I may not have been an innocent maid, but I was sure that the things that happened in a brothel were distinctly different than what I was used to.

Darius shook his head. "Won't happen. I'm not going to be working out of here. I'm just waiting here, and there's no possibility that Arturus can sense me. You'll be completely safe."

For the first time since she'd opened the door, she frowned. "Fine. You owe me, Darius. I'm taking a huge risk letting you stay here. Probably a bigger one than I should."

"I'm at your command," he said with a smile. "Now, if you don't mind, Orlana and I need to get cleaned up. We'll be in the bathhouse if you need us."

Kina's eyes ran over Darius's body, and I felt a twinge of anger at the way she looked at him. I didn't understand why, but it bothered me that she was looking at him like that, like he was a piece of meat. It didn't make any sense, though. I barely knew him, and I was sure that he would turn on me the moment that anything bad happened.

"Mind if I join you?" she asked. Her eyes seemed to get a little glassy, and my hand curled into a fist. Why did this bother me? I forcibly relaxed my hand and tried to ignore her flirting.

"Gods, if you weren't here, she'd probably drag him into that room and start ripping his trousers off." Shadow's words didn't help the emotions that were running through me.

"Not today, Kina. Orlana and I have had a very long journey. Maybe another time."

She frowned, and a part of me rejoiced. The last thing I wanted was for her to join us in the bathhouse. That was when I realized what he was saying. There weren't private baths here.

I'd read about public bathhouses, but I hadn't paid any attention to them. They'd seemed archaic and unnecessary when you had Binder magic to fill personal baths. But this wasn't an arden kingdom. This was the land of Kharn, and public bathhouses were the norm.

Shadow read my mind as he did so often. "Are you going to take a bath with him? I guess you won't have to convince him to show you what he's got under those trousers."

But I'd have to strip down as well. I didn't know if I could do that. I wanted to take a bath, but this was inappropriate in so many ways. He was the enemy, and I barely knew him to begin with. I wouldn't have bathed with Daphon even though we'd been friends for hundreds of years.

"Well, let me know if you get too stressed and need to unwind a little," she said. She reached out her hand, and, as if it were the most normal thing in the world, she ran her hand over his chest, her fragile human nails grazing his skin.

It was just a little too much, and I smiled as I said, "Thanks. Darius, lead the way." Darius grinned at me and nodded to Kina.

"Thanks again for the room, Kina. Have dinner with us tonight."

Darius turned around and walked down the hallway. Kina stared at his backside the entire way, and it infuriated me.

Still, I didn't understand why. It didn't seem to bother him at all. Why should it bother me? I already knew he was a liar and manipulator. What did it matter if he had a different woman in every city? I certainly wasn't going to be joining his harem, so why fault him for doing what he enjoyed?

I didn't know, but it bothered me more than I'd like to admit. At the end of the hallway, a blue scarf hung over the doorway, and he pushed by it. The bathhouse was empty, and in the center of the room was an enormous pool. Large enough to fit twenty people, there would at least be enough room between us that there would be no chance of touching.

Maybe if he turned around, I could get in without him

seeing me?

As soon as he walked into the room, he approached the bath, and without saying a word, he stripped his boots and trousers off.

Shamelessly, he turned around and said, "Aren't you going to get in?" I couldn't help but glance down between his legs.

I blinked a few times, and Shadow whispered to me, "You won't see that on an arden fae. You should ask if all solen fae are that big."

"No," I whispered to Shadow, but Darius heard me.

"You're not some innocent princess who's waiting until your true love comes to sweep you off your feet, are you? You've seen a man in just his skin before, haven't you?"

I nodded, and I tried to look him in the eye, but my eyes couldn't stop staring at his manhood. "I've been with a man before. Arden fae arcn't as... brazen," I said.

"Look Princess, either take a bath or expect to sleep on the floor. You will not get a pile of sand in the same bed as me."

I jerked my attention back towards Darius's face and said, "Why would we be sharing a bed?"

"It's a brothel, Princess. Not a lot of purpose in two beds in a room at a brothel."

There were too many emotions welling up inside me at the same time. Between that strange jealousy and his brazen nudity and now the idea of having to share a bed with him, my nerves were a little frazzled.

"Damn you, stop calling me Princess. My name is Orlana."

He shook his head, that obnoxious smile still on his lips. "Suit yourself, but you chose the last accommodations. I've chosen these. Either you can take a bath and share a bed with me until we leave, or you can sleep on the floor. Your choice."

He turned around and walked into the pool of water. It was me that stared at his backside this time. I'd known that he was muscular, but seeing his legs and backside made me realize just how different solen fae and arden fae were.

He could crush walnuts between those cheeks.

"Gods, Orlana. If you don't get into the bath, throw me in. Someone should get to spend a little time with him at least."

I continued to stare at Darius, but I responded to Shadow. "He's the enemy."

"No, he's not. He's the man who is helping you to defeat the real enemy. His father. Don't you remember how it felt when he was holding you?"

I shook my head, but I made a decision. I wanted a bed. I couldn't imagine sleeping on a sandy, stone floor. I stepped towards the pool hesitantly. I lay Shadow on the ground at my feet and kicked my boots off.

"Turn around," I said. Once I was under the water, he wouldn't be able to see anything.

"I don't think you understand what the word public means," he said as he settled against the wall of the bath. He wasn't going to turn around. He was going to force me to strip in front of me, yet he barely seemed to care.

I felt the anger rise inside me. "Fine," I said, spitting the word out. I pulled the tunic over my head and dropped it to the ground beside me. Then I pulled the soft leather trousers off and tossed them onto the pile.

"Are you happy now?" I asked with venom in my voice, not trying to cover up at all as I stepped into the water.

He shrugged. "We probably need to cover up those scales if you're going to be in a public bath."

I shook my head. "I don't think so, Prince. I think I can

manage to stay under the water if someone comes."

He leaned his head back against the wall of the bath and said, "Whatever you say, Princess. It's not as though our lives and our mission are relying on the illusions I weave. Go ahead and worry about your modesty rather than the thousands of lives and multiple races that depend on us."

The fact that he'd been right only made me angrier. I could almost hear Shadow telling me to focus on what mattered. I lashed out at him. "How did I get stuck with the most arrogant and obnoxious solen fae in the world?"

He didn't even look at me. "Because I'm the only one who can do what needs to be done. Just be glad that I'm an arrogant and obnoxious solen fae who also happens to be exactly what we need. I'm stuck with a Princess who is more worried about me touching her than about saving her people. I'd give anything to trade you for my brother. At least he would put the mission first."

Gods, I hated this man. He may be good at what he did, but he was the rudest and most arrogant person I'd ever met. I didn't want to work with him. All I wanted to do was wring his neck.

"Your brother? Which one? The brute or your father's mirror? Because neither of them would have half the capabilities I do. I've trained my entire life for this mission."

Still, he didn't look at me. "No, you trained your whole life to fight stone men. I asked your father what your qualifications were and how you trained. He assured me that you were the most capable fighter of stone men he'd ever seen. Face it, Princess, without me, you'd be dead by the end of the day."

It was too much. Everything that had happened. Instead of

turning to one of my meditations as I should have, I let my anger get the best of me. I lunged at him across the bath, my claws outstretched, and his head snapped up. He caught me by the wrists, pointing my hands upward.

I tried to jump backward, using his hold on my arms as leverage so that I could kick him in the stomach, but he pulled me to him and lifted me into the air. I snarled as he suspended me only inches away from his face.

"Princess, you need to understand something. I'm not a warrior, but I could kill you without thinking about it. I've been patient with you from the very beginning because I knew that you were in over your head."

"But you need to get your priorities straight. You're not a princess out here. You're a soldier. You have a single mission and absolutely nothing else in the entire world should matter to you. Nothing. Not your ego. Not your modesty. Not your comfort or even your health."

I didn't stop snarling, but as he looked me in the eye, I saw his eyes turn golden again. "You will not be the reason that we fail in our mission, Princess Orlana."

Then he tossed me. A gust of wind came out of nowhere and pushed me all the way back to my seat. Not hard enough to make me slam into the wall, it stopped as soon as the back of my legs hit the seat, and I stared at Darius. He could have hurt me. Hell, he could have killed me. But he didn't.

He sat back down and leaned his head against the wall, soaking in the warm water of the bath. "Now, when you've calmed down, I'm going to put an illusion on the rest of your scales. We're going to be here for a while, and the only baths in this part of the world are public baths."

I glared at him, but I didn't say anything. Just like that, he'd proven that he wasn't afraid of me at all. It would have been different if I'd had Shadow and been out of the water, but this still put things into perspective.

And I knew he was right. That was the part that bothered me. I'd spent my life running away from the title I was born with, but now that it was being tested, I wasn't acting like a warrior.

"Fine," I said, knowing that I couldn't back down completely, but I needed to say something.

I slid into the deeper part of the bath and began to rub away sand and grit that had found its way into every crevice of my body. When I felt like I was mostly clean, I dipped my head under the water and began to scrub at my scalp.

When I picked my head up, I saw that Darius was standing in front of me. A soft breeze flowed through the room, tickling my face. On that breeze, Darius's voice whispered, "Don't move."

Then I heard the footsteps. Two sets walking into the bath. "Ooh, who are you?" a feminine voice said with excitement.

"A friend of Kina's," Darius said. He'd been right. I couldn't get out of the water until they left now. Knowing that I'd made such a stupid mistake made me furious with myself. I would make sure that no future failures were my fault.

"Who's that behind you?" another voice said, and Darius turned, showing me to the two women standing completely nude only a few feet from the edge of the pool.

"Orlana," I said, doing my best not to show my surprise at how comfortable they were in their nudity. They were whores. They were used to being seen in only their skin.

Darius put his hands on my shoulders and pulled me to him as the women stepped into the bath. I didn't fight him. He knew what he was doing, and I assumed he would put the illusion over my scales quickly.

Instead, he pulled me towards where he'd been sitting. I looked down and saw the sparkle of the gray and red scales that ran all over my body. From the tops of my breasts down my sides to my shins and outer thighs, bits and pieces of my body were covered in the one thing that made it obvious that I wasn't human.

He was going to have to touch me almost everywhere.

"Are you two in the mood to play a little?" one of them asked. A woman with lighter skin than most of the women here. A foreigner with just the slightest bit of an accent.

Darius's hands moved up my waist and settled on my breasts for just a moment. Without any sexuality to it at all, his touch erased the scales. He had no idea where they were, but he slowly touched me everywhere. Everywhere.

And my body warmed to his touch. Not in embarrassment. Even as he pulled me tighter against him and I felt his manhood brush against me, I knew that the feelings that ran through me were anything but embarrassment.

"I'm sorry, ladies, but we're going to get out soon. I'm a one-woman kind of man."

"That's too bad. You look fun, and your friend does too."

As soon as Darius had run his hands over my feet and completed the illusion, he picked me up as a husband would carry a bride and stepped out of the pool. He didn't give me a chance to object to anything he was doing, and I stood completely naked in front of all three of them as he pulled two linen towels from a shelf.

When he handed one to me, I quickly wrapped it around myself, glad to be covered again.

He wrapped his around his waist and picked up all of our clothing and Shadow's sheath. He smiled to the whores in the bath as they stared at him, and then he led us past the blue scarf. Kina opened her door and looked at us as we walked by, her eyes stuck on Darius.

Gods, did any woman not want this man? Was that why he didn't think anything about sexually charged actions? He'd touched me everywhere, and it had been less invasive than me walking into the pool had been.

Though I was beginning to understand why the women were attracted to him. At least Kina. His touch had been different, as though he understood a woman's body as well as he understood his own. There had been no fumbling, no exploring. He'd known the curves of my body without ever having touched me.

He led me up a set of stairs to the third floor. One of the doors was slightly ajar, and he pulled me into it.

Chapter 8

⟨decorative ornament⟩

"That was close," I said as he handed me my things.

"Not really," he replied as he held out his trousers. A gust of wind flew through the room, but only seemed to touch his trousers. Swirling like a tiny windstorm, it pulled all of the sand away from the fabric, and then it stopped.

I was awed at the cleverness of his magic. Nothing in the arden Disciplines could have done that.

I handed him my tunic and trousers which he did the same thing to, and when he handed them back to me, they felt almost as clean as when the servants at the palace washed my clothes.

He dropped his towel and pulled on his trousers, not bothered by the fact that I watched him do it. That I saw all of him. Then again, there was little about his body to be embarrassed of. Not a single blemish marred his skin, and every piece of him was that of a warrior. The bit hidden by his trousers was just as impressive as the rest of him, and the part of me that had enjoyed his touch before wondered what it would be like to be in bed with him.

I took a deep breath and dropped my towel as well. He didn't so much as glance at me as I pulled on my trousers and my tunic.

A part of me was slightly bothered by how little he cared about me seeing him without his clothes on. And how little he cared about seeing me without mine. Was he simply not attracted to women? They threw themselves at him at every turn, but he ignored them for the most part.

"They were stupid whores without any knowledge of the arden fae," he said in a whisper. "I would have told them that your scales were a new kind of piercing if they'd seen anything."

I didn't know what a piercing was, but he seemed to believe that it would have fooled them, and that was good enough for me.

He walked across the room to lay down on the bed, and I realized just what a strange place we were in. On the one hand, everything else in the brothel had been simple and most likely very inexpensive. The bed was different, though. Made of stout wood, it had been decorated by an artist. This was a brothel, and the beds were where the money was made, so it wasn't all that surprising.

It was a large bed, and I wasn't all that worried about sleeping in it with Darius. Though he was massive, the bed seemed to have been made for people his size. I would have plenty of room.

I sat down in one of the chairs next to a simple wooden

table with Shadow laying across my legs. "I apologize, Darius. I should have listened to you earlier."

He rolled onto his back, and I wondered if it was uncomfortable having his wings pressed against the bed like that.

"Good," he said as he stared at the ceiling. "I spoke poorly as well, though. You may be a better partner in this endeavor than my brothers would be, but you're so young, so...immature. And I don't know what you can do."

I bit my lip and didn't interrupt him even if I wanted to argue with him. "I know what I can trust my brothers with. I know what I can trust most solen fae with. I don't know you, and I don't know if you're going to freeze in the middle of battle like you did the first time we flew. I don't trust your instincts because even if you've trained forever, you've never seen any real battle."

I looked away. He was right. I knew the feeling of not trusting people. None of the people around me seemed to have the same weight on their shoulders, and so they didn't push as hard as I did. Even Daphon needed me to push him to work harder, and he knew what kinds of burdens I carried. My father had been right that just because Darius's actions hadn't been written down, it didn't mean that he was unskilled. I needed to prove that I wasn't either.

"Then tell me what to do. Tell me what to expect. I have skills that your father and brothers won't expect. Things that had never been used before we went into hiding, and I can fight with blade and flame. I don't know if I'll freeze, but I do know that I'm more than a helpless little girl."

"I want to believe you, Princess, but I don't. Not until I see it. Otherwise, I'm hoping, and unfounded hope will get you killed."

"Then let me show you," I said. "Tomorrow, while we wait, I can show you some of my abilities."

How did we get to this position? Somehow, in the span of less than an hour, I'd gone from feeling confident in myself to feeling like I needed to prove myself. I slung Shadow over my back. I needed to hear his advice. I needed someone to tell me that Darius was an idiot and reassure me.

"He's right," Shadow whispered to me. "You can't be sure you're as strong as you are until you're tested."

Those words hurt. They shattered the image I'd had of myself. Darius saying that I was incompetent was one thing, but Shadow saying it was so much worse. He'd been with me for my entire life. He knew me. He knew how hard I'd worked. He'd seen nearly every moment of my life.

And even he didn't trust me.

"That's a good decision. We'll have to fly far enough away that no one can see us, though."

I nodded as the weight of doubt settled over me. The thought that I'd been wrong for so long was crushing, and though I tried to tell myself that all of my training had to be worth something, I knew that it was a pale comparison to actual battle.

"Have you ever been in a battle?" I asked.

Darius shook his head. "Not a large-scale battle. Not like this war will be. But that's not what we're doing. At least, I hope it isn't because we won't win that. I've spent hundreds of years ruining things and killing without being seen, Orlana. That's exactly what we're going to do. I've never done anything quite like this before, but I have an idea of how it should play out."

I nodded again, and he lay back in the bed. The minutes

passed in silence, and I thought about getting up and going somewhere that I could talk to Shadow. Then Darius spoke up. "We need some cards or something. This is going to be a long week if we have nothing to do."

"I've never played cards," I said. "Gambling is against the Disciplines."

Once again, I remembered the written records of the humans who frequently played card games, gambling their last coin away. Ardens weren't known to gamble in the old days because all of them had enough riches to buy whatever they wanted. Now they didn't gamble because the Disciplines preached against it, claiming that it led down a path of laziness.

That got Darius's attention. "You're telling me that you've never played Thief or King's Cradle?"

"I've never held a playing card."

He just stared at me for several seconds before saying, "I can't decide whether you're telling the truth, or you're trying to play me."

I shrugged. "Believe what you will, but I've never been known as a good liar."

Darius grinned and said, "Then do you want to try a hand or two?" His eyes seemed to light up at the thought.

"I doubt I'll ever be a lazy person, and we've got nothing else to do. I don't know where to get cards, though."

Darius jumped up, excited for the first time since I'd met him. "Stay here. I'll get a deck from Kina. There are always a few games of cards at brothels."

And with that, he left me alone in the room. Alone for the first time since we'd left the Emerald Caverns.

I took a deep breath and looked down at Shadow. "What is

66

happening?"

"You're realizing that you don't know as much as you thought you did. You're realizing that the world is a lot bigger than you thought it was, and you're not nearly as prepared for it as you thought. It's good you're realizing it now, Orlana."

"But how can I help if I'm not prepared? How can I do what I was commanded to do? We have to slow Azulus down, and I'm failing at every step of the way."

I felt frustration well up inside me. How could I be unprepared when I'd done everything I could to be ready for this moment? "Orlana, your training was valuable. You've just missed a few things, and now you'll have to figure out how to learn those pieces in a hurry." Shadow paused for a moment as I felt the crushing weight of my failure. "And solen fae are annoying. Especially Darius."

I chuckled even though I wanted to break down. "He's extremely annoying, but he's something else too. I question the way I feel around him. Everything about him is a contradiction. I should hate him because I always have, but then he touches me, and it feels wonderful. He doesn't seem to care at all about the way I feel though. The way he touches me is so impersonal that it's almost a chore for him. How could he touch me like he did in the pool and not care?"

"I think there's more to Darius than you're seeing."

I nodded and took a deep breath before I tried to relax my body. I couldn't let Darius see me this angry. He would notice it and question what had caused it. Darius may have been an ass, but he was extremely perceptive.

It was good that I did because he burst into the room holding a deck of cards and wearing a wide smile on his face. As soon as he closed the door, he started explaining the game Thief to me.

The goal was to find the Thief card and play it. All the other cards were to manipulate the deck and the other player's hand.

Except the Knight card. If someone played the Thief while you held the Knight, you won the game by playing that card. If you were forced to play it before the Thief card was played, then you would probably lose.

It was complicated and based almost entirely on bluffing and reading the other person, neither of which were things I was good at.

As soon as Darius was done explaining, he said, "Normally, we would gamble money, but all of our money is for the mission, we'll need something else to gamble."

"I don't have anything to gamble, Darius," I said.

His lip curled in a smile as he said, "You have favors, and you have your clothes."

I frowned and Shadow whispered to me, "What's the worst that can happen?"

I wanted to tell him that I had no idea what kind of favors Darius would ask for, and the way he looked at me made me want to put on more clothes instead of less.

"You only have a pair of trousers on. I have trousers and a tunic. That doesn't make for a very long game."

He shrugged and said, "Fine. We'll play for favors then."

I hesitated for a moment. I knew he would beat me. He'd been playing this game for a long time, and I was terrible at reading people and bluffing.

But a part of me wanted to know what he'd want from me. "Any rules on the use of those favors?"

"No. They're usable anytime and anywhere." A shiver ran through me. I knew what most men would use them for, and

I looked at Darius in a different light. I wondered what it would be like to be under him, but would he even want that? He certainly hadn't shown any interest up to this point.

"Do it," Shadow whispered. "I'll help."

I didn't know what kind of experience Shadow had with card games, but he'd been around for a very long time.

"Deal. The arden fae are very strict about keeping promises, so you'd better be willing to pay up when I claim my favors."

He gave me that sideways smile and began to shuffle the wooden cards. He slid five of them from the deck of thirty to me, and I stared at them. I didn't have the Thief card.

He still had that smile on his face as he stared at me. He played a card that let him look at the top three cards in the deck. I played a card that made him discard two cards. Back and forth it went, and the pile of cards dwindled until I pulled the Thief.

I glanced at Darius, and Shadow whispered, "Play it. He doesn't have the Knight."

But the deck was so low. There were only three cards left, and I had no idea what they were. I hesitated, and then decided not to play it. Back and forth we went until we were down to our last cards, and Darius smiled as I was forced to play the Thief on my last turn. He countered it with the Knight and won the game.

"It was the last card I drew," he said with a grin. "That's one favor to me. Want to play again?"

"I told you!" Shadow said.

I couldn't tell Shadow anything, but I felt a tingling run through my body. I owed Darius a favor. Any favor. Looking at the way that he was smiling, I knew that I was in a lot of trouble.

Though, that trouble might be exactly what I wanted.

"Play again, Orlana. You can win if you listen to me," Shadow said.

He'd been right the first time. Maybe I could win if I listened to him. "Fine. Deal them again."

His smile got even bigger as he shuffled the cards a second time. When he dealt the cards, I tried to watch his reaction. He barely even looked at them, and I played a card to pull two extra cards from the deck. He immediately played the Thief, and I tossed the cards onto the table in frustration. How could I beat that?

"Bad luck on that one," he said. "Not a lot of ways to win if the other person gets the Thief on the draw. That's two favors to me. Another?"

My stomach was twisting as fear crept into me. One favor was something I could handle. But two? How many was I going to let him collect?

"I don't think so," I said.

"Come on, Orlana. At least get one off him. As he said, that was bad luck."

"Are you sure?" Darius asked as he picked up the cards and began to shuffle them.

"Fine. One more, and then I'm done." This was a bad decision, and I knew it. Shadow was confident, but I wasn't. Not in the least.

He dealt the cards again, and we began to play. The deck dwindled again, and I drew the Knight. I knew how to win with the Knight. I had to force him to play his cards as quickly as possible.

Then Darius played the Thief, and I immediately trumped it with the Knight. I felt better knowing that I had at least one favor over him. This way, he would need to make sure that his requests weren't too extravagant, or I'd be able to request the same from him. I just couldn't use it until he used both of his.

Then a knock on the door sounded, and it broke me away from the game.

Chapter 9

Kina's voice came through the door. "Dinner is ready. Come and eat with me, Darius."

Darius huffed and stood up, setting the cards on the table. "Come on, Princess. Let's go eat and find out what's been happening in the world."

He opened the door and ushered me out to where Kina was standing in the same sela. She led the way down the stairs, her backside swaying in a way that most men would have been drawn to. Darius ignored it completely, looking straight ahead.

She led us to her office where three chairs had been set up around a black granite table, something that seemed foreign and very expensive in this part of the world. It would have been a very poor table back home. At the same time, the food on the table would have been something that only royalty would have eaten.

Braised lamb chops in a white sauce that smelled sweet was next to mixed vegetables covered in a buttery cheese sauce. This was food that would have rivaled the feast we'd been preparing when I'd left.

"Tell me what's been happening in Kharn," Darius said before he'd even picked up his fork and knife. Was this normal? It seemed rude to begin interrogating Kina before eating. Maybe food wasn't as important on the surface. It would have been silent while the feast was eaten in my father's castle.

Kina began to cut her meat as she talked. "Your father called all of the soldiers sworn to him about two weeks ago. There's talk of true war. Not just the little skirmishes that he sends Marcellus on. Real war. Like the old days when you were young."

"Yes, that's exactly what's happening. Do you know when they're planning on leaving Kharn?"

Kina shook her head. "I haven't heard very much about it, but there's someone arriving tomorrow that will know better. You're still friends with Rea, aren't you?"

Darius nodded, and she continued. "Well, she'll be here tomorrow. Says that she doesn't want to be in Kharn any longer. She's stopping here and then she's taking a ship all the way across the Windswept Sea."

Darius cocked his head as though he were listening to something that I couldn't hear. "She's traveling with a friend, isn't she?"

Kina nodded, and Darius began to grin. "Don't tell anyone else that she's coming. No one."

"What's so important about Rea and her friend?" Kina

asked so innocently that it was obvious that she knew the information was valuable.

"I grew up with the friend. Rea is doing me a favor by getting her out of Kharn while the soldiers are away. She has a very abusive husband, and I'd rather not have him hear where she lands."

Kina almost frowned at how lackluster that answer was, but she seemed to believe it. I wasn't sure if I did, though. "I won't rat out your friend. Gods know that I've had to deal with enough abusive men in my brothels. Surprised you didn't just gut him. That's my usual approach."

Darius's lip moved just a bit, just the tiniest quiver, before he said, "He has an important place in my father's Court. His disappearance would be noticed."

Kina nodded and looked at him again, her eyes seeming to glaze over just a touch as she focused on his mouth as he chewed.

It was strange seeing Kina look at Darius like she did. That hunger in her eyes. I wondered if she was remembering times past when he'd accepted her invitation to the bedroom or if she was just fantasizing.

I'd normally have been disgusted by the way she was acting. It was so drastically different from how a respectable arden fae would act, but I was quickly realizing that I wasn't in that world any longer. I'd said goodbye to the world I'd grown up in.

In this new world, I was the foreigner, and I couldn't judge the way that people acted by arden standards.

"How do you know each other?" Kina asked, finally seeming to recognize me.

"She's here to help me take care of some things," was all that

Darius said, and he gave me a quick glance that told me to stay silent.

Kina set her fork and knife down on the plate and crossed her arms. "You're so much less fun now, Darius. You used to tell me all sorts of things after a few rounds in bed." His head snapped up, his golden eyes glowing, and Kina's eyes went wide.

"Your mouth is getting you into trouble again, Kina," he said. I saw a glimmer of something in the air next to her neck. I couldn't tell exactly what it was because it was so clear, but something was there, and it was pressing against her flesh. Then I understood. He'd created an air blade, a blade made from crystalized air.

"I gave you what you requested in return for the favor that I needed. I paid you in flesh, and I told you to keep it to yourself. Remember to whom you speak."

His eyes were blazing gold. All traces of the honeyed brown illusion had vanished, burned away by the intensity of what he said. Kina didn't speak, but I saw a trickle of blood begin to flow from her neck.

Then she seemed to relax as Darius went back to eating. The room was silent for the rest of the meal, and Darius didn't look at me a single time. Kina kept her eyes on her food. I'd never seen him act like that before.

"He may not wield steel weapons, but he has weapons of his own," Shadow whispered to me. "Don't forget that, Orlana. That man may not be a warrior, but he's still a killer."

I gave the most imperceptible of nods to Shadow as I worked on finishing my plate in silence. When Darius had finished his plate, he pushed it away and stood up. "We'll dine in our room tomorrow night, Kina," he said.

I glanced at the rest of the vegetables and pushed my plate away as well. Darius needed to get out of here, and Kina needed him to leave as well. I would have more good food tomorrow.

I stood up and Kina kept her eyes on her plate as we left. As we walked, I could see how much stiffer Darius was than he had been. The relaxed air he'd worn this whole time was gone, and he seemed filled with anger.

As soon as we got into the bedroom, I shut the door behind me and confronted him. He was a keeper of secrets, but I needed to know if this was going to get in the way of the mission. As he'd said, we needed to have complete focus.

"What was that about?" I asked as I sat in the chair again.

"Kina needs to learn to keep her mouth shut," he said as he kicked off his boots again. "You don't need to worry about it."

I was tempted to leave it alone, but I couldn't. This was just as important as my scales. She was here. She knew he was here. I needed to know if we could trust her to stay silent about us.

"I'm sorry if it upsets you, Darius, but I need to know if this is going to jeopardize our safety here and the mission. You cut her with an air blade. Most people would look for retribution from an attack like that."

He closed his eyes and said, "She won't. If she does, she'll bring my father to her brothel, and she, along with all of her whores, will be dead in days. My father may want me dead, but he won't let any news of me being used by a whore get out."

This whole thing was so confusing. How could Darius owe Kina anything worth enough to force him into bed with her?

"What were the terms of your deal with Kina?" I asked.

76

"I don't see how this matters to you," he said. The anger was still in his voice, and I could see how tense his body was. We were on dangerous ground talking about this.

"She's a whore, and I slept with her. That's what you do with whores, and she's not the first whore I've slept with. I'm sure that's a terrible thing for ardens, but get over it. I'm not in the mood to explain why it's a childish issue."

I gritted my teeth and stood up. "You called me a child, Darius. You told me that I wasn't putting the mission first. I need to know why you were willing to put an air blade to Kina's throat, and I need to know why you lost your temper when she talked about your time in bed together."

Darius stood up and began pacing. His wings slowly spread and closed, making him look massive in the small space. I waited patiently as he waded through his thoughts.

He turned on me, his eyes blazing once again. "It doesn't matter to our mission, but I'll try to explain." His wings didn't stop their repetitive motion, but he tried to keep his voice calm.

"I traded a week with Kina to keep someone safe. It wasn't the first time I'd made a deal like that, but it was the only time I've made one with her. She..." The air seemed to swirl in the room as he paused. "She was not a pleasant bed partner, but I made the deal, and I stuck to the bargain."

His wings closed tightly against his back as he turned to me. "But it doesn't matter. That was years ago, and as with all deals that I make, she swore that she wouldn't speak of it again. My father has made it clear that he doesn't want me to be 'soft', and if he finds out the kinds of things I do, he'd punish all of us."

"She broke her promise when she made that comment. That

was why I was angry. Broken promises are not something I handle well. If anything, that's what you should get out of our dinner. Don't promise me something and then break your oath, and we'll probably be fine."

Darius took a deep breath as I watched him. I wondered who he had been willing to barter himself to keep safe. It seemed so out of character for him, but then again, I really didn't know the man. The only thing I was sure of was that it was not a good time to push him. He'd told me enough that I didn't need to worry about it compromising our mission.

"Thank you," I said. "I don't break promises, Darius. An arden's word is stronger than steel."

"Then we have that in common," he said as he turned around and lay down in bed.

"There's something more to that man than either of us sees," Shadow whispered to me. "It would be good to learn more about him. For better or worse, you are bound to him for the time being."

I nodded, knowing that Shadow would see it. Then I stood up and said, "I think I'm ready for some sleep. It's been a long day, and I'm sure that tomorrow will be just as long."

When I'd first met Darius, I would have opposed him being in bed with me, but not tonight. Not after what had already happened today.

I pulled the sheets back and got into the opposite side of the bed after putting Shadow against the wall next to me. I never let him out of my sight. Especially not here.

I turned to face the wall, and I felt Darius get out of bed. I turned to see what he was doing, and I was greeted by his naked backside as he pulled his trousers off. For just a moment, I felt a warmth flow through me.

He was going to sleep naked.

I should have known. He made no moves towards me, and I closed my eyes. It was hard to let myself trust that I wasn't going to wake up with his hands on me, but I had to trust him. Even if his actions made little sense to me. Even if he was like no person I'd ever met.

That was it, though, wasn't it? He wasn't an arden fae. He'd been raised in a completely different world than me. A world where the difference between life and death could be saying the wrong word to the wrong person. He'd lived with his father, the tyrant of the entire world. He'd grown up having to hide everything he did.

He was used to having his back against the wall, and I wondered how often he snapped as he had at dinner. How often did someone find a blade against their throat for a misspoken word?

Maybe he truly was my ally, but I didn't think he was a friend. And I certainly didn't understand him.

And he didn't understand me.

We would work on that starting tomorrow. We would learn each other's powers, and we would begin the process of planning how to deal with Azulus and his army.

It was strange to think of the man that I'd wanted to kill for so long being an ally, but every moment we were together, it felt more real. I was beginning to think that Shadow was right.

There was more to Darius the Silent than anyone knew.

Chapter 10

I stood on the sands several miles from Assama. Both of our illusions were gone so that we could both see what was happening. Shadow's sheath was on my back, and our bag of supplies was on the ground.

"Show me what you can do," Darius said.

I held Shadow up and jumped high into the air, using flames to push me higher. Then I flipped, spraying flames in an arc around me from the bottom of my boots. As soon as I landed, I made several fast strikes against the air with Shadow.

I pressed my hand to the ground, and a spout of flames rose fifteen feet away from us almost ten feet into the air. Then, I coated Shadow in flames and took a few more strikes.

With a thought, I extinguished the flames around him and focused on myself. Pushing the innate power of the arden fae outward from my skin, and with a pop, fire exploded into existence around me, several inches away from my clothes. I held it there for several seconds, and then let it go.

Darius nodded. "You're a Firebrand, correct?"

"Yes," I said, surprised at the fact that he knew the term. I wondered how much he knew about ardens then. He had been young in the last war, and Azulus had never truly been a part of arden society, so I doubted that he knew the inner workings of the Disciplines.

"Can you work with stone at all?" he asked.

I shook my head. "I was training to be an assassin, so flames were the only things that I focused my studies on."

He nodded again as he began to pace. "What can you do besides illusions?" I asked.

That made him stop, and when he turned towards me, he was smiling. "Most things."

Darius didn't move, but suddenly, the sand around us rose into the air and began swirling. More and more sand filled the vortex that he created around us. Without seeming to try, the sand became so thick that I wondered if anything could pass through it. I certainly couldn't see through it.

He raised a hand, and I felt wind rush under me, lifting me into the air for just a moment. I stuck my hands out to balance myself, but then the wind was gone, but I was still above the ground. Underneath me, it was solid, though.

I could see the sand beneath me, but then I saw something gleaming between me and the sand. I bent down and ran my hand across it, realizing that he'd solidified the very air, crystallizing it.

What I stood on was smoother than any glass, and even more transparent. Then, he dropped his hand, and with a puff, it turned back into air, and I fell several inches to the sand below.

The vortex ~~of sand surrounding us~~ suddenly stopped as well, and the sand fell to the ground as though it had never been touched by Darius's magic. "Solen fae are masters of the air and light. My connection to the light is what fuels my illusions. My control over the air is absolute, but my control of light is limited to what I have shown you."

"Are all solen fae able to do these things?" I asked.

Darius shook his head. "The solen fae culture focuses on physical combat. They train daily with the sword but rarely with air. I ignored the way that my father, brothers, and other solen fae trained, and I focused entirely on my magic. Just as you ignored much of your magic so that you could train with the sword."

I nodded. "Then we're a good match. I can't show you what the bound tools can do as I am not a Binder able to replenish them."

"I don't doubt the effects of them. If there's one thing that everyone knows of the ardens, it's that their magical items were the best of any race. It's why I requested that your father bring all of them that he could to my brother."

"So where do we go from here?" I asked.

"My father's army is massive, but the manpower is not what worries me. It's the djinn's magic. It's the solen fae. It's the ifrits. The elves can do some magic, but not on a grand scale like will happen. Their soldiers will be the best in the world for they've had nearly a thousand years to train, and from my experience with them, they're damned good."

"But the djinn will destroy them. Just as you have power over fire, they do as well. And they are trained to fight with it. How many of the ardens train daily to go to war with flame and stone?"

I shook my head. "None except me. We've spent the last eight hundred years leading normal lives, never expecting to leave the caves. There was no purpose in training for war with that mentality. Probably the only advantages they'll have are the Binders and Stonewakers. Though, most of the Stonewakers will be exhausted after only an hour or so."

Darius nodded. "That's what I expected. We need to even the odds here. We won't be able to slow them down in the sands since it's so open, but we can start dealing with the pieces of the army that give my father so much strength."

"The djinn tend to stick together in the center of the encampments. My father dislikes the idea of a raid catching them by surprise. I can get us inside, but as soon as we do anything to draw their attention, I won't be able to stop them."

It was my turn to begin pacing. I knew he wanted me to have a solution, but I wasn't sure what I could do.

Djinn had two real purposes in an army, according to the old reports. Sending streams of fire at defenders from the back ranks and interrogation due to their ability to manipulate the soul.

In this scenario, only the fire part mattered. I smiled and walked over to my bag of Binding tools. I dug through it for a few moments and pulled out a small square stone.

"Thermal disruptors," I said. "That's the answer. They will regulate the temperature of an area and everything in it. We use them for cooling and preserving food back home, but it's impossible to start a fire in its radius. If you can get us in and out, the djinn will be powerless if we put these down."

Darius smiled. "I was hoping you'd have a trick. Pack up your things. It's time to go back to Assama."

Chapter 11

I moved through the water of the public bath, enjoying the calm that filled me. It had bothered me when Darius had insisted that he replace my illusion, but I'd known that it was necessary. Just as he had each time before, his hands had been almost clinical, but he'd still brought a warmth to my body.

I still got nervous taking my clothes off in front of him, and it was embarrassing how easily he took his off in front of me, but it was becoming easier. Being in the bath with him wasn't hard, though. He barely looked at me as he leaned his head back and let his body soak.

"Tell me about yourself, Princess," he said.

I let the name wash over me this time. I was in too high of spirits to let something that small bother me. "What do you want to know?"

"Whatever you want to say."

I sighed and moved to the edge of the pool. I wasn't sure what Darius got out of these conversations. It seemed like every time we had one, we ended up fighting. We were unified by the mission, but we were too different, and my history of hating his family always got in the way.

"My father is King of the Emerald Caverns. My mother was killed by Arturus. I've spent my life training to be an assassin. I don't know what else there is to say."

He said, "I already know those things. Tell me about you. Not your parents or your training. What do you enjoy doing when you aren't planning how to kill me?"

"I work, Darius. Even when I'm not training, I'm usually working. On the rare occasion that I'm not doing either of those, I like to take walks through the caverns. Lazy evenings where I can let my feet dangle in the river and just not think about anything. Similar to what I'd be doing now if you weren't trying to get to know me."

"You don't do anything for personal enjoyment? You don't read or watch plays or paint?"

I gripped the seat and let my feet float upward, not enough for Darius to see anything, but enough to feel weightless. "No. I tried to grow seed crystals for a while, but there was too much math involved. I read old reports regularly because information is power. I only go to plays when my father forces me to."

"I think constantly, so the best way for me to relax is to just ignore everything and let my mind wander." What I didn't say was that I talked to Shadow in those times. We talked about his old life and about my life. He told me stories about the surface world. But Darius couldn't know about Shadow. For some reason, he was the only secret that I wasn't willing to give up.

I glanced at the sword lying within arm's reach. My best friend in all the world. The only "person" who understood me.

"You've never been pushed to find a man to marry? No courting at all? Isn't that what most princesses worry about?"

I chuckled at that. "My father wouldn't dare. You saw what I did when he tried to get me to go to a feast. No, I've courted a few men, but they wanted more than I could give them. The ones that were acceptable to my father weren't acceptable to me, and vice versa. My experience with men has been limited to stolen kisses and late-night tumbles, few of which were worth the effort."

It was Darius's turn to laugh. "Few late-night tumbles are worth the effort in my experience as well."

There was a sadness in Darius's eyes even as he laughed, and I wondered what it was that had hurt him so much.

"I'm boring. What about you? What do you enjoy doing?"

He smirked even as he looked up at the sandstone ceiling. "My normal response would be something something brothels, but after the last comment, that wouldn't make much sense."

He finally looked at me. "I enjoy reading and games. Especially when the games have real stakes. That's why I was excited to play cards yesterday."

His comment reminded me of the favors I owed him, and I wondered what they would entail. "Why do you let everyone think that you're spending so much time in brothels?"

He chuckled, and for the first time, he moved across the bath towards me. "I do spend a lot of time in brothels. I can relax there," he said as he got closer to me. "I like the people in brothels. At least the ones I frequent. The customers are free there in a way they can't be elsewhere. They don't have to pretend to be something they're not. The whores are treated well and don't have terrible lives like so many other women."

Then he smirked as he got closer to me. "Plus, it's nice to be around so many beautiful naked women."

The way he looked at me sent shivers through my body. He was so confident, and I knew that if he touched me now, it wouldn't be that cold touch he normally used on me.

And for just a moment, I wondered what it would be like. Would it be more than those late-night tumbles had been? Darius was not a young man just learning about the bedroom. He'd spent his life with women who were willing to do and be anything you paid them for.

He said, "Though, there are issues with the brothels I frequent. The women are humans, so I have to be far gentler with them. I wonder if ardens are as breakable as humans."

For that split-second, he seemed to be tempted by something, and then he turned around. My heart raced as I watched his bare backside move away from me. That man knew how to pull at the irrational side of me.

When he turned around, he caught me staring at him, and he smirked again. "Do you want to spend your favor?" he asked.

I realized just how easily he'd played me. He'd seemed interested, teasing and pulling at my senses with his tone and his words. He hadn't touched me, hadn't even said anything very sexual. Instead, he'd just seemed interested, and that had been enough.

And it hurt how easily he could manipulate me like that. I snarled at him. "It sounded like you were the one considering spending your favor."

"Princess, I don't have any need to spend a favor on you. If I'd even touched you, you'd have been begging me, much less if I'd tried to seduce you. There's no magic spell on Kina."

That hurt even worse because I knew it was true. He was still the same liar, the same trickster. While I'd spent my life doing everything I could to win battles with sword and flame, he'd spent his life learning to win battles with his tongue.

And body.

I didn't say anything. Instead, I climbed out of the bath. I could sense his eyes on me as I walked to the towels. I didn't care. Not anymore.

I pulled a towel from the shelf and wrapped it around myself. When I turned towards Darius, he was looking at me with that same smirk on his face. "I hope you enjoyed the view."

I picked up Shadow and my clothes and walked out of the bath towards the room. I couldn't stand the trickery and manipulation. It was everything that I'd hated about the negotiations my father did. Darius would have been at home there.

As I walked into the room, a piece of paper was on the floor with a single sentence written on it.

Your father's army has left Kharn.

Chapter 12

We were attacking Azulus's army tonight, but until then we didn't have anything to do, and I certainly wasn't going to be playing Thief with Darius anymore. Not until I knew a little bit more about how he was going to spend those favors.

We'd planned a nap for this afternoon so that we'd be well rested, but for now, we were going to relax in the tavern area. Darius was quickly becoming claustrophobic in our little room, and I didn't blame him for that. Standing out on the sands for days on end would have driven me insane. We were from two different worlds, and when you shoved one of us into the other's world, we didn't do well.

Darius leaned back in his chair and propped his feet on the table. He looked completely comfortable here, but I was nervous. Anyone could walk in and see us. I'd been sequestered under the Aedenian Mountains for so long that it was still strange to relax in a place that the enemy could see us on accident.

"So we just sit around doing nothing?" I asked.

Darius nodded. "My friends will be here soon, but the goal is to just waste the day away. Sometimes, the hardest part of being stealthy is the wait. Why don't you go get yourself a drink to help you stop thinking so much?"

I shook my head. "No way, Darius. I don't need to be hungover tonight."

He chuckled as he closed his eyes. "I didn't say that you should get drunk. I said to get a drink to take the edge off. Let your body and mind calm down a bit, Princess. Stressing will only make things worse."

I gritted my teeth. I still wasn't happy about the way that he'd manipulated me yesterday, and his constantly arrogant behavior annoyed me more than anyone I'd ever met. Why did he presume to know what was best for me?

But I couldn't pick a fight with him. Not now, at least. Tonight we were going to have to work together, and if we messed it up, we'd both die, and more importantly, the arden kingdoms wouldn't have time to get to Inoras.

So I held my tongue and tried to relax.

"You know what I miss about being a prince?" Darius asked.

I took a breath and tried to rein in my frustration with him. "No idea. I'm sure you're going to tell me, though."

"It's that I'm bored right now, and there's nothing I can do about it. You refuse to play cards with me, and I can't leave the brothel. If I were still a prince of Kharn, I'd be able to find something or someone to entertain me."

"I'm sure there's a woman or two here that wouldn't be against entertaining you for at least five minutes before you finish up with her."

Darius opened one eye and his lip curled up. "Is that what your late night romps have taught you about the bedroom? Maybe I should show you what it's like to be with a real man."

"Just because the people you pay applaud your attempts at pleasure doesn't mean that you're any good at it," I said before I remembered that I was trying to keep tensions low.

He chuckled instead of being angry, though. "Kina wouldn't be begging me to join her in the bedroom if I weren't good at what I did."

"Then why don't you go ask if she'd entertain you for a while. Maybe I'd finally get some peace and quiet to gather my thoughts."

A part of me instinctively hoped he wouldn't. I didn't like Kina in the least, but it was more than that. I wasn't sure why I'd said that other than to make him a little snarly.

"I don't think that'd help me relax at all, Princess. She's not really my type. Plus, I'm waiting for Rea."

The room quieted, and I wondered where Kina was. Was she still afraid of Darius hurting her? When I'd first met her, I'd have imagined that she'd try to spend as much time with him as possible, but after he'd cut her with the crystal blade, maybe she'd changed her mind.

Before I had any more time to think, the door slowly opened, and two women walked in. One had on a typical sela, but the other was dressed in trousers and a tunic not all that different from my own.

The one with the tunic and trousers would be Rea. She had run a brothel in Kharn for a long time, but now she was trying to escape. I didn't know why, though.

And who was the friend? Darius hadn't given up any

information on her. She was beautiful, but that word did her a disservice. There was something about her that drew the eye. It wouldn't have mattered if you'd put her up against every other beautiful woman in the world, she would have been the one that people would have stared at.

Long, shiny black hair ran down her back. Her cheeks and chin were sharp, but her eyes and lips were soft. The sela she wore made her look almost regal even though it showed off most of her body.

"Ona, I'm so glad you made it," Darius said with a smile. He pulled his legs off the table and stood up, his eyes sparkling.

Ona held out her arms, and Darius gave her a hug. It was the kind of hug that I'd give my father. Who was this woman?

When they broke away, Rea was grinning. "Told you I'd get her here. Took me a minute to get her out of the palace, but we managed. I hope you've got a good plan for getting us to the elven cities."

Darius said, "Ona, this is Princess Orlana. She's working with me to slow down Father."

She turned to me, and I felt something in the air. Just the slightest bit of warmth, and then she smiled at me. "An arden fae," she whispered. "Never thought I'd get to see a woman born of flames. It's nice to meet you, Orlana."

That comment made me pause for a moment. How'd she known that I was arden?

"Ona is part djinn," Darius said. Ah, that made sense. Djinn could read a person's soul, and there'd be no mistaking my race. "Do either of you two ladies want a drink? Kina won't mind if we pour ourselves a little drink in celebration."

Rea nodded. "A cup of wine would wash down some of the sand from the journey. We had to sleep out in the dunes for the past two nights. The number of troops on the roads wouldn't let us make very good time."

"None for me, Darius," Ona said as she continued to stare at me. "A djinn won't ever complain about a little sand. I might even take some with me so that I don't go crazy spending the next few months in a world without any."

Darius and Rea got up to get drinks, and I smiled at Ona. "You're an interesting woman, Orlana. The first arden fae to resurface after all these years. A woman with cracks in her soul that have been healed with steel and stone."

She grinned at me and said, "You and Darius ought to get along well."

I didn't know why she thought that. We were such complete opposites. "How do you know Darius?"

"I'm King Azulus's wife, and though I don't claim to have any parental role to Darius because he was a grown man when I met his father, I've spent a lot of time with the troublemaker."

That made sense. I hoped that Darius's trust was well-founded, but as I looked at Ona, I felt drawn to her. Like I was sure that I could trust her, that she only wanted the best for me.

"You're manipulating me," I said as I gritted my teeth.

She shook her head. "I don't have those kinds of powers, Princess. The only magic I have from my djinn side is a bit of healing and the ability to read a soul." Her voice was so soothing, though. I could imagine my mother's voice being like that as she held me.

"Then what are you doing?" I asked.

She smiled at me and put her hand on mine. "I'm not doing anything to you. But sweetheart, the soul knows what it's missing, and there are chips in your soul a mile wide. Just because you don't understand what your soul is trying to tell you doesn't mean that someone's trying to manipulate you."

"Why should I trust my enemy's wife?" I snarled as I pulled my hand back. "I've never met a djinn, but everything I've read says that I should be wary of them."

She began to laugh with a tinkling silvery sound. "You sit here with the greatest snake of them all, and you worry about me. Oh, that boy will be proud that I've made you nervous."

I glanced at Darius who was drinking at the bar with Rea and looking at us. "Why would that make him proud?"

"He always says that I'm too nice. I can't help that I like seeing people smile though."

Darius and Rea began walking to the table and when they were a few steps away, he said, "It doesn't count that Princess doesn't trust you. The first words she said to me were that she wanted to torture me and then execute me. She has a murder first, ask questions later attitude."

"Why shouldn't I?" I asked, completely baffled as to why everyone was surprised that I was nervous around strangers.

"Because we're all on the same side," Rea said gruffly. "We all want to see Azulus dead." I trusted Rea more than Ona. As far as I could tell, she didn't have a sneaky bone in her body.

I didn't say anything, but I still worried. Darius was one thing. He was a known entity, someone I'd gone my entire life knowing about, but these two women were strangers. Now it wasn't just me and Darius that knew what we were doing, and the more people that knew, the more dangerous it was that someone would catch us unprepared.

We already walked a razor's edge, and failure would mean the deaths of so many people. Why would Darius want to add more risk?

Ona said to Rea, "She doesn't understand. She hasn't lived in our world or known the man that we know."

"Sweetheart," she said to me, "the world is full of people who would give their last breath to see my husband burned on a pyre. You're not the only person who has cracks in their soul because of his actions."

She smiled at Darius, and his lips tightened. "But I'm sure that you two need to prepare for your night. I know that Azulus draws close to Assama."

Darius nodded and stood up. "Stay safe, both of you," Darius said. "Get to Kaladorei without stopping. You should have plenty of time, but don't take any detours."

"We won't, Darius," Rea said. "I have no intention of dealing with your father's soldiers."

He nodded to her, and I stood up. Ona reached out and took my hand, pulling my attention back to her. "Remember Princess, you're not the only person whose soul has cracks in it. Don't judge too harshly when you find out that some people have filled in those cracks with things other than steel and stone."

Chapter 13

I glared at Darius as we stood on the sands at sunset and surveyed Azulus's army. Gods, it was massive. The largest city in the world wouldn't have been able to house all of these people. For as far as the eye could see, there were tents. Different colors for different groups.

I was still bothered by the fact that he'd given my secrets to others, that he'd risked our mission by revealing us to strangers. Then there was the fact that he'd tried to manipulate me into wanting him last night in the bath. All in all, I was pissed at him. "Stop thinking about it," Shadow said. "You can yell and scream at him when this is done, but for now, focus on what has to be done."

Good advice, but not an easy thing to do. I slipped into the Flames of Peace meditation for just a moment, and I felt the frustration fade. Yes, I would deal with that after our mission was accomplished.

When I opened my eyes again, I was overwhelmed. How could we get to the djinn?

Darius held the bag of supplies. We'd left everything except the thermal disruptors further southwest in a sand dune we'd dug out. I had no idea how Darius planned on finding it again, but he assured me that he knew exactly where it was.

"How do we get to the djinn?" I asked.

"We become invisible," he replied without looking at me. "You'll need to move quickly once we're there because the djinn can see the soul. They won't expect us to attack this quickly, and they won't expect us to attack them specifically, so we have the element of surprise."

He turned to me then. "Don't ruin it."

"And what are you going to do?" I snapped back.

He grinned. "I'm the one who makes sure you don't die. Think of me as the gods watching over your shoulder."

What did that even mean? It didn't matter. I knew my job, and I had to trust that Darius would take care of the rest, and that included getting me out of there.

The truth of the matter was that I was terrified, and his comment weighed heavily on me. He stood behind me and wrapped his arms around my waist. I looked down and saw the sand where my feet should have been. He was right. We were invisible.

I closed my eyes as he took off. His wings were silent as we flew across the city of tents. When I finally opened my eyes, I saw that the tents were no longer single colors. Instead, each of them was dyed in strange patterns.

A large clump of them had white with red stripes, and Darius seemed to be headed towards them. My heart was racing, and for the first time, it had nothing to do with being in the air.

This was the first time that I'd kill someone, and I knew it. I thought I was prepared for it, but it was impossible to be sure. Then there was the distinct possibility that this would fail, and we'd become the first casualties of this war. I tried to push the nerves away, but it was nearly impossible. Even my meditations failed me. They could only do so much, and when I opened my eyes, the reality was still there.

But, like it or not, this was going to happen, and my skills were the only thing that would keep us alive.

As Darius landed without a sound, he thrust the invisible bag into my hands. It was strange to move without seeing anything, but I managed. The only things in the bag were the thermal disruptors, and I carried the bag in one hand while the other set the disruptors down around the tents.

I had no idea where Darius was, but I knew my job, and as soon as I'd set them down, I stepped into the first tent. Two tanned men with shaved heads lay on sleeping bags, snoring silently.

I slid Shadow from his sheath, and with a quick breath, I slid him through the first man's ribs to pierce his heart. His eyes opened wide, and his body convulsed as he gasped for breath.

And then he stopped, the spark of fire in his eyes completely gone. This was what it felt like to kill a man. The blood that poured from his chest was nothing compared to the lifeless eyes that stared at me. He'd seen me, seen my soul as he died.

He knew who had murdered him, and there was no way around it. I tried to push the feeling away, but it wouldn't leave. I didn't have time to feel, though. I turned to the other djinn who was beginning to toss and turn from the noise. Just as silently, I slid the blade through his chest.

He looked up at me with the same shocked eyes as his spark left his body empty and soulless. I turned away from this one. I knew I needed to move more quickly, and I walked into the next tent. Three men slept in this one.

One after the other, I murdered them in their beds, leaving their bodies lifeless as their blood pooled under them.

"Keep going," Shadow urged me as I slowed. The death of those men weighed on me. "You can't stop now. Your people need you to do this. The world needs you to do this."

I stepped into the next tent, and no one was sleeping there. One of the djinn looked up, his red eyes seeing me. He began to shout, and without thinking, Shadow slid across his neck. The other djinn raised their hands to me, but nothing happened, their flames consumed by the thermal disruptors. Shadow flashed out two more times, slitting their throats effortlessly.

I heard noises outside and still had no idea where Darius was. Djinn were stepping out of their tents now, and I slipped through them, cutting and stabbing as quickly as I could. I had to make sure that they were dead or nearly dead before moving to the next. Azulus had plenty of healers to bring them back to health by the end of the night.

More and more of the djinn raised their arms towards me as I cut them down, and I wondered how much more the thermal disruptors could handle. I'd never had anyone test to see how much heat they could absorb.

Dozens died in minutes as I slid through their ranks. Crimson covered the ground as Shadow and I danced invisibly through the crowd. Human soldiers began to step into the ranks, and we cut them down just as quickly because they couldn't see me.

Then I heard the roar of flame before it hissed out of existence. The thermal disruptors were failing, and I had no way out of this army, so I continued to cut djinn down. They'd picked up blades at this point, stealing them from the soldiers who couldn't see me.

But they were not trained in the art of the sword. They hadn't needed it. They'd trusted to their magic instead. Another burst of flame raced towards me, and I split it with Shadow.

He groaned as I felt him absorb it. Steel was able to absorb the magic that fueled the flames, but it didn't absorb the heat, and I felt Shadow begin to heat in my hand.

With a thought, I dismissed the heat in a simple warding gesture as prescribed by the Disciplines. Something taught to even the youngest of Firebrands.

The djinn were capable of battle with flames, but they were not what Darius had described. They held none of the advanced techniques that firebrands learned. But there were so many of them. I couldn't deflect their flames for long.

One stream of fire nearly caught me, but I rolled out of the way. As soon as I was away from the crowd, I felt strong hands jerk me upwards. I held Shadow out, and as one ball of fire was hurled at us, I focused on it, forcing it back towards the group of djinn on the ground. It exploded as it connected with them, and screams filled the air.

"Good job," Darius whispered to me. "Now don't do anything. No sound. No motion. The solen fae will be out soon enough, but they can't see us. They'll be listening, though."

And so I waited as I watched the tents disappear from underneath us. They were replaced by sand dunes. The wind was strong, and little swirls of sand ran along the edges of the dunes, making them look fuzzy underneath us.

The world was so quiet up this high. Those djinn's eyes going dark filled my mind as I stared at the sand. The blood that coated Shadow's edge should have bothered me, but it was those eyes that I couldn't get out of my mind.

I'd killed at least a hundred people. Living, breathing people. They'd had families. They'd had lives and friends and goals. I'd snuffed them out like candles in a storm. Half a second had been all it'd taken for each of them. One quick movement, and their lives had ended.

And that explosion at the end. How many people had died to that explosion? A fireball the size of Darius would have coated dozens of people in flames. How quickly would healers have been able to put out the fires?

I knew that it was the right thing to do. I did. There was no doubt in my mind that the arden fae were on the right side, and those djinn would have had no problem killing my friends and family. That didn't change the fact that I had murdered them in their sleep.

I was the reason that their children would no longer have fathers. How many people would grow up dreaming of killing me?

I very well may have created orphans on this night, and that was the most terrible thing I could imagine. It had been right, but that didn't mean that it was good.

"I'm sorry, Orlana," Shadow whispered to me. "War is a terrible thing, and I wish that you'd never had to learn that."

I said nothing, and Darius slowly descended to the sand

below. I had no idea how he knew where the rest of our supplies were, but I trusted him. I had to.

As we approached the dune, he put his hand out, and the illusion covering the doorway disappeared. Inside the dune, a thin layer of air had been crystallized, and a hollow waited for us to hide in. He walked in first, and I followed him. There were no pillows or blankets, no comforts at all.

Just the hard, crystallized air below us.

He lay down on the ground, and with a snap, the illusory wall appeared behind me. We were safe. We'd survived. We'd accomplished the goal, and Azulus's army had taken a very significant hit to its strength.

But when I lay down, I didn't feel like we'd done a good thing. No, I felt like I was becoming a monster. Like Azulus himself, I'd done what I'd needed to do to get the results I needed.

Even if that left orphans in my wake.

The dug out hole in the dune was small, barely large enough for us to both lay down. I curled up and held Shadow in my arms. I didn't want to let him go tonight.

Then I felt Darius behind me. He didn't turn away from me as he normally did. He wrapped his arm over me and pulled me tight against him. Normally, I would have pushed him away, but tonight I would accept the comfort. He knew what I was going through. He knew the soul-crushing feeling that filled me.

He whispered to me, "Go to sleep, Orlana. What we did had to be done. Those men had to die. Tonight, the world is a terrible place, but when you wake tomorrow morning, the world will not be quite so dark."

Chapter 14

I watched as the dunes turned into grass which turned into forest. It was a fast transition, and I wondered what it was that changed to allow plants to grow here when they were so rare only a few miles away.

Darius held me tight to him as he flew through the air. Something was different now. Was it that I'd proven my worth to him? Did he find that I was valuable now?

He still didn't say anything, though. He'd been mostly silent since we'd left our hideaway at dawn. Flying as quickly as he could, we were headed to our next stop, a small village not much bigger than Steras named Borlet.

Azulus would not come close to it unless he was going to commandeer food and supplies. We weren't going to wait for him to get that close.

I knew of an orphanage in Borlet as well. We would be safe

from prying eyes, and I'd be sure that we had a hearth in this room. It was time to report back to my father.

Darius set us down a few miles away from Borlet, and I looked up at him. He was so serious. Gone was the mischievous smile that he'd held this entire trip.

"What is it? Why are you so serious?" I asked.

"Nothing, Princess. You said you had a contact here?" he said as he began to walk through the woods. The oak trees and canna ferns made it difficult to see very far in front of us.

"Yes. Another orphanage. This one should be quite a bit larger, and there will probably be better food. No one begrudges the children having decent accommodations here."

The oak trees were mature here, and acorns littered the ground. Grateful for the solid boots on my feet as one crunched under me, I pushed a canna fern out of the way.

As I moved it, I pulled two of the little fruits that clung to the bottom of the giant fronds. Soft crimson berries that were slightly citrus. Before they were pollinated, they were very bitter and white, but the deep red showed that they were nearly ready to fall on their own.

I tossed one to Darius, who caught it. "Thank you," he said quietly. I put the berry to my lips and felt the soft citrus juice explode in my mouth as I ate it. A nice treat.

It felt strangely lonely here. As though we were all alone in the world, and each of us was walking the same road, but we were separate. No longer the team that was going to stop Azulus from winning the war, we were simply two travelers who had seen things that they wished they hadn't.

The songs of birds were constant here. Tiny little ruffs and the larger doves flitted from tree to tree, probably gorging themselves on the ripe canna berries.

I looked at Darius again, wondering what was going through his mind. Finally, when we weren't far from Borlet, I reached my hand out and touched his shoulder. "Please tell me what's wrong," I said.

He pulled away from my touch. "That's my father's army, Princess. I knew some of those men, and though they'd never have turned on my father, that doesn't change the fact that I will never see them again."

I frowned. "But you were the one who explained how to fight them. You told me how to kill them best. Why would you have me kill the men you knew and cared for?"

He snarled at me as his wings stretched out. They were invisible, but I knew the stance by now. "Because that's what had to happen, Princess. I told you that nothing mattered except the mission, and I wasn't lying. I know the costs of war. I know that many of my friends will die. On both sides. And I'm prepared to pay those costs. That doesn't make it any easier."

He turned around and continued walking. I hadn't thought about that. I hadn't realized that he'd known those men. I'd thought that I was the one who was hurting worse because of what we'd done, but I'd been wrong. Could I have watched Darius kill people in the Emerald Caverns if I knew that it would help the war?

I didn't know.

He'd made that sacrifice, and he was hurting because of it. Now I understood, and I wouldn't push him anymore about it. We would both have our own soul wounds by the end of this mission. I just hoped that I could bear them as well as Darius was.

We walked onto the path of dark soil that was as close

to a road as Borlet had. Grass grew up on either side of the pathway, and flowers brought color to the scenic village. People wandered in the village, but it was tiny in comparison to Assama or even Steras.

That was a good thing for us, though. Nothing important happened in Borlet. No one important visited. It was a farming village on the outskirts of a kingdom. The most important man that came was the tax collector who showed up every year around mid-winter.

Then there were the merchants who came once every two months like clockwork. They were coming for one reason only. My emeralds. Ms. Addie took care of her children and spread the wealth amongst the poor of the village. My father's emeralds were the reason that this entire village thrived.

We turned off the main path and headed down a slightly beaten trail into the forest. Wagon wheels had worn ruts in the path, and I smiled. Ms. Addie was a wonderful woman who had spent the last fifty years of her life caring for her children and her village.

It wasn't long before we arrived in front of a huge white building. I smiled. A painted building in a tiny village was such an oddity. She'd spent her inheritance to build the orphanage initially, and everyone knew it. Now, my emeralds were just the remnants of her inheritance in most people's eyes.

I stepped up to the door and knocked.

A child that barely reached my waist opened the door and smiled at us. "Ms. Addie's coming," the little boy said before stepping back. "Come in and wait here. She was in the garden."

We stepped inside, and I looked around. Unlike the

orphanage in Steras, everything here was beautiful. It had a sense of cheer to it all, and I knew that the effort and emeralds were changing lives.

"This is an orphanage?" Darius whispered to me.

I nodded. "I pay for its upkeep. Looks like they're putting the funds to good use."

Ms. Addie walked in from a door on the opposite side of the room. She had dirt on her knees and was wearing a gardening apron. She brushed her hands off on the thick, jute fabric.

She was an older woman, nearing seventy years old, but unlike so many other women her age, she stood tall and had a smile on her face. Her gray hair had been pulled back in a bun, and several children trailed behind her as she walked into the room. Their hands and knees were just as dirty, but they didn't seem to bother with wiping it off.

"Hello," she said. "I'm Ms. Addie, and I'm sorry for the wait. I wasn't expecting guests today."

She crossed the room, and I said, "Hello, Ms. Addie. We've known each other for a long time, but this is the first time we've met. I'm Orlana."

She gasped and put her hands to her mouth. "Orlana? The one from the fire?"

I nodded with a grin. "My friend and I need a place to stay for a few days. Is there any way we could stay here?"

"Oh, of course. I'd feed and house anyone who asked, but I'd give up my own bedroom to you. You have no idea what you've done for so many children. Then there are the villagers you've helped. You've given Borlet a safety net, and it's saved so many lives."

"We need a room with at least a large bed and a hearth. Food would be nice as well."

Ms. Addie nodded. "There's a visitor's room in the North Wing. No children are in that wing, so you'll sleep a bit more soundly. It has a fireplace, though there's nothing special about it if you understand my meaning."

She was talking about the sigils that were carved under the ash of her own hearth. They were only needed to receive messages, not send them. "No, we don't need a special hearth."

"Then it's yours for as long as you need it. Would you like your food brought to your room or would you prefer to eat with the rest of us?"

I glanced at Darius, who was looking at the children playing. They were filthy, but they were happy.

"I think we'll dine with everyone. It'd be nice to see the children."

She turned to lead us to the room, but then she stopped and turned around. Without warning, she wrapped her arms around me. "You have no idea how grateful everyone is for what you do. Even if they don't know who to thank, in their hearts, they know that someone has been there watching over them. And they're grateful."

I patted her shoulders, feeling awkward as I saw a smile creep across Darius's face for the first time. When she pulled away, she didn't say anything else. Darius and I followed her down a hallway. Paintings adorned the walls, not of famous people, but of young men and women.

"Who are these paintings of?" I asked.

"The orphans," Ms. Addie said. "When they find their purpose and move out of the orphanage, we have a painting done in their likeness. Helps me remember what I work for. Each of these paintings is of a child that would have died without me, and you of course, and now they're each living a

108

happy life somewhere."

She stopped at a set of double doors and pulled them open. Inside was a massive bedroom. Why anyone would need a room this large was incomprehensible to me. "If you need anything, please let me know," she said.

"Thank you for the room and meals," I replied, dismissing her.

Darius grinned as he looked at the bed. "That's a lot fancier bed than the brothel. Though, I doubt it's as sturdy." He shook the bedpost and the whole bed shifted slightly. "Definitely not strong enough for a solen fae bedroom. Oh well. Not like we'll be testing that."

I squinted. I didn't understand what he was getting at. Was it that he was too heavy?

"All this space and no bath," he said. "Typical humans. I guess that's normal when you don't live in the sand."

He wasn't talking to me. He was just talking. Just thinking about something other than the price he'd paid.

He turned to me. "Well, what are we going to do this evening?"

I shrugged. "Sleep? I feel like I could sleep for days."

"Lazy arden fae," he said with a grin. "You could sleep. Or…" he pulled out the cards he'd gotten from Kina.

I sighed, but Shadow said, "Yes! Time to avenge our losses!"

I chuckled and said, "Fine. I don't want to go too far in debt to you, though."

"We could play for clothes instead," he said with a smirk. "Or other things…"

A shiver ran through me at what he could mean by "other things".

"No, I think favors will do just fine."

Chapter 15

"Damn! Damn! Damn!" I shouted as Darius played the Knight over top of my Thief.

"I'm done," I said as I stood up. "Arden fae are not meant to gamble. I'm being punished by the gods for breaking the Disciplines."

Darius leaned back in his chair and began to chuckle. "You're not being punished for gambling," he said. "You're being punished for gambling against someone who has spent their life playing games of chance and winning."

He'd won seven games, and I'd won a measly two. That meant that I owed him nine favors, and he only owed me three. Even with Shadow's help, I hadn't been able to beat him often, and Shadow was far older than Darius.

"He's cheating," Shadow whispered to me. "That's the only way he could have won a few of those games."

I turned on Darius. "You cheated, didn't you? You put an illusion on the cards, didn't you?"

He smirked. "Would be tough to tell if I had, wouldn't it?"

A cheater. I'd known he was a liar since the beginning, but I'd still played the damn game. "Then those favors aren't valid," I said with a snarl.

In a flash, Darius was on his feet and moving towards me. "I didn't say that I cheated, and even if I did, you accepted those games as losses. Do not try to wiggle out of your agreement."

I bared my teeth at him. "It's not wiggling out of an agreement if you cheated," I said.

He smiled. "I never said that it was against the rules to cheat, but I didn't. I didn't need to. My favors are mine."

I growled at him, but I knew that he was right even if I hated him for it. Any arden would have told me to be sure to know all the rules beforehand. I wasn't used to playing with a damned liar, though.

"I hate you," I said. "You're the opposite of what a good man should be."

He shrugged and turned around. "That's fine. There are thousands of people in the world that hate me. It doesn't change the fact that you owe me nine favors."

I glared at him as he walked back to the bed. The same bed that I was going to have to share with him. He lay down on his side and stared at me. "Why did you have to cheat?" I asked, ignoring the fact that he'd told me he hadn't cheated.

"I didn't cheat, Princess," he said with a sigh. "It's funny that you think I did, but I didn't. I've cheated other people for things, but there was no upside on this to cheating. I already knew I was going to win."

I shook my head. This was why gambling was a bad decision.

This was why ardens didn't gamble. We weren't meant to be good at it.

"What are you planning on using your favors on?" I asked.

I needed to know. Nine favors were terrifying.

"I don't know. That's the great thing about favors. I can use them whenever I want something. Is there something that you're planning on using yours on?"

I shook my head. I'd been so focused on what he could make me do that I'd barely thought about what I could make him do.

"Does it bother you knowing I could make you do whatever I wanted at any time?"

His voice had an almost bored tone to it, but I knew that was false. He enjoyed having this power over me. He enjoyed the thought of controlling me and the rest of the world around him. That's what manipulators did.

"Yes," I said softly.

"Fine. I'll spend one. I'm sure I'll earn more back eventually since you're not going to get any better at cards."

He stood up and walked towards me. When he was only inches away from me, he raised his hand, and air blew around my body. Slowly, I floated into the air, but it felt like I was still standing on solid ground.

I glanced down, knowing what to expect, and saw the faint shimmer of the air under me that was the telltale sign of crystallized air. When I looked back at Darius, he was smiling.

"I'll spend my favor on a kiss."

The words were so simple, but they made me question everything. I'd wondered if he'd been interested in me at all from the beginning. The way he'd touched me, the way he'd seen me and ignored me. Even the way that he'd slept next to me without clothes on had suggested that he had no desire for me.

But this told me the opposite.

"Why a kiss?" I asked.

His eyes seemed to glow as he talked. "You never understand a relationship until you've kissed someone. It's the one time that there are no lies. That simple act of pressing your lips to mine will tell me more than your words have since we met."

"What do you think they'll tell you?" I asked.

His eyes sparkled as he said, "That you want to make the same kind of deal that Kina did."

I felt the anger inside me begin to burn, and I had to make sure that I didn't manifest it outside of me. I would never make a deal to force someone into bed with me. I'd never even use a favor to do that.

"I'd never do that, *Prince*."

He smirked and said, "Maybe. Maybe not. I didn't say that you would. Just that you wanted to. Now, I said that I wanted a kiss."

The rage inside me began to boil even stronger with the way that he waited confidently. The way he dismissed my reaction as though I were a maiden who knew nothing of men and bedroom games.

I smirked this time and gave him a peck on the cheek. "Funny," he said.

"You never said anything more than a kiss. You should have been more specific."

As I stepped backward, off the block of crystallized air, I watched as Darius's eyes blazed with bright gold. A gust of wind lifted me into the air and forced me against the opposite wall.

Then the wind was gone, but I remained pressed against the wall. I felt as though I was bound, but there was nothing there. Until I saw that glimmer next to my body. He'd bound me in place with air.

At first, I was furious and did my best to struggle against my bondage, straining with all my strength against the invisible ropes that held me. No amount of straining or moving would loosen them in the slightest. The crystalline bondage was just as solid and smooth as any emerald or ruby.

He walked across the room without any rush, his hands in his pockets. "Fine, Princess. I'll use another favor, but this time you won't be able to cheat me out my kiss. You agreed to the gamble. Now you'll pay your debt to me. You should be thankful that I only requested a kiss."

There was no hint of the mischievous grin on his face any longer. Gone was the man that you could dismiss as being childish, and in his place was a man that exuded a strength that I'd never seen matched.

He moved his hand, and I felt my tunic begin to shift upward. "I could have requested far more." The wind that blew under my tunic caressed my body in ways that no man could have. Teasing my skin, I felt my body warm to the gentle touch. Another wind blew, slipping past the tops of my trousers and running between my legs. As soft as a lover's kiss, it made me shiver.

"Now, you'll kiss me, or I'll consider our agreement a farce, and you'll receive no trust from me again."

The wind continued to blow through my clothes, teasing my body, and though it didn't wash away the anger, it transformed it. I still wanted to lash out at Darius, to fight and claw at him, but I also wanted him to press his body against mine. He was so close to me that I could feel the warmth radiating from him, and I wanted his hands to touch my skin.

When he pressed his lips against mine, I felt that same warmth. Behind it was a passion that I'd never experienced. He'd been right. There were no lies when lips touched.

He was not harsh, but he was not gentle, and as his hand reached around my head to pull me to him, I didn't pull away. Then he released my head and took a step back. His eyes roamed over my body, and even though I was fully dressed, I felt more vulnerable than I ever had when I'd been naked before him.

This was more than demanding a kiss. This was overstepping a line that I would allow no one to cross. It had nothing to do with the mission, and it had nothing to do with his favor.

His gaze was on me rather than ignoring me this time. "Interesting," he said. "Not what I expected at all."

I wondered what he was thinking, but I didn't say anything. He put his hand to his chin and smiled. Then the winds that caressed my body stilled, and the crystalline ropes disappeared. I landed easily and adjusted my clothes before approaching him.

He'd done the one thing no one else in the world had ever done. I felt so vulnerable. He'd made me feel weak and manipulated me for the last time.

As soon as I was a foot away from him, I swung my fist. Just as fast as if I'd been using Shadow to strike down an enemy, my fist connected with Darius's jaw. He didn't crumple as an arden fae would have, but I knew that there would be a bruise tomorrow.

"Don't you ever do that again without my permission," I

snarled. "You are not my lover, and though you may hold favors over me, you will not force me like that. I am not your toy, and you will treat me with the same respect that I deserve."

He grinned. "Fair. I'll ask permission before I tie you up next time." As I turned to go to bed, I saw him rub his jaw out of the corner of my eye. It made me feel a little bit better.

But then Darius said, "I'm going to use another favor," and I stopped moving. Slowly, I turned around with anger in my eyes. He was still grinning as he said, "It's just a simple question, so no punches are needed."

"What do you want to know, Prince," I responded. His words hadn't diminished my anger in the least.

"I just want to know if hitting men after they kissed you was a normal thing for you, or if you reserved it only for me. I like the idea of being special."

"Just you, Prince. You're also the only man I've ever kissed that may end up on the sharp end of my sword."

I kicked my boots off and crawled into bed. I didn't turn around when I heard Darius undress, but when he got into bed beside me, I felt that warmth fill the space we shared under the sheets.

And I remembered the warmth that he'd brought to my body.

Chapter 16

The days passed uneventfully. Darius and I scouted out areas that we guessed would be places that Azulus and his army would pass through, but we wouldn't know for sure until they came closer.

The solen fae within the army were the next target. They would be far more difficult to deal with, though. Their wings would keep me from doing the same thing to them, and their hearing and skill with swords would allow them to fight me even if they couldn't see me.

As we landed in the forest outside Ms. Addie's orphanage, Darius stopped me. "Your illusion is fading. Turn around."

I looked up at him as he put his hands on my cheeks. His fingers pressed just a tiny bit more against my skin as he moved over my scales. "Are you unhappy that you don't get to see me without my clothes on anymore?" I asked.

He grinned and said, "I could if I wanted to. Remember that I still have six favors. Maybe I should use one to take your clothes from you tonight."

"Maybe I should use one to force you to wear trousers tonight," I snapped.

He huffed. "That's just rude."

"Well, it's rude to force someone to sleep naked too." His hands moved over my arms, and that warmth flowed through my body as it always did when he touched me.

"What kind of favors do you ask of other people?" I asked.

He chuckled with that mischievous look in his eye again. "All sorts of things. I've requested things just to see some people squirm. I could have you give me your clothes and then give you an illusion of clothing. Then we could go shopping in the village. You'd feel like everyone could see you even if they couldn't."

I shrugged. "I'm not as afraid of that as I once was. You've taught me that at least. I've tried to think of what I'd require you to do, but I can't think of anything."

"You just haven't decided what you want from me is all," he said. Without saying anything, he ran his hand under my tunic. He was hiding the scales along my sides. It sent shivers through me, and then, without warning, his hands tightened at my waist.

"What are you doing, Darius?" I whispered as my breath hitched in my throat. Just as I'd felt that day that he'd forced the kiss on me, I felt vulnerable. But this time, it was a good kind of vulnerable. The kind that could make a woman weak in the knees.

"I..." he paused for just a moment before releasing me. "Never mind, Princess. Let's go back to the orphanage. I have a date with a seven-year-old. She has a painting she wants to show me."

He turned around and began to walk towards the orphanage, but I stopped him. "What were you going to say?" I demanded.

He turned and smiled at me. "You can spend a favor if you want to know."

I chewed my lip. Another trick? Or was he trying to make me think that it was another trick? That man was infuriating. I'd felt something. It was unusual, something that didn't fit with the way that he was normally.

"Yes. I'll spend the favor. Tell me the truth of what you were going to say."

He shrugged and turned back to me. "I was going to say that I wished that I could actually use my favors how I desired."

"And how would that be?" I asked.

"Another favor? That would leave you with a single favor left." Gods, I wished that I'd won more hands of Thief. This was the most open he'd been since I'd met him. I needed to know what it was that was going on in his head, and I was sure that he would be honest.

"Yes, damn you. I'll spend the favor. Now, tell me what you want to use the favors on."

He smiled then. "I'd spend them all if you would just stop fighting what you felt. I can't force that, though."

I knew what he was talking about. He meant that I wanted him, that I wanted more than just our working relationship. I wasn't sure how I felt about him, though. He still infuriated me in ways that no one else in my life had. He still made me question whether I should help him or stab him.

But I couldn't ignore the way his touch made me feel.

119

Not any longer. That kiss, though it had been forced, had cemented the feelings in me. There was something there.

"What if you're wrong? What if I'm not feeling what you think I am?"

Darius's lips curled up in a smile. "I'll answer that for free. I'm not wrong. I'm never wrong when I've tasted a kiss. That's the difference between the solen fae and the arden fae. I was born to be free." He spread his wings to put additional emphasis on the difference between us. I couldn't see his actual wings because of the illusion, but I knew the way his shoulders moved by now.

"You're taught to control every little thing. There's not a single bit of you that's free. Right now, if I told you that you could do anything you wanted, if there was no war and no mission, what would you do? Probably exactly the same thing that you were already planning to do."

"That's why you live in caves instead of in the open air. Your people don't want freedom. They want to put little walls everywhere. Do this. Don't do that. Magic can do this. Magic can't do that. Your people didn't fight being caged, not really, and though the solens accepted chains, they chose the longest chains possible."

His words hit me hard. They were exactly what I'd said to my father time after time, but now that I did have some freedom, I hadn't done anything with it. I'd seen the sun and stars. I'd walked in the open air, but I hadn't enjoyed any of it. Not the way I should have.

"What if I agreed to do what you said? What if I stopped holding back? Would you go along with what I asked?"

Darius chuckled. "Princess, to see an arden fae lose control, I'd give a great many things."

"Then take me to the nearest river. I miss our baths."

The gold in Darius's eyes blazed for just a moment, but he wrapped his arms around my waist. "I guess that I'll have to look at Elana's painting tomorrow."

* * *

I looked at the lazy river that ran through the forest here. We were close enough to the mountains that it was crystal clear and reminded me of the Emerald River. "Take off your trousers," I said without looking at him.

I could already feel the tingling in my body, but I pulled my tunic off and dropped it on the bank. "No more favors, Darius." I turned around and looked at him. I knew the scales that ran over my breasts were gleaming in the sunlight for the first time in my life.

I pulled my own trousers off as I looked at his naked body. "And no more lies. Not with me. That's the trade I'm willing to make."

He grinned as he looked at me. "I'm not entirely sure what to think of this deal. You haven't told me what I get."

"You get me without the cage. You get a free arden fae."

He seemed to weigh the thought in his mind for a few moments and said, "Deal."

He raised his hand, and a gust of wind carried me through the air towards him. He caught me in his arms, and without hesitation, he kissed me. His lips only lingered on mine for a few moments before he pulled away from me and set me down.

"And the deal is sealed. Go play, Princess."

I ran my hand over his chest as I looked up at him. My nails dragged across his skin, and I wondered if he was afraid. With just a little pressure, I could force that sharpened point into his chest and pierce his heart.

"I didn't ask to come to the river to go for a swim, Darius. I asked so that you would come for a swim *with* me."

He cocked his head and grinned at me. "Why don't you lead. I enjoy looking at your backside."

I laughed and turned toward the river. Not bothered at all by him seeing me, I sashayed just a little bit as I walked, and as the cool mountain water ran over my calves, I turned to see him staring at me.

I grinned and dove into the water. It was barely deeper than the bathing pool in Assama, and as I stood up, my shoulders rose into the sunlight. It felt good to be wet again, and as Darius moved into the deeper water, his hand ran over my stomach.

"Why didn't you take advantage of touching me when we were in Assama?" I asked. "Any man I've ever met would have either been ashamed or would have done more than a little groping."

"I know it may come as a surprise, Princess, but the female body does not turn me into a fool. If I'd 'done more than a little groping', it would have pushed you away from me. You were barely accepting of me seeing you or touching you."

"And now?" I asked.

He didn't say anything, but his hands wrapped around my bottom and lifted me into the air. I wrapped my legs around his waist, and one of his hands ran up my side.

That tingling feeling rose inside me. His touch was wonderful and had been since the beginning. Since that very first time he'd run his hands over my body to hide my scales, I'd enjoyed his delicate touch. I looked into those golden eyes and saw more than the mischievous smile. Darius looked happy.

"Now, I might do a little more groping."

I smiled back at him and said, "Now that I know you won't lie to me, I want to know something."

"Ask away, Princess."

"Why do you enjoy spending your time in brothels?" I'd questioned it from the beginning. He had turned away every opportunity to spend time with other women, and I was sure that it had nothing to do with me. In fact, he hadn't said a single good thing about another woman. Yet, he obviously enjoyed brothels.

He pulled me away from him and set me down. "I already answered this question. Why ask it again?"

"Because I don't believe what you said."

He nodded and raised his hands. Air rushed into the water and lifted him into the air until he was sitting above the waterline on a block of crystallized air. His legs were spread and nearly all of him was visible except his feet, which hung in the water below him.

"What part of me do you notice first?"

The illusion around him disappeared. His black wings spread out around him, and even though most of him was impressive in comparison to most men, it was the wings that really drew my attention.

"Your wings," I said as I looked up at him.

He nodded. "Exactly. I'm the only person in the world with these wings. They mark me as a prince, and they mark me as dangerous. I can hide my wings and walk into a brothel. Everyone still knows me as Darius, but they forget the wings. They forget that I'm a prince. They forget everything about me except that I'm funny and enjoyable to be around. Nowhere else in the world can I do that."

"It doesn't hurt that the women are there. Just as I said before, I enjoy seeing a woman's body. More than that, I enjoy the way that people behave when they're in a tiny world outside of the normal bounds of society. Yes, I may see people that work for my father there, but they don't treat me any differently there. They still drink and fondle women. They still laugh too loudly and say things that may be taken wrong."

"Everyone there is free to be themselves except the whores. And when the whores are with me, I make sure to push them to be themselves. I go to brothels because brothels are the only place that I can be me and still be free."

Was he ignoring the fact that he enjoyed sleeping with those whores or did he simply not do it?

My lips curled in a smile this time. "How many nights do you spend with a woman in your bed when you stay at those brothels?"

"Ah, the arden princess is jealous," he said as the crystallized air disappeared, and he fell into the water, landing on his feet and splashing me just a little. "Do you want to know? Truly, what does it matter?"

I looked at him. He was everything that was against the arden way. A man who craved freedom. A man who did as he wanted without thought for the others around him.

"Yes. I need to know."

He smiled and said, "I have always slept alone, Princess. I've fucked a whore or two in my time, but I learned long ago that whores and I are better friends than lovers."

I blinked in confusion. "Why?"

"So full of questions today, Princess. I'm not going away anytime soon. Enjoy the water and ask your questions later when you're not standing next to the most beautiful man you know in a cool mountain river."

I laughed at his arrogance and dove under the water. He was right. There would be plenty of time to ask questions of him later. I saw fish as long as my arm swimming lazily, and, like a child, I began to chase them. They were quick, but I'd spent many days in my childhood swimming in the Emerald River.

I caught one by the tail without too much trouble and held it in both my hands. Turning to see where Darius was, I saw him sitting in the shallows with his long, sandy hair floating in the water just like in the bathhouse. With an impossible-to-remove grin, I made my way back to him.

The fish squirmed in my hands, but my claws held it tight. Not injuring it, but still holding in within the tiny cage.

As I got close to Darius, he picked his head up and smiled lazily at me. "Enjoy your swim?" he asked.

I didn't answer, but I crawled up in front of him, not wanting to let him know what I was doing. His eyes went to my backside as it stuck out of the water, and my grin got even wider.

Without any warning, I tossed the fish at him, and it hit him in the chest. He jumped out of the water, his wings flaring up around him as he rose into the air.

As soon as he was in the air, I couldn't hold back the laughter any longer and began rolling around in the shallows.

He slowly lowered himself back to where I was laying and laughing. "What did you just throw at me?" he asked.

"A fish," I said in between bouts of giggles. "No idea what

kind though."

"Why would you do that?" he asked as he sat back down, a smile beginning to appear at the edges of his lips. "What would possess a princess to throw a fish at someone?"

"I'm only a princess in title," I said, as I got the giggles under control. "I don't act like a princess, and I told you over and over again to call me Orlana instead of Princess."

"You said you wanted me to be an arden uncaged, and this arden fae thoroughly believed that you needed to be hit with a fish." The giggles almost started over again as Darius smirked at me.

"Why do you always call me Princess?" I asked as I lay backward, propping myself up on my elbows.

His fingers traced the scales that ran over the top of my breasts, and my breath began to come out more shallowly. I could already feel the blood rushing between my legs. It seemed that he'd become uncaged as well, no longer asking before he touched me.

"Because it pissed you off," he said. "And because you still act like a princess constantly."

"How would you prefer me to act? Like one of your whores?"

He raised an eyebrow. "Like someone who hasn't had the world given to them. Like the person you would be if you didn't get to choose what you did every day."

His hands moved down my stomach, and without asking, he pushed my legs apart. "You're still a spoiled princess. You've gotten better." His hand didn't stop where I'd expected it to, instead tracing the soft skin of my inner thigh.

"A princess wouldn't let you touch them like this," I said.

"Maybe not an arden princess, but a solen princess would.

You're all too prim and proper for this, but we solens enjoy the pleasures of the flesh enough to embrace them."

He pulled his hand away and stood up. "It's getting close to dark. We should be getting back to the orphanage. My father's army will be close tomorrow, and we have things to do. I've come up with a plan on how to defeat the solen fae, but we'll need to get a good sleep tonight."

And just like that, he slid the wall back up between us. I didn't know what I'd done to push him away from me, but as my heartbeat slowed and my breathing became normal again, I realized that he was right. The pleasures of the flesh may have been enjoyable, but we had a job to do, and no amount of touching would be worth a bad night's sleep.

I stood up and walked over to where Shadow and my clothes lay on the ground. As soon as I had my clothes on, I slipped Shadow's sheath over my shoulder.

"Gods, did I miss anything good? What did you do with him? Was he as sexy as he looks?" Shadow's words made me smile, but they also made me wince. I still wasn't sure if Darius was interested in more than touching. He seemed to believe that intimate touching was normal, but he'd never pushed for anything more. Even when it was obvious that I wouldn't have pushed him away.

And did I even want that? We had a good working relationship right now. Sex changed things. I enjoyed his touch, and I enjoyed his openness, but I wasn't sure if I wanted anything more.

"Not now, Shadow," I said softly.

"You can't just leave me waiting in anticipation like this. That man is hotter than fire, and you just went swimming with him. Naked. Your heart's still pounding. What'd you do?

I live my entire life vicariously through you, so you have to tell me what happened!"

I chuckled and whispered, "When we get back to the orphanage, I'll tell you all about it."

"What was that?" Darius asked as he approached.

"Nothing," I said. "Just talking to myself."

"Well, are you ready to go?"

I nodded, and he reached his hands around my waist. This time, he slid his hands under my tunic. Things had changed between us today, but I wasn't sure just how much. And I wasn't sure how much more I wanted them to change.

Chapter 17

"I'm going to take a walk," I said as I slung Shadow over my shoulder.

Darius sat up in bed and gave me a confused look. "Stay close to the orphanage, Orlana. My father's troops are close, and you won't see the solens flying, but they'll see you."

I nodded. "I just need a bit of air before I go to sleep."

I walked out of the room and down the stairs, staying as quiet as I could. When I slipped out the front door, I heeded Darius's warning. I moved to the well and sat under the roof.

"Finally! You could have talked to me before dinner, you know." I hadn't felt Shadow this excited in a very long time.

"We went swimming, just like when we bathed together," I said. "It wasn't really all that different. Though, he did touch me. It didn't get very exciting though. Just a few soft touches."

"That's it? He touched you? No more kissing? You didn't

climb on top of that mountain of a man?"

I chuckled. I was sure that Shadow hadn't been an arden fae in his previous lives. He wasn't nearly prim and proper enough, as Darius would have said.

"No, I did not climb on top of Darius. I did throw a fish at him, though."

Shadow began to laugh so hard that I could hear the sword rattling in the sheath. "What did he do? Was he scared? Did he throw one back at you?"

I shook my head. "He jumped out of the water, but as soon as the surprise was over, he settled back down. I don't think that solens are as at home in the water as I am. He probably couldn't catch a fish."

"Wow. A man that couldn't catch a fish. No wonder you didn't climb on top of him. Maybe I need to rethink whether I approve of him or not."

"Approve of him in what way?" I slid Shadow out of his sheath and looked down at the gleaming metal. It had only been a few days since I'd had to clean the blood of all those djinn off him.

"I was considering him for your husband, of course. He's a prince. You're a princess. He's beautiful. Especially that hair and those arms. I bet he could do all sorts of things that the other men you know couldn't dream of with those muscles."

"I don't see why you wouldn't consider it. It's not like you've been interested in any of the other princes you've met. Probably because their hair wasn't as nice as his."

I couldn't help but laugh. "I'm not going to marry Darius, Shadow. He doesn't seem to be the kind of man who would marry an arden fae, and we fight constantly. You saw me hit him just the other day."

"Well suit yourself. I'd marry him if I weren't in this blasted sword. I wonder if he'd ever consider marrying a sword."

"Doubtful. I don't think you have the right parts to keep him satisfied." Shadow had a way of helping me to work through my thoughts since he was always tapped into them. Even when I wasn't wearing him. He could talk to other people, but he was only bound to me.

But mostly, he just understood me because he'd always been there for me. "Do you think he actually wants more than what we have? I think that he simply enjoys being intimate with people. I think it's one of those differences between us."

"How much time have you spent on your mission versus time spent with each other playing and being intimate?" he asked.

I sighed. "It just doesn't make sense, Shadow. He hasn't made sense from the very beginning. Everything he does makes me question him."

"That's because you try to understand him. Maybe stop doing that. You said that you'd be free, so maybe you should do what you want and throw caution to the wind when it comes to Darius."

That was a more difficult thing for me to do than to take off my clothes and go swimming. How could I just stop worrying about all the little quirks about Darius? How could I ignore the things that didn't make sense? That was like asking me to wear a dress. It was against my very nature.

"I can try," I said. "That's all I can do."

"Then that will have to be enough." I stood up and slid Shadow into his sheath, closing the top clasp to hold him in place. "But Orlana, you've never felt like this with another man. Don't ignore it. That's me being an ancient soul who is doing his best to guide you, so don't ignore me either."

"I'll do my best to follow my heart at least a little more."

Chapter 18

The hearth roared to life, and I picked up the flux. I thought about the Emerald Castle's communication center, seeing the specific script carved above the hearth. I'd put this off for too long, and if I wasn't careful, my father would leave the Aedenian Mountains before I'd had a chance to speak to him.

Darius sat beside me as I threw the flux into the fire. The flames roared for only a moment before I said, "This is Princess Orlana. Please get King Finneon."

A voice answered from the flames, "Yes, Princess. Give us a few moments. Your father has been expecting you."

I was sure that he had been. I shouldn't have waited this long, but I'd been wrapped up in the doing rather than talking about it. I glanced at Darius, and he smirked. I wondered what he was thinking, but I didn't linger on it too long. He'd promised to be silent while I spoke to my father.

"Don't worry about it," Shadow whispered to me. "You caught him in time, and you've given him plenty of time to come to solid conclusions about what the other arden kings will do. There's no reason to stress about it."

I knew that Shadow was right, but it was difficult to keep from letting my mind focus on my tardiness. It wasn't like me.

My father interrupted my thoughts. "Orlana, I'm so glad to hear your voice. I was worried that something had happened to you."

Surprisingly, I was glad to hear his voice as well. Even though we fought, we'd never gone more than a day without speaking, and it had been weeks since I'd heard him.

"We have news," I said as I glanced at Darius again. The smirk was gone, and it had been replaced with a serious expression. "We've eliminated a significant portion of the djinn. We caught them in a surprise attack, and at least two hundred of the estimated two hundred and fifty are dead."

"Gods, Orlana. That's fantastic news. Both you and Prince Darius are safe, then?"

"Yes. We're safe, and tonight we plan to attack Azulus's army again. We're targeting the solen fae tonight. We can't slow them down yet, but we have plans on how we'll do that."

"Be careful when you deal with the solen fae, Orlana. Arturus will be with them, and we all know how dangerous he is."

I took a sharp breath as the realization washed over me. Arturus might be there tonight. I would have my chance at revenge. "Yes, Father. I understand how dangerous he is."

"I have news as well. All of the arden kingdoms have agreed to join the fight with the exception of the Ruby Plateau.

They've always been antagonistic to us, and I think they're choosing to stay out of the fight purely to spite me. That means that twelve thousand ardens will start the journey to Inoras in four days. All the Binders in all the kingdoms have been working day and night to make weaponry. We'll be ready."

Now that was a surprise. Arden fae were like bears. Until you poked them with a stick, they tended to stay in their comfortable dens, and everyone remembered the aftermath of the last war. This was a very un-arden thing.

"How did you manage to get them all to agree?"

"I told them that any kingdoms that stayed out of the fight would be dead to the Emerald Caverns. Even if we were forced back into hiding, they would never have any trade with us, and therefore, they'd have no trade with the outside world."

"Are you telling me that all of your trade deals and political maneuvering was preparation for this moment?"

Father began to laugh. "Orlana, I hate politics as much as you do. I swore to myself when I saw your mother die on the battlefield, that I would make sure that Arturus and his father died. I couldn't do that alone, and so I had to have some kind of power over the other kingdoms. That meant that I had to become a politician."

Shadow whispered to me, "See. Your mother wasn't wrong about him. He simply held his thoughts close to him just as you have. You're not all that different."

"Thank you, Father. I'm sorry that I doubted your purpose."

I could almost see him smiling through the fire. "It was better for everyone to think that my daughter was the only one of us who was striving for revenge, and there was no keeping you quiet about it. It played into everything perfectly."

There were whispered from the fire, and Father said, "I have to go now. There's still so much to get done. Good luck, Orlana, and stay safe. Stay away from the shadows if you do end up seeing Arturus. May your spark ever find tinder."

"And may your flame forever burn," I said back.

The fire went out and I stood up, shaken by the fact that my father had used my relationship to further his goals. It seemed cold, but would I have done anything differently? Hadn't it worked splendidly?

Like everything else I was learning, war was terrible, and sometimes you had to do what was necessary even if it hurt the people that you cared about. Could I accept that I'd been a tool if we'd had a common goal?

I thought I could, but then I turned to Darius, and there wasn't a smile on his face. Something that my father had said bothered him as well. He stood up and began to pace. His wings didn't extend and retract, so he was just thinking. There wasn't any anger in him.

I would let him think. I had enough to worry about on my own.

At the same time, I knew that the arden fae were committed to the war. They would make victory possible. We were still significantly outnumbered, but numbers didn't matter when you had strength and skill on your side.

Things were working out, and we didn't have to slow Azulus down by much. A few days at most, and the ardens would have time to get to Inoras. We needed to deal with the solen fae and the ifrits though.

One step at a time. Tonight, we would decimate the solen fae. Then we'd deal with the rest.

Chapter 19

I looked at the rigging we'd made. We'd woven hundreds of vines together to cover the area with just enough space for a head to fit through, but not enough to fit a man's shoulders. It had taken us all day long to run them together into the massive mesh. Thin ropes we'd bought in the village ran across the outside edges and held the vines together.

The woven vines hung almost fifteen feet in the air from the branches of the trees on either side. The two ropes had plenty of slack on my side, and plenty of slack on his side as well. I pulled mine, and the entire mesh slid as if it were on tracks, opening the area up. Darius did the same on his side, and the mesh slid closed over top.

I only had to cut two ropes and the whole thing would collapse on top of the solen fae when they landed. It was a good plan as long as I could move fast enough.

"When do you want to go?" I asked.

"Let's wait until nightfall. If they see me flying in the daylight, they'll know they're following us into a trap, but they might move without thinking as much if they see me flying at night without an illusion. It's still stupid and may not work, but it's more feasible at night."

I looked up at the sun and saw that it was hanging low. Only a few hours until sunset now. I wiped the sweat from my brow and said, "Well, what do you want to do until then?"

He reached into his back pocket and pulled out the deck of cards. "A game?" he asked with a smirk.

"I thought we agreed no more favors."

He shrugged. "We don't have to play for favors. We could always play for higher stakes."

I arched my eyebrow at him and said, "I don't think anything good will come from me playing that game with you."

Darius shook his head. "That's too bad. Maybe another time then."

"Yeah, maybe another time." The last thing I needed was to end up angry at Darius for winning again.

"You're an odd man, Darius. You enjoy the gambling more than the spending of your winnings."

He grinned. "Caught that, did you? I play for money all the time, but money means so little to me that I don't care. Favors matter, and outside of me and you, there is at least some purpose to having them. Most people are willing to risk being in my debt at the possibility of me being in theirs. It makes the game interesting."

"But you don't enjoy that power over people. That's what I mean. Most men would hold the debt over someone, but you didn't. Not really."

He shrugged. "That's not me. I don't want people to dislike me even if they owe me. They stop playing my games if they hate me." He grinned. "If I'd held those favors over your head, would you have gone swimming with me yesterday?"

"No, I certainly wouldn't have." He turned around and began to pace.

"I hate the waiting part," he said. "It's frustrating that everything's ready and we can't do anything to hurry it along."

I sighed and said, "Fine. Come play cards with me, but there are no stakes. Teach me how to play better so that maybe you can convince me to play for stakes later. I might even be convinced to play for higher stakes."

He turned around immediately with that childish grin on his face. "This is your first lesson. Thief, and most card games, aren't about what cards you get. They're about what cards you project and about how much information you have on your opponent. Just now, I knew that you wanted to do something, but there was nothing to do. I just had to continue to make you think about it, and you decided on your own to play."

"So you're admitting to manipulating me?" I asked.

"Absolutely." His expression told me that he thought that was the stupidest thing he'd ever heard.

"Now, come sit down and I'll teach you how to be a good card player, but first, let's be rid of these illusions."

With a wave, both of our illusions disappeared. "I'll put yours on again after the game, but it's easier to see what I'm saying if you can see yourself."

He closed his eyes for a second, and I felt a strange warmth flow through me, and then an exact replica of myself appeared from thin air next to him. "Watch your face," he said.

My eyes widened as I realized that he hadn't just made

an illusion, he'd made a mirror of me from nothing. The illusion's face changed just as mine did. "You can never understand what you're giving away until you see it on your own face. When I was younger, I played cards with my brother Marcellus, and I placed a mirror between us so that I could see what I looked like."

"That's incredible," I whispered. "You could do so much with this in battle."

He shrugged. "I prefer to use it when teaching cards. Focus, Orlana."

And so the lesson began in how to trick people while playing cards.

Chapter 20

The world was coated in silver as the full moon shined down on us. A perfect night for him to be seen. Darius handed me his Binding pendant and said, "Now, I'm going to lead the solen fae back here. As soon as they land, spring the trap. If you miss a few, it doesn't matter, but if you take too long, they'll spot the trap, and we'll be dead."

I nodded to him. He took one more step towards me and put his hand on my arm for just a moment. "Stay hidden until the trap is sprung, Orlana. They will kill you if they find you before that."

I looked down and saw that he'd made me into shadows. "He doesn't have to touch a spot to give it an illusion," Shadow whispered.

I grinned at him, but I didn't mention Shadow's words. "Fly safe and fly fast, Darius the Silent. I'd prefer that you didn't die tonight."

He bowed his head and said, "May the wind be at your back, Princess Orlana."

And then he leaped into the air, leaving me huddling behind the bushes. He'd never seemed to be the brave one, but I knew what kinds of powers the solen fae had. He'd have to be a fool to be ignorant of the dangers, but he seemed confident.

We'd been incredibly successful with our first attack. But we'd taken them fully by surprise. No one had been expecting arden Bindings in any attack, and they probably didn't expect us to attack at all. Now, I was sure that they'd be more prepared for us. There were people that could sense Darius. At least when he wasn't wearing his pendant. That's how they tracked everyone that used magic. Especially elves.

The minutes turned into hours as I sat next to the tree that held the first rope I had to cut. "Are you ready to do this?" Shadow asked.

"I don't know," I whispered back. "I think so."

"This will be harder than the last time. Focus on the Flames of Sight." I nodded. Emotions couldn't be involved. I turned inward and let the sound of a bonfire fill my mind. Not the gentle crackling of the Flames of Peace.

Fire was purifying. Sometimes, healing could only happen after something was destroyed, and this meditation reminded me of the purpose. Yes, these men had to die, and though it was a tragedy, it couldn't be stopped. More death would follow if they were allowed to live through the night.

I opened my eyes and scanned the skies again. Darius said that he was the fastest of the solen fae, and I believed him. Though he was arrogant, he knew where he stood in relation to the world around him.

A glimmer of movement. Black against the silver sky. He was coming. I climbed the tree without any trouble and unsheathed Shadow. Darius hit the ground hard, his wings flaring around him to slow him just enough to keep him from breaking bone.

But no dust rose into the air around him. This was an illusion. Darius would be on the other side of the trap already. I looked up and saw white wings in the night sky, gleaming silver in the moonlight. Hundreds of them. They dove just as he did, and as the illusion began running for the tree cover, the solen fae dove around him, hitting the ground with audible thumps.

I saw the trap closing over top of the solen fae as most of them landed. Several were still circling in the sky, and a call went out from them as the vines slid over the heads of the rest.

Initially, the illusion of Darius had stopped as the solen fae surrounded him, but then, when the call of surprise came, the solens hesitated. I cut the rope before it was all the way across and leaped through the trees until I was on the other limb. Shadow sliced through the second rope, and the whole netting fell on top of the solens.

Several of them had moved quickly enough to get out from under it, but they were still far from me. I dropped to the ground and grabbed an edge of the netting. Using one of the more difficult Firebrand techniques, I forced fire to spread across the netting.

The entire thing roared to life in an instant. The feathers of the solens caught fire first, and gusts of wind rose in all directions as they tried to put it out. Most of them had never fought a well-trained Firebrand, though. The winds only fanned the flames as I continued to push my power through the vines. Screams rose in the air as the fire began to burn flesh.

Several of the solens cut themselves out of the flaming net, but their wings were already too burnt to fly, and crystal shards of air found homes in their chests as Darius ended their lives quickly.

I finally had to let go of the vines as four of the solens who had escaped found me. The ones that had circled had landed as well. Each of them brandished their weapons as they circled around me.

This was what I'd trained for all of my life. I reached down and sent flames to two of the solens, forcing the fire to flare from the ground around their feet. The tips of their wings caught, and they rolled on the ground.

The other ten rushed at me, but they were too big. I put out a hand, and flames streamed from my fingertips, catching two in the shoulders. They screamed as the rest of the solens reached me.

I dove, using the only Stone Discipline I knew. Stone rose up in a tube that I slid through. It was ugly work that no Stonewaker would have been proud of, and as the solens beat on the tube, it crumbled.

I slid past the circle and was on my feet in the blink of an eye, flames roaring from my fingertips towards the huddled group of solen fae. Most of them caught fire, and the ones that didn't catch fire rose into the air, no longer feeling as confident in their ability to defend themselves against me.

I raced to the solens who were rolling on the ground, trying to put out the fires that covered their charred wings. Without hesitation, I slammed Shadow into their chests just as I'd done to the djinn.

A group of solens hovered in the air above us out of range of my fire. On the ground were more than a hundred dead and dying solens. Groans were suddenly ended as Darius walked across the charred ground invisibly ending their lives one at a time.

Then a shadow hit the ground outside of the netting, and I knew who I was looking at. Arturus the Hunter. The one man I wanted to kill more than anyone in the world.

He stared at me with eyes that glowed yellow even in the darkness. I knew his power over shadows. I watched as the dark bits of the world began to come to life. I swept out and felt the strange tingling fill my arms as Shadow absorbed the magic that gave them life.

"Watch him. Tell me what he's doing," I whispered.

"He's just watching right now. He's trying to kill you without having to get close. He's afraid of the fire."

And so I swept through the shadows, burning his magic up as I went. He was powerful. I knew that. It would take a long time before he'd be forced to fight me.

"Darius, call off your bitch," he said. "I would prefer it if I wasn't forced to kill you both."

"You chose father," Darius's voice said, and Arturus glanced toward it.

"I chose life, brother. You should have as well."

A shimmering light flashed just behind Arturus, and he spun, the giant two-handed sword coming down as a shard of crystallized air flew towards him. The sword crashed into the crystal, and it shattered, turning back into air immediately.

Hands gripped my waist, and I saw that my body was invisible instantly. Without a sound, Darius lifted me into the air and left Arturus on the ground behind us. The remains of the solen army were circling above us.

For the first time in my life, I'd seen the man that I wanted revenge on more than anyone else. And now Darius was taking me away from him. Why hadn't he fought him? Why hadn't we worked together to kill him?

A whisper on the wind came to me. "Don't make a sound, and we'll survive. You cannot win a fight with my brother."

I had to bite my lip not to lash out at him, not to reveal us both. Darius must have his reasons. He must. Maybe we were outmatched, or maybe he knew something that I didn't.

So, I followed his directions and waited silently until he brought us to our next stop.

Stormcrest.

Chapter 21

Stormcrest was a city unlike any I'd seen. Walled in gray stone with a keep, it was the port city of the Caston Kingdom. The keep was the home of the Duchess Aleera, and she ruled with an iron fist. Two different husbands had died early in their marriage, and she'd had no suitors since.

Darius landed in an alley. We'd flown the entire way completely invisible, and seeing him again was jarring. He was covered in blood from the solens he'd killed. Thoughtfully, he'd picked up our bag of Binding supplies.

He flicked his hand, and when I looked down, my scales and claws were gone. Just one more thing that bothered me about the whole thing. "We need to find a place to hide for a few days. My father will be furious, and if there's not solen fae over the city now, there will be. They won't engage us. Not after what we did to the rest of them, but they'll let my father

147

know where we are, and he'll burn this city to the ground."

I bit my lip. It wasn't the right time to have it out with Darius. But that time was coming, and it would be soon. "A tavern?" I asked.

He nodded and took a breath. The blood that covered his body disappeared, but I knew that it was an illusion. Over his chest, a tunic hung, and his hair had become short brown hair. I was sure that mine was long and brown just as it had been elsewhere.

He led the way out of the alley, and I followed him, Shadow on my back beneath an illusion. Even Shadow was quiet. He knew how angry I was, how much I wanted the chance to go back to that clearing and end the man who'd killed my mother.

Darius didn't walk long, turning into an old building made of dark wood with a creaking sign that read, "The Dancing Pig Tavern", with a crude painting of a pig on it.

Unlike the brothels, the men who drank here were quiet. There was no splashing ale as people sang songs or gambled. Too many of the men stared with nearly empty eyes, and my hand itched to draw Shadow from his sheath.

Darius walked to the bar and said, "I need a room."

The barkeep looked him up and down before saying, "That's twelve bits for the night. Comes with dinner for the two of you."

Darius dug into a small pouch at his side and pulled out a few bits of silver. Where he'd gotten any bits was beyond me since they were only used in this part of the world.

The barkeep dug under the counter for a key and slid it to Darius. "Bar yer door while yer sleepin'." He glanced at me and said, "Stormcrest is in an unruly state these last few weeks. You look like a fella that can take care of 'imself, but wouldn't want the missus getting hurt."

"I'll be sure to do that," Darius said and took the key from the barkeep.

"Second door on the left at the top o' the stairs," the man said as he went to fill another mug with ale.

Darius immediately turned and walked towards the stairs. They creaked as we walked up them.

When we slipped inside our room, Darius closed the door behind him. Now was the time to find out why we'd left.

I turned on him and said, "Why'd you run away?"

"Not now, Princess. Not now." He turned away from me and went to a chair at the tiny table that rocked on crooked legs. In his hands, a bottle of wine and two cups appeared. He'd stolen them from the bar, and he poured us both a cup filled to the brim.

I didn't touch mine, and I didn't sit down. "Why not now? Arturus was right there. We could have killed him. He hasn't fought an arden fae in centuries. Between the two of us, he'd be dead."

Darius drank the entire cup of wine and poured himself another. "Don't you think we did enough tonight? Don't you think that there's enough blood on both our hands for one night?"

I thought back to how those solen fae had screamed, how the smell of charred feathers and flesh had filled the air. Yes, it was terrible, but I'd found my purpose in it. We would be the ones who would accept the pain of what we'd done so that those that we loved would survive. "Our mission is to kill, Darius," I snarled. "Are you no longer up to the task?"

He poured the second cup of wine down his throat before

throwing the cup at the wall. I'd never seen wood shatter before, but this cup exploded into splinters as it hit the opposite wall. He stood up and faced me then.

"You want Arturus dead. I understand. He killed your mother, and he ruined your life. Remember, Princess, you're not the only one that matters. He's my brother, and it's not his fault that he's in this war any more than it's your sword's fault that it's in the war."

I snarled at him again, the sound coming from low in my throat. "You're choosing your brother over the mission? He chose his side. How many times has he chosen that same side? How many times has he chosen the side of evil? He may be your brother, but he's just as at fault for this war as your father is."

Faster than I could blink, Darius was in front of me, his hand gripping my neck. He continued moving until my body slammed into a wall. "My brother is not like my father, Princess. He's been twisted and broken in more ways than you can imagine, even worse than I have, and I will not be the one who holds the sword to his throat."

Flames coated my skin as he pressed me against the wall, leaping from my skin to Darius's hand. He pulled away as pain shot through him. This would not go the same way that it had in the bath.

I kicked him in the chest, making him stumble backward. "You're a coward, Darius. That's what it is and nothing more. The only solen fae who does not wield a blade. The only solen fae who is not a warrior. The child who will never grow into a man. Even the female solens become warriors, Darius. Only you refuse the path. A spoiled prince who has survived on his father's power."

Darius glared at me with rage in his eyes. "You don't know what you're talking about. You call me spoiled, but what have you done with your life? What have you done for anyone?"

"I prepared myself for this moment in my life. Unlike you, I was ready to kill. How many people have you fought since we started this mission? It seems like all you're good at is getting into women's beds and hiding."

In a flash, he crossed the distance between us, but I was ready for him. My fist flashed forward, fire coating it, and he ran into it. But he didn't stop moving. My fist pressed against his chest, burning his skin, but he forced me backward until I hit the wall again.

I could smell the charred flesh of his chest, but he ignored the pain that I was sure was shooting through his body. He stared into my eyes as the flames moved across his skin, consuming it. "I am anything but a coward. I have lived a life of pain like none you could imagine. Where you were given chance after chance to grow, I was punished for not being like my father and my brothers. I was beaten bloody every day. I had no one to trust except my brothers. That includes Arturus."

"And I learned that pain and sadness and the rest of the shit in the world were endurable as long as you had a purpose."

His hand went to my neck, and his fingers wrapped around my throat, tightening until I couldn't breathe. I lashed out with my other hand, claws outstretched as I sliced at his wrist and arm. Stripe after stripe of crimson rose along its length, but he didn't seem to notice it.

Those fingers didn't let up as they threatened to crush my throat. He stared at me with those golden eyes as my body used every bit of air left in me to try to escape his grasp, but it was no use.

"My father is that purpose, Princess. Not Arturus. My entire life has been filled with nothing but pain, and even it doesn't compare to Arturus's, so no, I will not help you with your vendetta against him."

My fire went out as my vision began to blur. He released me, and I fell to the floor in a crumpled heap. When I had finished gasping for air, and my vision was clear again, I looked up at Darius who was drinking the wine straight from the bottle.

His arms were still dripping blood onto the floor, and his chest was scorched from one side to the other.

My anger wasn't sated, but I knew that there was nothing I could do to him unless I was actually going to try to kill him. I glared at him as he set the bottle down, empty this time.

"What could you possibly have to complain about, *Prince?*" I snarled at him. "You grew up with all the freedom in the world. You've had nothing but a life of luxury."

He picked up my wine cup and downed it as well. "My mother killed herself when I was barely a man because my father was so horrible. Your mother died in battle, but both of your parents loved you. My father hated me from birth, and he set out to show it."

I didn't know that, and I wondered how bad Azulus must have been. What kind of terrors must Azulus have brought to their family?

"When you were learning to fight, did you get a mentor, Princess? Did you have someone teach you to use your abilities?"

"How else is someone supposed to learn?" I asked.

"My father handed me two daggers and fought me. Every day. He didn't teach me. Didn't train me. He fought me every single day for two hundred years, and he hurt me bad enough that if there hadn't been a healer standing nearby, I would have died. Every. Single. Day."

"No mentor or teacher was allowed to help me. No one understood my powers because I'm the only person in the world that only has a touch of umbran fae in me. Every solen fae bit of me has a tinge of difference. That's why my wings are black, and dear Father told me that only I could learn my powers. Until I did, I would nearly die every day."

I thought of my father. I'd fought him with words and actions my entire life because our ideology of how to help the arden fae differed so much. I couldn't imagine having him hurt me. Especially not like that.

"That's terrible," I said.

Darius shrugged. "I had it easy. Arturus had it worse than me or Marcellus. Father believed that Arturus was too soft when he was young, so not only did he force him to train with him, he also brought him down to the dungeon every day."

"Each day, Arturus, at the ripe old age of ten, was forced to execute a prisoner in a new way. The one thing that never changed was that the prisoner was never executed slowly. Can you imagine how broken you'd be if your own father had forced you to flay a man when you were ten?"

I turned away in shame. He'd always been the enemy in my mind. Always. The very thought of him had brought flames of hate to the surface, but now that I knew what he'd gone through, I couldn't think of him the same way.

"He's still the enemy, Darius. He may be broken, but we're all broken to some degree, and he chose the other side."

Darius shook his head. "No, he didn't. He can't choose something different. He doesn't know how. Arturus is bound to my father just as much as you're bound to the arden race. There's nothing in the world that would convince you to fight for anyone else, is there? Even if it was the right decision, you'd always choose your people. Well, Arturus's people is my father. He'll never turn away from him until my father is dead."

He looked down at me then. "My goal when I joined this little rebellion was to kill my father to free all of us. Arturus may fight against us if he's forced, but he doesn't want to. And I won't force him to choose between me and my father because he can't make that choice."

I understood why Darius was making this stand, but I couldn't accept it. I couldn't accept that the one man in the world that I wanted to kill was the one man Darius wouldn't.

"You'd let our mission fail to save your brother?" I asked. "You say that you won't make Arturus choose, but what if I made you choose? Would you choose him or the rebellion?"

Darius didn't answer, and I stood up slowly. "There's only one right answer, Darius, and you know it. If he's that broken, then the only answer is to put him down. Eventually, you'll have to make that choice because one day, we're going to fight your father, and Arturus will fight beside him."

Darius stared at the wall in front of him and said, "I think that I'm going to need more wine." Then he stood up and walked out of the room.

"What am I going to do?" I whispered.

Shadow spoke up. He'd been strangely quiet this entire time. "Don't make him choose, Orlana. Not yet."

"How can I accept that decision? How can I just wait?"

"Don't push him away by forcing that decision on him. Could you kill your father to save the world? He loves his brother as much as you love your father, and though you're right, that doesn't make it any easier."

I tried to trust Shadow, but this was something that needed to be worked out sooner rather than later. He needed to know which side he chose if it came down to a fight. Would he let Arturus kill me rather than fight alongside me?

I took a deep breath and let it out slowly as the crackling Flames of Peace washed over me. "I will give him time, but not long. When we make our next move, I need to know where he stands."

Chapter 22

I woke the next morning after a fitful sleep to see Darius sitting at the table dressed and ready for the day. The scent of something hung in the air that I couldn't place. When I rolled out of bed, I saw he had two cups sitting on the table, and he was sipping out of one. Steam rose from the cup.

The first thing that ran through my mind was the beautiful warmth from a cup of ignas tea, but when I approached, I saw that the drink was black rather than crimson.

"What is that?" I asked.

Darius chuckled as he took another sip. "Coffee," he said. "It's hot, so don't burn yourself."

He continued to stare past me at the simple wooden wall as I sat down across from him. I picked up the cup and inhaled a bit of the steam. Strangely earthy, it didn't smell like any tea I'd had before.

As soon as the first drops hit my mouth, I set the cup back on the table. "What kind of sludge do they make that out of?" It tasted like someone had burned a bowl of dirt and run hot water through it. Actually, that would probably taste better."

"Guess that I get two cups today," he responded quietly as he pulled my cup to him without looking at me.

"We're going to wait for my father to cross into the Marshes of Sorrow before we attack again. They'll be on high alert now, but that will be the best place for an ambush, and it will be the best chance we have of slowing them down. You can't cross the Marshes without bridges, and that big bag of explosions will go a long way in isolating the troops on the islands."

After last night, he was already focused on what to do next. I wanted to apologize, but he was letting it go. The last thing I wanted was to bring up the emotions that had pushed him to leave last night. He'd said that the only thing that mattered was the mission, and I would fall back on that.

"I don't know anything about the Marshes of Sorrow. I saw them on the map, but they're not talked about much in any reports."

Darius nodded and said, "They never are. Everyone goes around them whenever possible, but my father won't. He's grown so cold that even the remnants of the past don't break through the ice around his heart, and it's the shortest route to Inoras."

He drank the last of his cup and picked up mine. "I apologize if I hurt you last night, Orlana. I shouldn't have allowed myself to become as angry as I did. It was hard killing those solen fae. I knew far more of them than the djinn. They were my brothers, after a sort. Like if you were forced to kill your own

157

people. That's no excuse, though. I won't let it happen again."

I glanced at Darius's chest then and noticed that it and his arms were already healed. "I shouldn't have pushed you as I did," I said. "I need to know where we stand, though. I need to know where I stand compared to your brother. What happens if it comes down to me or Arturus. Who would you pick?"

Darius shook his head as he drank the disgusting coffee. "I don't know, Princess."

I nodded in understanding. I didn't blame him. Not really. Not after last night's conversation. It was important to know where I stood, though. Even if it hurt more than I liked to admit. Darius had grown on me, but even if he enjoyed my company, family was different from friendship. He'd murdered many of his friends last night.

I stood up and said, "Well, let's go see these Marshes of Sorrow. It sounds like we need to decide where to place the explosives and where to attack the ifrits."

Darius finished his coffee and nodded.

* * *

Darius's hands held me as they had the first time we'd flown. Fingers on the outside of my tunic. There wasn't even the slightest bit of inappropriate touching as we flew through the sunlit sky.

The marshes were laid out below us. Covered in fog and mist, they were exactly as the old texts had described them. A place of unimaginable sorrow. A place where a man's greatest fears and nightmares came to life.

Broken and dead limbs rose above the mists like skeletal

fingers begging for rescue. Dark spots in the mist represented the various islands. There would be small wooden bridges from one island to the next that crossed the swampy water that no one dared to enter.

"The Marshes of Sorrow are nothing like what your books describe, Princess. The arden fae are wonderful at many things, but exploring the world and understanding the magical places in it is not one of them."

He descended as he continued to talk. "They are not haunted, as the villagers say, and they are not possessed by evil spirits, as the priests say. My mother told me the true story of them."

"Before they were filled with magic as they are now, it was a simple swamp. Nothing menacing or terrifying about them other than the insects and the terrible humidity. But then there was a battle between two kingdoms. This was before my father had come to power, and kingdoms warred constantly."

"They clashed in this swamp. As is the case in most battles, the most casualties occur when the opposing sides are evenly matched. In this battle, two kingdoms had brought their entire forces, and the battle took two days. Each king fought to secure island after island while maintaining their own."

"During those two days, a terrible storm blew in from the sea. The waters rose, and all the men on those islands were trapped as the bridges were flooded. The waters continued to rise, and eventually, the battle was forgotten as two hundred thousand men and elves were drowned."

"When the storm had passed, elves gathered from all over the world and came to this swamp. Five thousand elves had died in that battle, a tragedy that had never happened on such a large scale in all of history. The elves that had come created a monument in their way."

"So that no one would forget the sorrows of those two days, they cast a spell over this swamp. Forever, it would be hallowed ground, and any who stepped on those islands would watch as their greatest sorrows came to life. This way, any of the elves who had loved ones that had fallen in that storm could come and see them again any time that they wished."

I stared down at the mists as we approached them. I didn't doubt Darius. I had no doubt that he was telling the truth, and it terrified me. There was only one memory that I had that could be called sorrow.

And what would the mists hold for Darius? What would be his sorrow? I would soon find out.

Chapter 23

The islands were broken and dead things. The entire world seemed to be made of browns and grays except for the black water that surrounded the islands. Mist swirled like phantasms, but it wasn't as thick as I'd thought, and I could see to several other islands, though they looked even grayer because of the mist.

"Time for the show to begin," Darius said, with a hint of sadness in his voice. He looked around for a moment and then wrapped his arms around my waist again. When he jumped, it only took three flaps of his wings before we landed on a thick branch from one of the dead trees.

I scooted off Darius's lap, feeling none of the warmth that I'd felt before, and I looked down. The mist began to thicken below us, and Darius put his hand on my thigh. "I'm sorry for whatever you see. This place is terrible, and there's a reason that people go weeks out of their way so that they don't have to cross the mists."

I shrugged. I'd accepted my past. I knew the greatest trauma I'd ever experienced.

"I'll be fine," I said. "It's just memories, right?"

Darius shook his head, but he didn't say anything. I looked down and saw a beautiful arden woman. Dressed in the silversteel armor of an arden warrior. She crouched with a long sword in her hands. I knew the position. A basic defensive stance.

The figure began to change from the gray of the mist. Colors blossomed in the woman. The armor shined. Her long red hair blew in a non-existent wind. The scales that ran across her face were deep blue and crimson.

Just like my mother.

I looked closer and saw the sword for what it was. Shadow Soul. "Gods," Shadow whispered to me. "I'm sorry, Orlana."

Then, Arturus was formed from the mist on the other side of the island. Wings of shadow. Eyes of gold. A massive two-handed sword in his hand. I'd heard the story of how this fight went.

But I'd never seen it. Never experienced it.

Darius's hand gripped my thigh tightly as my mother faced down Arturus.

"Why wouldn't you just leave us in peace, Arturus?" she asked with nothing but sadness in her voice.

"I do as my father commands. You know this." His eyes burned, but they didn't seem to be the hateful eyes that I'd always pictured.

"We were friends, Arturus. You showed me Kharn the first time that I came to see your father's kingdom. We ate and drank. We danced and sang. Nothing has changed between us, yet you stand prepared to kill me."

His eyes burned even brighter. "Yes, we were friends, Sorchna. That doesn't change the fact that I cannot disobey my father. I cannot turn from my duty any more than you can turn from yours."

"I don't want to fight you, but I will. Turn around. Take your people. Hide in your mountains, and I swear that I will never hunt for you there. If we fight, you will lose, and you will die."

My mother's eyes darkened, and I knew the expression. The Drums of Pain. Each scream from her fellow arden would fill her with fire. A meditation that I'd never felt the need to use.

"Being caged in the mountains would be as good as being dead. I'll never allow you to cage my people." She raced towards him. Even knowing how strong of a warrior Arturus was, she didn't turn away from the fight. I was my mother's daughter.

Dark shadows rose from the ground around him, transforming into vines with bladed tips. My mother leaped, fire propelling her upward into the sunlight and away from the shadows that would fight against her.

Arturus was ready, though. Two hounds grew from his own shadow, and low growls rumbled from their throats. The Hunter's hounds were legendary. Massive creatures whose shoulders rose to a man's waist with gnashing teeth that could pierce steel and who feared nothing.

And whose only purpose was in causing death.

My mother seemed ready, though, and with a quick lunge, she thrust Shadow through one of them. Arturus immediately lashed out with his sword, but my mother was faster. A stone pillar rose from the ground, and Arturus's sword crashed into it with a loud clang.

Mother rolled around the pillar, flames spouting from her fingertips. Arturus was fast enough to get out of the way, but the hound wasn't, and with a pitiful wail, it dissipated into nothingness.

Arturus began his assault then. Quick strikes that my mother deflected deftly. They were safe strikes that didn't leave him open, and I watched in horror as he began to push her backward across the stony clearing. Each time she tried to use fire, his sword would move to block it, the steel drawing the magic from the attack.

On and on, they danced, Arturus constantly gaining ground, and my mother taking one step backward at a time until she made a fatal mistake.

She stepped too close to a large rock. Its shadow twisted out into a vine with a blade for a tip. Impossibly thin, and impossibly sharp, it slid under her cuirass, and without a sound, it pierced her back, severing her spine.

She screamed as she fell, and after Arturus gave the battlefield a quick glance, he said, "I'm sorry that it has to be like this, Queen Sorchna."

I felt myself tear up as I watched my mother writhe on the ground, her legs no longer functioning. Pain was in her eyes, but anger was there as well. "Damn you, Arturus," she snarled. "You know your father is evil. You know that you're decimating an entire race of fae, and for what?"

"For loyalty, Sorchna. For family. There is nothing greater than those." He raised that wicked sword of his over my mother's breast. She reached out with her hand, but before she could spray him with flames, he thrust the blade through her breast.

"I'm sorry," he said to her before pulling his blade from her body. "I counted you as a friend, but when it comes time to decide between friends and family, I'll always choose family."

He turned to walk away, and a scream of rage filled the air. Materializing in the blink of an eye, my father ran toward Arturus, but shadows wrapped around his ankles, trapping him.

He turned his sword to them, but he stopped when Arturus spoke. "Take your dead, and go to the mountains, King Finneon. Take your wife and burn her body. Mourn her. Do not make the mistake of continuing this battle."

"You monster!" my father shouted as he cut through the shadowed vines and began his charge again.

Arturus's head hung low, but he didn't give up. New shadows attached themselves to his legs, and another rose up, a blade on the tip. As my father moved to sever the ones that were attached to his legs, the blade pressed against his neck.

"You have a daughter, King Finneon. Do not make her an orphan. Accept defeat and go back to your mountain homes. Hide. Survive. If you continue this battle, I'll be forced to kill every single arden fae. Accept this kindness that I give my friend's husband and her child."

My father shook, but then he looked around at the massacre of his people, and he dropped his sword. "I hate you, Arturus. I will never stop fighting you and your father, but I will retreat. For my people and my daughter."

Arturus nodded and took to the sky on wings of shadow. This was how my father had survived when my mother hadn't. Arturus had given them the chance to retreat. Arturus hadn't wanted to kill my mother, and even when given the chance, he hadn't killed my father.

I took a deep breath as all of my feelings about Darius's brother were broken inside me. He hadn't been the enemy. He'd only been the sword carried by the enemy, and a sword does not choose who it slays.

I looked at Darius whose eyes held plenty of sadness. "I'm sorry," I said.

"You don't know my brother. I don't blame you for hating him. He's a horrible person who has done horrible things. He's broken, and broken people do what they have to do to survive."

The mists dissipated for a few moments. Then they became thick again, and it was my turn to put my hand on Darius's thigh. "I'm glad I understand better now," I said.

I turned to watch as new people grew from the mists below us. King Azulus was the first one to appear. I would know him anywhere, even though I'd never seen him. He was the only umbran fae in the world. Skin as black as night with white lines of powers like djinn that ran over his entire body.

Darius appeared next, standing in front of Azulus. Beside him, a beautiful woman stood wearing a sela, the traditional dress of Kharn. "Damn," Darius whispered, "I should have known this was what the mists would show."

"Father, I'd like to ask your permission to marry Yasmin." He seemed so scared yet excited, and I wondered what this scene was about.

The woman stood up straight, but she was afraid. Everyone was afraid of Azulus. Her long black hair hung down to the middle of her back, straight and shining. Her tanned skin matched Darius's, and her body curved in ways that would make a man hungry for her. She was beautiful but standing

166

as she was, she looked like she could be royalty.

Azulus approached them without saying a word. "A human," he said with a sneer. "What sort of power would she bring our house? When she dies in a few years, you'll have nothing to show for what you gave her."

"Father, I have never asked for anything before. I have done everything you've asked. Please, just this once, will you allow me to do something purely for myself?"

Azulus turned to her, and I saw Darius begin to visibly shake. "I love her, Father."

"So this is the whore you've been spending all your time with?" Azulus asked. "Yes, I know you spend all of your time in that brothel rather than training with Marcellus."

Darius paused for a moment, but he didn't let Azulus fluster him very much. "Yes. Yasmin is the reason I've ignored my training."

Azulus nodded and turned around to look into the mists. "Darius, you have been a failure your entire life. A miserable warrior. A liar. Dishonorable in every way, you make a mockery of your mother's bloodlines."

"Now, you bring me a human whore and tell me you want to marry her. The same whore that has kept you from becoming even the slightest bit better at fighting. Why would I agree to let you marry her? The last thing that you need is more of a distraction. Especially from a whore. No, I do not give my permission to marry her. You will marry a woman who is respectable and has value. Not a piece of trash like this one."

And Darius snarled. "You will not speak like this about the woman I love, Father."

Azulus turned back to him and said, "Finally, a bit of spine from my snake of a son. I suggest you rein that temper in, boy."

"I'm going to marry her, Father. You can't stop me."

Azulus stared at his son and slowly smiled. "You're right, Darius. I can't stop you from marrying a woman. You're a grown man, and all men are allowed to marry whom they wish by law."

He raised his hand, and Yasmine's hand immediately went to her throat. "But, it will be difficult to marry a dead whore."

Azulus turned and walked into the mists leaving Darius to hold Yasmin as a river of crimson ran through her fingers. He began to sob as he held his fiancé.

"No, no, no." His words were broken as he looked down at Yasmin. Her eyes were wide with terror, and both of them knew that she was going to die. The river of red continued to run as Darius ran his hand through her hair.

"I love you, Yasmin. I love you so much," he whispered to her. "I'm so sorry."

Her eyes glazed over, and her hand fell from her throat as Darius pulled her to him. As her body went limp and her eyes lost the last spark of life, Darius bent down and kissed her one last time. "I will always love you, Yasmin."

"And I will kill my father. I don't know when, and I don't know how, but I will kill him."

"That's terrible," I whispered as the mists cleared once again, the phantom images turning into nothing.

"That's my father," Darius said, as a few tears ran down his cheeks. "He's the monster that needs to die. Everyone has their own stories of how he's ruined their lives."

"I didn't know that you'd been engaged." The thought of Darius caring that much about someone else was surprising. He'd been so aloof since I'd met him. He'd pushed me away, and though he'd chatted with me and teased me, there seemed to be no way that he'd ever cross into any kind of relationship with anyone.

"It was a long time ago. After that, I swore to myself that I'd never love another woman. My father would hurt them if I became too close to anyone other than my brothers. All of us felt the same way. Only Marcellus was ever married, and that was someone that my father had chosen for him."

I looked into those eyes of his and saw the sorrow there. The spark in him had faded, and behind the sorrow was a determination. "I thought that you wanted to kill your father because he'd hurt you."

Darius shook his head. "I've been hurt by many people, Orlana. The only one that I've ever hated was my father. Yasmin was the only woman I've ever been able to be myself around."

He sighed and said, "But she died a long time ago. The pain's mostly gone now, but the realization that happened that day isn't. I'll never know happiness until my father is dead."

"I understand what you mean. My life was set in motion because of my mother's death, but I don't lie awake at night filled with sadness. It's been too long, but it doesn't change the fact that my life can't be what I want until I'm free from the fear of your father."

Darius put his hands at my sides and lifted me up. It was amazing how strong he was. He slid off the dead tree branch, and I didn't fight him as we rushed to the ground.

His wings flared out and gave a single flap before his feet hit the ground. When he set me down, I turned to look at him. "We're going to fix this. We're going to win this war, and then we'll both be free to do what we want."

Darius shrugged, and I put my hand to his chest to stop him from walking away. "You're already free of him, Darius. We're already going to die if we lose, so you're free." I gave him a crooked smile and said, "And you don't have to hide yourself from me. I know you're an ass already, so just be yourself. No more masks, Darius."

He grinned a little wider and said, "Maybe I'll try that, Orlana. Maybe I'll try to be free for once. It might be nice."

Then he turned and said, "Well, I guess it's time to make a plan for how to win this fight."

Chapter 24

I was exhausted as we flew under the illusion of shadows into Stormcrest. Once again, Darius landed in an alley to shed the shadow illusion. He snapped his fingers, and the shadows that covered me disappeared, and I was looked just like a human.

"You lied to me in the beginning, didn't you?" I asked.

"What do you mean?"

I took a step towards Darius and said, "You said you had to touch me to create an illusion. You touched me everywhere. Everywhere. And you didn't have to."

Darius grinned. "Caught me. What can I say? I hadn't touched an arden's scales before, and I needed an excuse. They're similar to Marcellus's wings, though they may be just a bit harder."

"You really have gone through life living on lies and manipulation, haven't you?" I asked. I'd already realized it, and at this point, it didn't bother me that much. I'd still needed to confront him about it, though.

"And you've gone through life as a spoiled princess. We're both changing a bit. I haven't lied to you since I made that promise, but I haven't really seen you act like an uncaged arden in a while."

I huffed. "You can huff all you want, Orlana, but that doesn't change the facts. I paid for an uncaged arden, and I'm not getting it. We have about three days before we can spring this trap, so what are we going to do until then? What do you *want* to do?"

I looked at Darius and really saw him for the first time. I'd noticed what he looked like plenty of times before, but now I was seeing him. The real him. He was a master of illusions, but the real illusion had nothing to do with his powers. It was his ability to cover up pain and sadness. It was his ability to convince people to think about something else, to see something else.

"Let's get a few bottles of wine and then let's talk. I want to understand you, Darius the Silent. Tomorrow, I'll be the uncaged arden you've wanted to see."

He chuckled and said, "Fine. I expect payment for my services as your bard."

"Payment? What do you want?" This was obviously not about money. There was only one other thing we'd wagered before.

"A favor. Just one, and I'll use it before the night's over."

I nodded. "Done. Now, let's get some wine."

* * *

I sat down at the table in our room and Darius poured the cups. He passed one to me, and I took a sip as he sat down. "This is terrible."

"Sure is. This is what the common people drink, Princess, but it does the job. Now, what do you want to know?"

I looked Darius straight in the eye. "What was the deal that you made with Kina, and why did she want to get you into the bed?"

He chuckled and sipped his wine. "Again with this question? Fine. I'll tell you the story. It's a simple one, actually. One servant in my father's palace, a young girl, had pissed off one of my father's djinn because she refused him a night in the bed. She was a nobody, and the djinn was important. The girl had no money and no place to go, but he began to torment her in ways that only a djinn can do."

"She had emotional outbursts and was punished numerous times for them. She was overcome by deep depressions. Then there were nightmares that kept her from sleeping. It was as close to torture as the djinn could come without physically harming the girl. Then, he approached her and made his offer again, telling her it would fix all her problems."

"She refused him again, and I found her crying in a hallway. When she recounted all of this to me, I took her to Rea who smuggled her to Kina. Kina was supposed to put her on a ship with some money and send her out of the sands towards a greener part of the world. But she refused until I accepted her agreement. For one week, I was hers in the bedroom."

"I took the deal for a few reasons. The most important was that Kina had friends in other cities outside the sands that would take the girl in. Secondly, I realized that at some point, I may need Kina's help, and her lust would only further my ability to use her. There were other factors, but those were the important ones."

"Now, as to why she wanted that deal, well, that's a trickier answer, and it may offend your royal sensitivities. Are you sure you want to know?"

I grinned at Darius. "I'm not too worried about it. Continue your story, bard."

He finished his cup and poured himself another before standing up. All the illusions faded from him as he looked down at me. "Women lust after me for many reasons, but the simplest is this," he said with a smirk. "Everyone knows men will do many things to convince a pretty girl to come to bed with them. Princess, I'm going to tell you from experience that women will do many things to get a pretty man into bed with them as well."

I knew exactly what he was meaning. I'd been drawn to him even when I'd wanted to gut him.

"But that's only half the reason, Princess. The other is a little less simple. Solen fae crave physical intimacy. Not sex. Simple physical touch. We need it for our emotional stability. I had no one, and I couldn't trust anyone. I learned that if I could pleasure a woman in ways that no one else could, they would want that touch. As you trained with a sword, I trained in a bed with a different woman every night. Different wants. Different desires. There were no emotions involved, but they gave me what I needed, physical intimacy and practice."

He took a sip of his wine, and I wondered what he'd been like all those years ago when he was younger and less experienced. Would he have been as frustratingly obnoxious when he was still learning?

"I learned how to play a woman's body like a bard plays a

lyre. I didn't need to know the woman to draw the pleasure from her. I could see what she wanted just by the way she moved, by the way her heart beat, by the very way she breathed when I touched her."

"Kina knew that, but I'd never given her a chance in the bedroom. She was too greedy, so I couldn't count on her to reciprocate and give me that physical affection."

I took a long drink of my wine as what he said ran through my mind. That was the most arrogant thing I'd ever heard a man say about his bedroom skills, but truthfully, Darius had proven repeatedly that his arrogance was almost always well-founded. I wondered what it would be like to let him show me that side of him.

"I hope your whore friends gave you a title to go along with those boasts of yours," I said with a smile.

He chuckled and asked, "Is that all you wanted to know?"

It was my turn to stand up. "Why did you want to marry Yasmine? What was it that made you want to marry her when women were probably throwing themselves at you as Kina did?"

For some incomprehensible reason, I wanted to know more about Darius. Not just about his family or how to fight them. I wanted to get to know him and understand what made him act the way he did.

"You're very stuck on my relationships with other women," he said. "Kind of makes me wonder about your intentions. I promised that I'd tell you my stories, but you'd better be willing to be very uncaged tomorrow."

I grinned at him. "I'm positive that you won't be disappointed with me. Just keep answering the questions, and you'll be paid."

Darius turned around as he talked. I wasn't sure if it was because he was a little embarrassed or if he was trying to think.

"Yasmine didn't judge me for the way I acted around other people. She saw through the masks I wore, and she understood why I wore them. At the same time, she refused to accept them when it was only us. She pushed me to let go of the pain that had built up for so long inside me instead of pushing it deep down."

He turned back around to face me, and I knew that he'd been thinking about her fondly. He'd wanted to forget that I was in the room while he let thoughts of her run through his mind.

There was a softness in his eyes that was so out of place for him. He'd grown harder through the years. When he'd known Yasmine, he hadn't been the same as he was now.

"She was the first person who wanted to know the pain that I felt, and she didn't run from it. She wasn't disgusted to see me weak, unlike solen fae women, and it was nice to be treated like a human man with all their fragility. I enjoyed being able to be vulnerable with her, and it's probably the reason that I never really broke after everything my father did. When I met her, I was close to the breaking point, but she helped to wash away the pain of my childhood and of my mother taking her life. She helped me to forgive Arturus for giving up and becoming so similar to my father."

He shrugged. "She was important to me, but my father was right. She wouldn't have been a good wife."

I sat down on the table next to Darius's cup, my legs swinging right next to his chair. "I almost married someone once," I said.

"It would have been a terrible match, but I was important, and they wanted to climb the social ladder. My father pushed the match as he hoped I would be drawn more towards the court. It's always been his hope that I would be more involved with kingdom issues."

Darius reached out and put his hand on my thigh with no question of whether I'd accept his touch. Relief washed over him as his fingers ran over my inner thigh. Even though I was fully dressed, that simple, intimate touch seemed to let him breathe easier.

"He wouldn't have been able to see me vulnerable without thinking less of me. Ardens aren't supposed to allow their emotions to flow freely like that. They're supposed to bottle them up and let them dissipate through meditations. I'm not built for that. I need to let go sometimes and just let my emotions control me."

I grinned at Darius as I looked into his golden eyes. "Luckily, I get to break things every day, so that helps."

He chuckled as he stroked my inner thigh. "Breaking things was the last thing I wanted to do back then. My life felt so overwhelming. The one man I wanted to die was the only man that I couldn't hurt. No one could. He was impossibly strong and impossibly powerful. No, back then, the only thing I wanted to do was crawl into a hole and die."

He pulled his hand back as he leaned backward in the chair. I loved how he touched me even if it was through my trousers, and when he pulled away, I wanted to ask him to put his hand back.

"Now it's not so bad. I've worked hard to prepare myself for this rebellion. I've done what I could to perfect my abilities so that I'd be ready when the time came to end him. It took

Yasmine to help me see that there were things I could do. Maybe that was what it was all along. Maybe I was missing something I could work towards, and when I found it, I didn't feel so overwhelmed."

I nodded. I knew exactly what he meant. We'd been working towards the same goal for our entire lives. That was our bond. Our determination helped us to make sense of each other when we were so different.

"Thank you, Darius," I said.

He grinned up at me as he sipped on the wine. "Now, my favor," he said.

"What do you want?" I asked, not even slightly frightened by him anymore.

He raised his hand, and when I looked down at my arms, I saw my red and gray scales. He'd removed the illusion. "Another kiss."

Chapter 25

I smiled down at Darius and said, "Fine. Take your kiss. I won't fight you this time."

He stood up, and instead of standing in front of me, he stepped back and raised his hand. The very air seemed to carry me towards him. His eyes never left mine as they lifted me to eye level.

I waited patiently as I floated only inches in front of him. He stared into my eyes for just a few moments before I felt my arms being lifted into the air. I tried to pull them down, but they were locked into place by crystalline ropes that pulled them upward.

His lips brushed my ear as he said, "You say you won't fight me, but I don't trust you." I could feel the warmth of his breath on my neck, and it sent chills through me. He'd been this close to me before, but for some reason, it was different now.

There was a connection between us now, and when that warm breath brushed my neck, I didn't panic and try to fight back. It was as though the crackling sound of the Flames of Peace meditation were running through me.

But they weren't.

His warmth brought that calmness to me. If I'd been this helpless in front of anyone else, I would have fought as hard as I could until I was free, but not with Darius. Not now.

His hand moved to my neck, and his nails grazed my skin. They were sharp. Like an arden nail. I glanced down and saw that telltale shimmer at the end of each nail. He'd made them into arden claws, and the touch was exquisite. So gentle, yet dangerous.

His hand moved to my tunic, and he slowly brought that nail down the front of it, slicing through the soft leather. As the air began to swirl around me, teasing my body in ways that no arden could ever have done, I felt my body react to his touch.

That was when he finally pressed his lips to mine. They were hungry for me, and just as they'd been the first time he'd kissed me, they pulled at me, urging me towards something.

Something beyond the wonderful electric sensations that rushed through my body as he kissed me. Something that no man had ever done before.

His clawed hands ran over my body, teasing at my skin, and when he pulled away from me, I saw something I never expected. Softness in his eyes like when he'd thought of Yasmine.

I questioned it for only a second before he put his lips to my ear and whispered, "Let go, Orlana. Stop being the caged arden fae. Stop trying to control everything, and just let it all go."

His lips moved to my neck, and I didn't tell him to stop. Each kiss brought a warmth to my body that made me want to beg him to never stop.

But I couldn't let go. I watched him as he moved down my body, his clawed fingers finding soft flesh between hard scales. Another rush of air ran over my body, slipping between my trousers and my skin. Slowly, my trousers slid down my legs, and I made no move to stop them.

Darius pulled away from me, and he seemed to be breathing just a little deeper than he had been only moments before. He looked at me with a hunger in his eyes that I knew. I was sure that it was in mine as well.

He stared at me, and I saw that something had changed in him. His eyes had become just the slightest bit darker. "Let go, Orlana," he whispered again.

"Then let me go, and I'll show you what it's like to be with me without a cage," I whispered back. A shiver ran through Darius, but he grinned back at me.

The ropes that held my arms up disappeared, and I fell to the ground, catching myself with ease. I took off the torn tunic, dropping it on the floor, and stepped towards Darius. I could feel my fingertips itching to release the flames that were building just under the skin.

"Are you sure you want me to let go, Darius? Those feathers don't do well with flames." I ran my claws over his chest, and thin white lines appeared in their wake.

"I told you that was the only thing I wanted."

I felt the self-imposed bindings around me begin to bend and crack. Arden fae had to be in control. Our powers were too destructive otherwise, and I looked into Darius's eyes. My entire body pulsed in time with my heartbeat, and my hand found the waistband of his trousers.

Smiling, I pulled them down to his ankles and looked at his manhood as it hung in front of me, already hardening.

I knew what I wanted, but there was no need to rush to that yet. Instead, my fingers ran over it as I stood up, gently caressing it. "I'll only ask one more time," I whispered. "An arden in bed is dangerous. An uncaged arden is deadly."

Darius grabbed me by the back of the head, wrapping his fingers in my hair, and kissed me harder than before. When he pulled back, he said, "A solen fae is deadly too."

Heat and fury raged inside me at the pain. He was goading me, and my body knew it. He was pushing me with pain to let down the walls that every arden, and especially every Firebrand, grows up learning. I gritted my teeth and wrapped my hand in his hair, pulling him back to me. My nails dug into his scalp as I forced him to me, and his other hand went to my breast, squeezing it tightly in his massive hands.

The winds picked me up once more, but there were no ropes to bind me, and I clung to Darius as he pulled me towards him. My legs wrapped around his waist as the hand on my breast moved to my backside. His nails were still shaped into claws, and they dug into me, pushing my body to give up the control that had been ingrained in me since birth.

He dropped me onto the bed, and he bent over to wrap those lips of his around one of my nipples. He was standing beside me, and I reached out and took his manhood in my hand, slowly squeezing it and feeling it swell. Moving lower, he kissed only the soft skin between the scales of my stomach.

When his lips slid down my inner thigh, I put my hands in his hair and pulled him back between my legs. Without hesitation, his tongue flicked out, and I sank backward. It was wonderful, and I felt that cage that I'd build around myself crumble even more.

Darius ran his hands under my backside, and they dug into the soft flesh of my inner thighs as he pulled me to his mouth. I moaned as he sped up, and that seemed to urge him on.

But this wasn't what I wanted. This was a tease just like everything else that Darius had ever done to me, and I stroked the soft skin of his manhood. It swelled in my grip, and I could feel it pulsing.

Darius's grip on my thighs tightened, and I felt his claws pierce my flesh. Heat boiled just inside my skin. Gods, I was going to lose control. Part of me was desperate to just let go as Darius had said, but the other half was terrified of what might happen.

I gripped Darius's hair by the roots and pulled him away from me. He grinned at me, and I whispered, "I need you."

I felt the air in the room begin to gust, and dust swirled around us as he created a whirlwind. When he climbed on top of me, his lips pressed hard against mine, and my body threatened to explode. My claws ran over his back, but he didn't pull away. I couldn't control myself. The pressure inside me was desperate to escape, and destruction was the only thing that it knew.

When he finally pulled away, I saw that golden fire burning in his eyes. The winds sped up as I felt pressure between my legs. "You're almost there, Orlana," he whispered into my ear before he bit my neck. He thrust into me at the same time, and I felt the fire explode outward.

And it was whisked away from our skin into the vortex that swirled around us. I screamed at the release of everything.

The tension that had built between us in these weeks finally had an outlet. The worry and doubt that I'd felt were washed away as that outpouring of energy pulled everything out of me.

Darius began to thrust as flames whipped around us. I watched their reflections dance in his eyes. "Gods," I whispered as he forced himself in and out of me. The flames continued to pour from my body and were immediately swept into the ever-growing whirlwind that spun around us.

I pulled myself closer to his chest, lifting myself off the bed, and I pressed my lips against him. Darius didn't stop thrusting as my teeth grazed his skin, and it somehow pushed my body towards another release. It didn't matter. How I felt at that moment was utter perfection.

I'd craved freedom my entire life. Freedom from a cage, from my father's rules, but more than anything, I'd craved this. I simply hadn't known it. The weight of constantly reining in my emotions was a heavier burden than I'd ever known because I'd carried it my entire life.

Now, it was gone, lost in the waves of pleasure that coursed their way through my body. And as I looked into Darius's eyes, I knew that this was what he'd meant. Break the cage. Shatter it and be free.

The cage wasn't the rules or my environment. It wasn't my father or Azulus or anything else in the world. It was me.

Another explosion of passion left my body as I screamed out my release. Flames leaped from every inch of my body, and Darius groaned out his own. Breathlessly, he smiled down at me, and I knew that this was just as much about him as it was about me.

A roaring inferno raged behind him, blocking out the rest

of the room. He ran his hand over the scales over my breasts, and I shivered. My entire body was so sensitive to his touch. "Any way you could let those flames die down a bit?"

I grinned at him, and with a slight gesture, they blinked out of existence. I glanced around me and realized that the vortex had kept anything in the room from burning. There were tiny burns on the sheets, but other than that, the room was intact.

Darius let the winds die down, and he rolled over next to me. "That was incredible," I said, still feeling the weightlessness of being uncaged. "How did you know that would work?"

"I didn't," he admitted. "But I didn't have many other ideas if you caught fire. Fire goes where the air goes, so I figured it might work."

His hand brushed against the soft skin of my inner thigh, and I remembered what he'd said about craving physical touch. I turned onto my side and curled up against his shoulder, laying my leg over his. My hand ran over his chest and down to his stomach, tracing the muscles of his body with my nails.

Darius sighed and ran his hand through my hair, gently massaging my scalp. "That feels wonderful," he whispered.

"You'd better be careful, or you're going to make me fall asleep," I said. Darius lifted his other arm, and the wind blew once more, picking up the crumpled blanket that had fallen on the floor. It was carried into the air before it finally settled on top of us.

"That's a handy trick," I said as I closed my eyes.

"Took me a while to get the hang of it, but it's worth it." Darius shifted, and he brought his long arm across his body. His hand ran over my backside, and I didn't pull away. I didn't think I'd ever pull away from a man who could make me feel like this.

"Sleep well, Orlana," he whispered.

I gave him a smile as I let myself fall asleep. I hadn't felt this relaxed in my life, and I wasn't going to argue with the man who'd made me feel like this. Everything else in the world may have been terrifying, but right then, I didn't care. Tonight, I just wanted to be happy.

I'd found a man who could handle me without a cage.

Chapter 26

"Wake up, Orlana," Darius said with an urgency I hadn't heard before.

My eyes snapped open, and I saw him standing in front of me holding my Nullifier pendant. The cord had burned, and I hadn't noticed that it had fallen off. He was tying the rope back together, and I sat up, pushing the blanket off me.

He slipped it over my head, and then he wrapped his arms around me, pulling me into a dark corner. I snatched up Shadow as he moved me, but I didn't fight him. When I looked down, instead of seeing my legs, I saw the floor. He'd made us invisible.

A soft breeze blew by me, and his voice whispered in my ear, "Don't move. Don't breathe. Be absolutely silent. Arturus is coming."

As though Darius could see the future, the window shattered in an explosion of glass and shards of wood. Arturus landed in the middle of the room and slowly turned. He sniffed as he tried to find us by our magical scents.

"I know you're here, Darius," he growled. I didn't move, but my body tensed as I watched him. If he drew his sword, I would attack. I may have understood why Darius didn't want to kill him, but I wouldn't let him fight me in this dimly lit room filled with shadows. He'd win that fight.

"Turn away from this foolishness and go back to Marcellus, brother. You've done what you could, but if you attack Father's army again, I'll be forced to fight you. Neither of us wants that."

Darius didn't move as Arturus continued to turn around, trying to find the barest hint of our scents. "This is your last warning. I've let you live twice now. I won't be allowed a third time. Father will know if I fail to kill you again."

And with that, Arturus walked to the window. He looked back one more time before he leaped through the remnants of it.

Still, Darius didn't move. He held me to him, his arms tightly wrapped around my body. I should have been tensed and ready for battle, but now that Arturus was gone and I was pressed up against Darius, I felt myself relax.

Seconds turned into minutes, and when almost half an hour had passed, Darius stood up silently. He handed me my trousers and boots and whispered to me, "Carry them." He picked up his own clothes and our bag of supplies and wrapped his arms around my waist. All of this was done through a sense of feeling as we were still invisible.

He picked me up and whispered to me, "Don't scratch me. This will be scary."

I squeezed his arm with my fingertips, and then he leaped through the window. Every ounce of me wanted to panic, but I'd flown with Darius enough times that I wasn't quite as terrified as I had been, and I kept from clawing him. I stared down as he plummeted, but then his wings spread, and we leveled out, sailing across the city.

The night was silent, and if I weren't half naked with the chance of Arturus finding us weighing heavily on my mind, I would have enjoyed the peaceful view of the city. Instead, I was doing everything I could to forget that the enemy had caught our scent.

We'd escaped, but it had been by the skin of our teeth. How had Darius known that Arturus was coming?

That was the question that hung in my mind as we soared across the rooftops. As we crossed the castle wall, I felt a little better. The tree cover was safety in a world of flying men, but I hoped Azulus wouldn't turn his anger on Stormcrest.

* * *

Darius set me down on soft grass, and our illusions faded. "It's safe to talk now," he said. "I haven't seen Arturus at all, and he can't track us with these pendants on."

"I'm sorry that I didn't realize that it had fallen off. I wasn't very focused on little things like that after..."

He grinned at me. "It's fine. This is our last stop before we go to Inoras if everything works out. I'll just have to make sure you don't get too worked up until we get there."

I chuckled at him and sat down on the grass. "At least it's a beautiful night to sleep under the stars," I said. "I've never slept on the ground before."

"It's miserable, and I hope we don't have to do it long," Darius said with annoyance. "But, it could be worse. We could be in the mountains sleeping on rocks. You'd probably like that, though. Do you ardens use rocks as pillows?"

"No. Do solens use chickens?"

Darius laughed and pulled me to him. The lightness of his mood helped to break up the storm clouds that were gathering in me. "It's too bad I didn't get a blanket when we were rushing out of there."

I shrugged as I curled up on his shoulder again. "You're warm enough for me. How'd you know Arturus was coming?"

Darius sighed. "I didn't. Not really. It's one of those extrasensory things you develop when you do things you'll get into trouble for. I woke up terrified that something was wrong. I must have noticed that your Nullifier was missing without realizing it. When I looked around, I saw that you'd dropped it onto the floor, and that's when I woke you up."

"Oh. Well, that was lucky. Do you think that Arturus would have killed us if he'd found us?"

Darius bit his lip. "I don't know. I hope not, but I can't be sure. The thing I know is that he didn't try very hard to kill us when he realized we were there but were hiding. He could have used shadows to find us. He's caught me with them before, but he didn't try at all. That says something, doesn't it?"

"It does," I said as I ran my hands over Darius's naked body. "Can we try to get a little more sleep now?"

"Sorry I ruined your beauty sleep, Princess. You just use me as a pillow, and I'll endure the rocky ground for you."

I slapped his chest and smiled at him. "Oh hush. Be the big strong solen fae for me for once. No snarkiness tonight."

Chapter 26

"Fine. No snarkiness until morning," he said as he ran his hand through my hair. "Sleep well, Orlana."

And I did.

Chapter 27

Darius slowly turned the two pheasants over the fire. The smell filled the air, and I had a hard time threading the crystal needle through my tunic. Darius had created the needle for me from the air. The day of our attack on Azulus's troops in the swamps was fast approaching, and the thought of doing it with my breasts on display was terrible.

Everything was quiet this evening as we took care of our little tasks, and I looked over at Darius as he slowly spun dinner. We'd become comfortable with each other. Comfortable enough that I could sit topless across from him and not feel a bit of insecurity. He'd made more than a few jokes about my torn tunic, and I'd made a few back at him, but all of it had been in good fun.

I thought back over all the fights we'd had since we'd begun our little adventure together. Nothing had really changed other than that we'd begun to understand each other a little more.

Darius didn't think of me as a spoiled child any longer, and I didn't see him as my enemy. Though I still wondered why he never picked up a weapon, I didn't fault him for not being a warrior like his brothers.

There was only one real problem that hadn't ever been dealt with. Darius would choose his brother over me. Maybe even over the mission. I couldn't fault him for his loyalty to his brother, but I also couldn't accept it.

Eventually, we would have to deal with that stumbling block. For now, I could be happy. We weren't done fighting, and the worst of it was still to come, but for now, I didn't have to think about it. For once in my life, I felt free. There was nothing to do except enjoy my time in the open air with Darius.

"What are you going to do when all this is over?" I asked.

He turned to me and cocked his head. "What do you mean?"

I tied off the stitch and held up the tunic that was once again mostly whole. "What are you going to do if we win this war? You said that you'd never be allowed to be happy as long as your father was alive, so what will you do once he's dead?"

Darius chuckled. "You know, I haven't really thought about it. Probably go back to Kharn and help my brothers rule. Though, I guess Marcellus will have to stay in the elven kingdoms since his woman isn't long-lived outside of the elven kingdoms. I don't know what Arturus will do. Well, now that you mention it, I may end up having to rule Kharn."

He chuckled again as he turned back to the pheasants. "Maybe we should let my father live after all. The only thing worse than dealing with him would be having to become a king."

I stood up and pulled the tunic on, testing the stitches I'd made. "Really? You'd hate sitting on your father's throne?"

"I'd hate sitting on any throne. I'm the youngest. That means that I was never supposed to sit on a throne. Being forgotten about is what I'm good at. Not being in the center of everything. Give me a library and a pretty woman, and I'd be much happier than deciding how everything runs in Kharn."

"A pretty woman and a library. That's what you want from life? I'm surprised you didn't say a whole brothel of women. That's what most men want, isn't it? Especially one who frequents them as much as you do."

He shook his head and pulled the spit off the fire, setting the two cooked birds on a rock. "Not me. Like I've said so many times. I enjoy the atmosphere of brothels. Freedom was what I craved. Now, I won't have the same problem."

"Truthfully, I think I'd like to settle down once all of this is over. Find a woman who doesn't want to claw my eyes... or arms," he said with a smirk towards me. "I've always wanted to raise children. My brothers and I were my mother's only joy, and I have enough of her inside me that I think that I'd find some happiness in it."

His lips tightened, and I saw a twinge of sadness cross his face before he replaced it with a mask of happiness. "At least, that would be the fantasy. It's doubtful that anyone would be willing to put up with me long enough to marry me or give me children. More than likely, I'll become a drunk while Arturus rules Kharn."

I grinned at him. "I doubt you'd have very much trouble finding a woman who would marry you. There's always Kina if you're that desperate for them." Darius laughed at my comment, but there was still a sadness in his laughter that he couldn't hide from me any longer.

"I think I'd like to run an orphanage. Gods help us, there will be enough orphans to go around after this war ends. Maybe I could see raising a child as well. It's been a very long time since an arden fae was born. I just hope that they're nothing like me. I've been the bane of my father's existence."

Darius laughed as he said, "Oh, I have too. You know what they say, don't you? Your children will punish you with threefold as much frustration as you gave your parents. Your spawn will probably blow your house up with you in it. And they'll probably refuse to wear anything but dresses."

"And yours will probably be warriors who never learn to read."

"Kill me now. Maybe I don't want to have any children," Darius said as he pulled one pheasant off the spit. "I couldn't imagine trying to raise my brothers." He shivered at the thought.

When he handed me the pheasant, I said, "It would be nice to be around children again, though."

"It would," Darius said in agreement.

"Especially ones who hadn't been forced to live in a world with King Azulus."

Darius took his pheasant and held it out to me with a grin. "Cheers to that." I tapped his pheasant with mine with a laugh. It was easy talking to Darius. Easier than it had ever been to talk to other men in the Emerald Caverns, even though I'd known them for so much longer.

He sat down on the ground and began to eat. "He'd make a good husband," Shadow whispered to me, and I turned my head to the sword which lay on the ground next to me.

Shadow had never spoken to me when I wasn't holding him. I didn't know he could.

I almost said something, but then I glanced at Darius. It was hard to imagine explaining that my best friend in the world was my sword. I would tell him another time, though. Shadow was my last secret, and I would tell him. Just not now.

I focused on the words as I took a bite of the pheasant. I wasn't sure if Shadow could hear me or not if I wasn't speaking the words. "When did you start talking without me touching you?"

"I've always been able to, but you always held me before, so I didn't bother. Now it's different. You don't even wear clothes half the time." A soft rattle came from within the sheath, and I knew that he was laughing at me. "It was time to tell you we were bound, and we could speak without touching. Darius would make a good husband. He makes you happy, Orlana."

I said nothing. I didn't want to think about us past right then. There were still too many unknowns. Darius had admitted to being able to manipulate women, and there was no way to tell if he was just making our time together as pleasant as possible. Maybe he truly felt something more towards me, but there was no way to be sure. Then there were the issues with Arturus.

No, at any time, whatever we shared could be ripped apart, and the more I let myself think about Darius as anything more than a friend, the worse that change would hurt. "Not now, Shadow," was all I thought, but I knew that he already understood what I was thinking.

I looked at Darius who had noticed my odd behavior and was watching me as he ate the pheasant. He said nothing, though, and I didn't try to make an excuse for the way I was acting.

But Shadow was right. Darius would make a good husband to someone. Maybe not me, but for some lucky woman, he would. He was kind, funny, and more intelligent than anyone I'd met. That wasn't even speaking to his skills in the bed.

"I have a request," I said.

Darius grinned as he finished his bite and said, "What does the beautiful Princess Orlana ask of me?"

"I want to bind myself to you." Darius recoiled immediately, taken aback by my request.

"I'm not saying that I want to marry you. I'm saying that I trust you. Completely. We've bickered, and I think we'll always bicker, but I trust you to do what's best, and I think you trust me to do the same. More than anything, I don't want you to die."

Darius nodded, and I could see the hesitancy in his eyes. "Once upon a time, the arden fae had warriors. Groups of men and women protected their kingdoms through the strength of arms and magic. These small groups bound themselves to each other with an ancient magic."

"When one of them was wounded, this bond allowed them to draw on their bondmates' magic to sustain them until they could be healed. I want to bind myself to you so that if you're wounded, my powers will keep you from dying."

He sat back and pondered what I'd said. "You know that there are still unresolved issues between us. Can we break this bond?"

I nodded. "Yes, a simple cut across the mark of binding, and you're free of it, but I don't think it happened very often. The bond… does things to people. It lets them understand the other one just a little better. It brings them closer together." I hesitated for a moment before saying, "Their souls are tied together, and it's difficult for them to be separated."

Darius was quiet as he thought about what I'd said. "It would be helpful in battle, but is that really what you want? Do you want to be bound to someone like me?"

"I was the one who brought it up. I think it would be a good idea, but I understand if you don't want to do it."

Darius stood up and set his pheasant down on the rock. "Orlana, you don't want to bind yourself to someone like me. You... you don't know how broken I am. I wouldn't wish anyone to understand that side of me."

"Don't push him," Shadow whispered in warning. "A bond cannot be pressured."

Shadow hadn't needed to tell me that. I remembered the explanations my mother had given me when she'd explained the burn across her shoulder. Even at seven, I'd understood how close a bond like that was.

"It's fine, Darius. It was just something I'd been thinking about. We'll just leave things as they are."

His pushback hurt me. It had brought our confusing relationship to light. I didn't know why he tried to blame it on his brokenness when I knew it was because I was just another woman to him. He cared about me, but he'd also cared about all of the solen fae and djinn he'd killed.

"Let's eat our dinner and get some sleep," I said. "Tomorrow, we have a lot of work to do."

I was a friend, and I was his partner in this mission. That was all. I needed to remember that.

Chapter 28

Explosives had been laid. Screaming traps had been placed to cause confusion. I was hidden, and Darius was scouting overhead. Azulus's army would be here any moment. Miles of swamp would be swarmed by his troops as they tried to cross the Marshes of Sorrow as fast as possible.

"You get to see your father as soon as this is done," Shadow whispered to me.

I was hiding in one of the top branches of a dead tree near the center of the marsh. I couldn't see anyone, but I still whispered. "Yes. Hopefully, we'll both have good news for each other."

I was trying my best to forget about the rift between Darius and me. In only a few days, we'd be in Inoras, and what we'd shared on this journey would be a part of the past. Just another story for us both to tell. We'd remember the nights we'd spent huddled together. We'd remember the days in the rivers and baths. The fights. The moments where we'd connected over our shared anger and misery.

But the trip would be over, and the bond between us would shatter as soon as we were back amongst other people. These would be fond memories, but that's all they'd ever be.

Darius and I weren't meant to be anything more.

"There's more to Darius than you realize," Shadow said, reading my thoughts.

"What more could there be? He isn't interested in bonding with me, and he would choose Arturus over me. I'm just a pretty girl he's entertaining himself with."

I needed to accept the truth of the matter instead of living in some sort of fantasy where everything turns out happily ever after. This was the real world, and the reality of it was that I didn't matter to Darius in any genuine sense. My mother had been friends with Arturus, but he'd killed her anyway. If it came down to saving his brother or me, Darius wouldn't hesitate to slit my throat.

"You're more than that. He bared his soul to you. That may not matter much to you, but it matters to him. You can see it in his eyes."

I shook my head. I couldn't believe that. Hope would only hurt me worse in this matter.

"It doesn't matter, Shadow. He's made his choice."

The branch shook, and I knew Darius had landed next to me. I wondered if he'd heard me talking to Shadow, but he didn't act like it. "They're rushing the bridges. It shouldn't be too much longer before they get here. Are you ready?"

I nodded to him as my heart raced. It was time. There could be a thousand emotional problems to deal with, but now that we were on the edge of battle, all thoughts of them fled my mind.

Tonight, life was standing on a razor's edge. Death waited below, and there was no time for anything beyond action.

"Do you remember what I said about the ifrit?" I asked.

Darius nodded. "I never thought I'd get to control one of them. Kind of crazy. It's a good plan, but I'm glad I'm only the diversion. I don't think I'd be able to actually fight with one."

I smiled at him. "This is what arden fae were meant to do." The truth of the matter was that I was terrified. An ifrit was the greatest combination of Flamewaking and Binding any arden had ever done, and it had taken the only master of both to manage it. Anyone could make an ifrit fight, but only a Flamewaker, Binder, or Firebrand could turn it into the truly awe-inspiring weapon they were meant to be.

Darius's only job was to take control and draw the attention of the army. They would swarm the ifrit, using bows and magic to take it down. The remaining djinn would be useless against it, and the solen fae were abysmal with their magic. The army wouldn't be using steel arrows which were required to defeat an ifrit. It would be pure insanity.

And I would sweep in to decimate the army and the bridges.

Darius whispered, "I'm going to see where the ifrits are headed." I nodded and prepared to wait.

* * *

The sound of steel-covered bodies marching filled the air, a sound I'd never heard before. Hundreds of thousands of soldiers moved across bridges only wide enough for a horse-drawn wagon onto islands big enough to fit a hundred people at a time.

The ifrits waded through the water, steam sizzling from the water around their legs. Gods, they were beautiful. I watched them as Darius carried me through the air.

We'd placed explosives along many of the bridges, and Darius knew how to arm them. He set me down in a tree on one of the islands in front of the ifrits. They'd been split apart, but they couldn't be too far apart, or the sorcerers that controlled them wouldn't have the backup they needed if the one controlling the ifrit was killed.

I smiled as Darius began to arm the explosives. I couldn't see him since he was invisible, but I knew how fast he was. It would only be a few more minutes. I watched as my ifrit and the sorcerer controlling it stepped onto my island.

I drew Shadow, and he whispered, "No mercy, Orlana. Not tonight."

The explosions began one right after the other, only seconds apart. I dropped to the ground cloaked in an illusion of invisibility and began cutting through the troops on my island. A blast of moonlight shot through the air, and I blocked it with Shadow, who groaned.

I rushed to the sorcerers as soon as the soldiers were dead. The ifrit began moving closer to me, but the sorcerers didn't know where I was, and I didn't hesitate to kill the three on my island.

Then I focused on the ifrit. There had been screams as I'd killed the soldiers and sorcerers, but with all the explosions and screamer boxes going off, the army was in chaos, and I didn't feel the hail of arrows that should have filled the air if they'd known what they were doing.

I spoke the ancient language. Sorcerers didn't use the ancient language, instead using a corruption of it. Even the ardens didn't speak it very often, but ifrits required it for only those words could bind two disciplines together like this.

I knew these ifrits. They'd been named by the Master Binder who had created them, and their descriptions had been placed in the Disciplines as the greatest achievement of the arden race. When I called my ifrit's name, no one else would have control of it.

And then I waited. I focused on the stone in the ifrit's chest, knowing the inscription by heart. "Let this living flame burn forever."

I listened for the chaos that Darius would be creating. The twang of bowstrings filled the air, and I hoped Darius was flying high above the ifrit. Eventually, someone would find a way to destroy it, and I mourned the loss of such a beautiful creation, but it was necessary. We couldn't take them with us.

I finally glanced to where the ifrit was ravaging an island full of troops. It was so awkward with Darius controlling it, like watching a child wield a sword for the first time. Yes, this sword was sharp, and the air was already thickening with the ash from the dead soldiers, but it was nothing compared to what an arden could do.

I focused on my ifrit once more and felt my awareness expand. I couldn't *see* through the ifrit, but I had a vague sense of my surroundings. It was time. Everyone was focused on Darius's ifrit.

With a single word, the ifrit ran through the marshes, slamming its fiery legs into as many bridges as possible. The fifteen-foot arms extended, and as I passed islands, I swung them in broad strokes, incinerating dozens of men in each sweep.

I spoke another word in the ancient tongue, and instead of red, the ifrit burned white-hot. It flew through the water, filling the air with steam that scalded the men that survived my powerful swings. Crisscrossing from island to bridge, I crushed hundreds of men and stranded even more in minutes.

As I moved, I heard Darius's ifrit's death scream. The telltale rattling meant that the fire had turned to crystal. I gave it a glance and saw Arturus flying away. He'd used magic to strike the ifrit's heart, but he hadn't turned his attention towards mine.

And no one had seen what an arden fae controlled ifrit could do in almost a thousand years.

My ifrit leaped into the air, soaring over the mists of the swamp. I could feel the sunlight through the ifrit, and when it crashed through the dead trees of an island, they came to life in a blaze of flames.

Arturus stopped in mid-flight. He was close enough. Unprepared and airborne, he would be an easy target.

Darius's ifrit exploded, and shards of crystal flew through the air as I looked through the flames at Arturus. The world was strangely quiet for how much death we had caused. Men were never wounded by ifrits. They either survived or they died instantly. Quick and clean deaths that transformed a flesh and blood man into a pile of ash in the blink of an eye.

Arturus knew it as he stared me down in the silence. I knew what my father expected of me. I knew what my people expected of me, and I even knew what I would have done only a few weeks ago.

But now?

Now, I hesitated. I glanced to where Darius stood, his

illusion gone as he stared at me. Not the ifrit. Me.

I should kill him. He was Azulus's sharpest sword. He killed my mother and who knew how many of my people? He'd kill even more in only a few weeks. But what would that do to Darius? He'd said that he wasn't as broken as he could be, but this would break him completely. The only people in his life that he cared about were his brothers.

I closed my eyes for only a moment, and then I felt a shock run through me. When my eyes flashed open again, an entire web of shadows had crossed through the ifrit, and I was sure that its heart was shattered.

The white turned to red and then to black. The flames stopped roiling across its massive body and became sharpened points. I pulled away from the ifrit as I watched one of the last of the most magnificent arden creations shake itself to death.

I'd been bound to the ifrit. I knew how close to living it was, and for just a moment, I mourned it.

Until I heard boots on the ground behind me. Seven solen fae touched down on my island, and all the bridges to this island were destroyed. They were staring right at me, and I knew they were listening for the only things that would give me away: my heartbeat and my breath.

They knew where I was, and as one of them raised its hand, I prepared myself. I raised Shadow in a defensive position, and a shard of crystallized air flew towards me. I blocked it with Shadow, and he absorbed the magic that had given the crystal its form.

I put out my hand, and flames spouted from my fingers, but the air in front of the solens hardened in front of them, blocking the flames. They'd learned not to fight me with swords because, unlike them, I had no problem combining swordplay and magic.

Without saying a word, another solen raised his hand, and I tried to move back to a defensive position, but I couldn't. Glancing at my sword hand, I saw the shimmering in the air.

He'd trapped me in crystallized air.

Just as Darius had done, I couldn't twist away, and unless I could bring steel to my bondage, I was dead. The rest of the solens raised their hands and shards of air rushed towards me.

There was nothing I could do except watch them in slow motion. My breath hitched in my throat as I realized that this was the end. We'd accomplished our goal, but there was no way I was getting out of this alive.

In that half-second, I made my peace with myself. These shards would hit me, and then the solens would attack me with swords. I'd be dead in less than a minute.

And I could accept that.

I'd done everything possible to save the arden fae. I'd done the impossible and nearly eliminated all of Azulus's strongest forces. The only thing I regretted was the fact that I wouldn't be able to experience the world without King Azulus in it.

And Darius. I regretted not being able to spend more time with Darius. He'd been a bright spot in my life. Brighter than any other.

The shards pierced my body in a dozen places. I felt my hipbones shatter at the impact. My spine, my shoulders, and even my cheek were torn apart by the explosion of crystalized air as all the solens attacked me.

My bondage evaporated, and I fell to the ground. Shadow hit the dirt next to me. "I'm sorry, Orlana," he said with more sadness than I'd ever thought possible. "Thank you," I whispered as cold flowed through me. "You've been a good friend."

And then a shadow filled my vision.

Chapter 29

Darius the Silent stood beside me, his black wings blocking out my view of the mist above me. "Don't give up on me, Orlana," he said as he bent down and picked up Shadow.

I couldn't move my feet, and I couldn't feel anything other than numbness. I knew I was supposed to be hurting, but my body had realized that it wouldn't survive. It was giving up.

I smiled up at Darius, glad to see him one more time, but Darius didn't whisk me away to safety. Instead, he stepped in front of me, wielding Shadow. That was right. If there was anyone that should inherit Shadow, it should be Darius. I had no children, and I had no siblings. If Shadow was going to leave my family, it should go to the only person who had ever understood me.

Darius glanced back at me and grinned. "Ready to see one of my last secrets?"

I tried to smile back at him, but the wound on my cheek had ripped away the muscles that let me.

Darius turned to the seven solen fae who had stopped advancing on me. Several of them raised their hands towards me, but Darius crystallized the air around me, protecting me from stray magical attacks.

And then he was gone.

Silent as ever, he didn't even stir the dirt into the air as he moved, and a solen fae fell to the ground. Darius's illusion disappeared as he pulled Shadow from the solen's chest.

He moved faster than I'd ever moved, and he was certainly faster than any of the solens expected. Like the wind, Darius whirled around, and solens died before they'd even had a chance to recognize what was happening.

How could Darius have gone all this time without being considered a warrior with how he moved? The first solen had barely hit the ground when the last one's head was severed from his body.

I couldn't have done that even on my best day, and I was the fastest arden. As soon as the solens were dead, Darius approached me covered in solen fae blood. "I'm going to get you out of here, Orlana. We've done what we came to do, and now it's time to get you fixed up."

"No." The word came from behind Darius, and when he turned, I saw Arturus standing there, his sword in his hands. "I told you to go back to Marcellus. I told you I couldn't go back to father with any more failures. Let me have the arden, and I'll let you escape. Father will accept that you abandoned the arden to make your escape."

I lay back. This was where I died. Darius had already told me that he wouldn't fight his brother, and Arturus was giving him a way out.

"I'm not leaving her." A snarl rose from Darius's throat.

Darius lifted his hand, and hundreds of shards of air flew towards Arturus. Arturus pulled the shadows from the ground upward in a wall, and the shards crashed against it, shattering upon impact.

I could see the shadows growing from the ground, climbing into the air, and as they tried to wrap around Darius's legs, they passed through as though he weren't there. An illusion.

Where was he?

More crystal shards flew through the air, coming from all directions, but Arturus's shadow wall covered him. The shadowy vines wrapped around the crystal shield protecting me, and I saw cracks begin to appear as they squeezed tighter.

I was paying attention to that when I heard a scream, and my eyes were drawn back to Arturus. Darius stood behind him, and Shadow was sticking through Arturus's wing, the steel piercing the writhing blackness that was his greatest weakness and greatest strength.

All the shadowy vines that had crawled across the ground puffed back to their original places, no longer controlled by Arturus's magic. Darius pulled my sword down, ripping through Arturus's wing, and Arturus collapsed, writhing in agony.

Darius was by my side in a moment, lifting me into the air as he fled the Marshes. There was no need for an illusion any longer. All the soldiers in the area were dead.

"You chose me," I gasped.

"I decided a long time ago that I was the only one allowed to kill you for being so obnoxious, Princess."

I looked up at him, but my body was fading. "I think you'll

get your wish. I can't move my legs." A cough rose in my throat as we passed through the mists and into the open air.

I could feel the blood that ran down the side of my cheek. "Doubtful," Darius said as his wings continued to pump faster than ever before. "I heard ardens are too dumb to die when they're supposed to."

I knew my smile was broken by the wounds, but I kept smiling. I'd thought I was going to die alone in those Marshes. I would probably still die, but at least I could die in the sunlight. In Darius's arms. He'd chosen me over his brother, and that meant something.

There wasn't any more time to tell him the one thing I'd questioned for so long. I closed my eyes as I felt the coldness fill me. "I love you," I whispered.

And then the blackness took me.

Chapter 30

I woke up in a place I'd never been before. A palace of some sort with walls made of beautiful white stone that I couldn't place. Stone that I'd never seen before? Where could it be from?

I tried to roll onto my side, and pain shot through my entire body. Then everything that had happened came back to me in a flash. I thought I was going to die. We hadn't had a healer, and we were five days away from Inoras. I should have bled out.

I ran my hand over my cheek and felt the tiniest scar. Just a thin scratch. How had I survived? I looked under the blanket that covered me and saw that I was wearing a white nightgown. What could have happened?

I gritted my teeth and pushed myself to roll over regardless of the pain. When I sat up, I looked around the room.

Everything in this bedroom was beautiful, but it was so bright. The elegantly carved furniture was made of white ash, and the sunlight poured through the open windows.

A gentle breeze flowed through the room, bringing hints of living forest and cooking foods. Calm scents. Scents so similar to my time with Darius. Then I looked around and saw that Shadow Soul was nowhere to be found. Darius had carried him with us when we left the Marshes of Sorrow. Where was he?

"I'm so glad that you're awake," Shadow's voice whispered to me. "And I'm sorry."

"Sorry for what? I survived, and we accomplished our goals," I whispered back.

"Sorry for this," he said as the doors burst open.

My father. Dressed in his finest robes. The crimson and black ones he wore during talks with other kings.

"Gods, Orlana. You had us all worried sick. You're lucky that there are plenty of healers here."

He carried Shadow, and I grimaced as I stood up. I needed to hold Shadow. "How long have I been asleep?" I asked.

"You were unconscious for the entire flight here. That was three days. Then you were unconscious for another three while the healers worked on you. They had to cut and re-knit your wounds. Prince Darius had cauterized them, and they'd already begun to scar, so the scar tissue had to be cut out and healed correctly. It's a much slower process of healing."

I nodded to him. No one in the arden kingdom could have done that. A scar was a scar forever. Otherwise, there would have been many ardens who had been maimed in the old wars that would have been able to be healed.

"I'm grateful for your insistence," I said formally. "May I

have Shadow Soul back?"

My father looked me over and shook his head. "No."

I stared at him in shock. No one had ever tried to take Shadow away from me before. Why would my father suddenly do it now?

"I don't understand," I said as calmly as possible, even as panic overtook me. "Shadow is mine, given to me by Mother. I am bonded to him, and you have no right to take him away from me."

"You disgraced your mother's memory," my father said. "You didn't take revenge when you had control of the ifrit. After everything that I've done to instill the purpose of your training, you ignored it the first time that you had the chance."

Every muscle in my body tensed in anger. Who was he to question my choices? I knew what he'd done all those years ago, and I knew what Arturus had done for him.

"Shadow is mine," I said as rage pushed flames to the edge of my skin even though pain filled me. "You have no right. My mission was successful. Nowhere in your commands did you tell me to kill Arturus. Return my sword to me. Now."

Every inch of my body ached, but at that moment, I would have fought my father to get Shadow back.

That was when a monster of a man walked into the room. I knew him instantly. Marcellus the Black. At his side was an elven woman. Talia was the name that Darius had said.

He glanced at my father and then at me, and I was sure that he realized the tenseness between us. He just didn't care. Instead of walking back through the door, he said, "It's good to see you a little less bloody, Orlana. According to my brother, you're one hell of a warrior princess."

"I'm glad your brother approves of my skills," I said as I

continued to stare at my father. I knew what I had to do to get Shadow back. "But until my father returns my sword, I will refuse to contribute anything to this war effort. You may want to have a chat with your newest ally, Prince Marcellus."

My father may have been a diplomat by necessity rather than because he'd enjoyed it, but all those years had instilled in him a need to keep from being embarrassed. Marcellus raised an eyebrow to him to show his confusion, and Father decided to prevent the explosion he knew would come in moments. Not willing to be embarrassed in front of the leader of this rebellion, my father tossed Shadow onto the bed and walked out of the room without saying another word.

Then Talia cracked a smile. "Clever," she whispered. She glanced backward and said, "He doesn't understand what you know. You did the right thing, and I think that we'll all be glad you did it when this is all over."

Talia was an elven prophet that had been the key to starting this war, but I knew little else about her. Her words resonated with me, but my mind was still very foggy after my six days of sleep. I didn't have the energy to puzzle out the exact meaning of what she'd said, and I was glad when Darius walked into the room. As soon as he saw me, he said, "I guess that letting you nearly die is the only way I'll see you in a dress."

I grinned back at him. "Any way you could find me a tunic and trousers?"

"Not a chance. I could find you a tighter fitting dress though. Or a sela."

Before I had a chance to argue with him, Marcellus interrupted, "I'm sure you're hungry. Would you like food brought here or would you prefer to eat in a dining hall?"

I looked at Darius and said, "In my room so that Darius can

tell me what happened while I was busy nearly dying. I'm still more than a little confused about it all."

Marcellus grinned and somehow still looked so serious. "I'll leave you two to talk." He glanced at Darius and said, "But remember that the healers say that her internal wounds are still barely stitched together. Don't get too excited."

A normal healing would take minutes. How bad had I been when I'd been brought here for it to have taken days? I was grateful that I'd been asleep for it because I was sure that it would have been pure agony if I'd been awake.

"Me? Be excited? You mistake me, brother. I'm not you or Arturus."

Marcellus chuckled as he turned to go, shaking his head. When he closed the door, I went back to the bed, pulling Shadow to me. I felt better knowing that he was with me again. I'd been in a panic when I'd thought that he'd been lost.

Darius pulled up a chair and sat next to the bed. "I thought that we'd agreed on no more lies."

I lay my head back. "I don't have the energy to try to understand your cryptic questions."

"Why didn't you tell me you had a talking sword?" I looked at him and grinned. I'd thought about telling him, but it seemed almost too personal.

"I almost told you. But the battle was hanging over our heads, and I didn't want to worry about how you'd react to finding out that my best friend was a sword. Plus, it was only you who agreed to not hide anything. That was never part of my deal."

Darius leaned back, putting his hands behind his head as he lounged in the straight-backed chair. How did he always look so lazy? "Well, your dear friend Shadow Soul had plenty to say while you were sleeping."

I glanced down at the sword, and I imagined him blushing. "Kind of rude, don't you think, Shadow?"

"It's not rude at all. He's far more talkative than you. It was nice to be around someone who wanted to talk for once. I'm your friend and guide, not your servant."

Darius chuckled, and I glanced at him. "Did you hear that?"

"Oh yes. Shadow and I have an agreement as well. But that's between the two of us, so don't even bother asking. One of our agreements is that he can talk to me now."

I blinked at him. How was that possible? Shadow could only speak to people who were holding him other than me. "How?"

"We're bonded as well. But that's between the two of us." Shadow's words were infuriating. How could he bond someone else? He was my friend. My sword. I didn't want to share him.

I tried to let the Flames of Peace wash through me. Marcellus had told me not to get excited, and I was at the point of lighting him and the entire room on fire.

The meditation didn't work. I heard the crackling fire in the back of my mind, but it did nothing to dull the anger that was rising to the surface. Darius watched me, but then he turned in the chair and pulled the waistband of his trousers down to reveal his hip.

A small symbol had been burned into his flesh. A single figure from the ancient language. I knew what it was instantly. "Where's mine," I whispered.

"I was thinking about putting it on your breast so that only I could see it, but Shadow recommended I make it public as it was done in the old days. Look at your left arm."

I glanced down and saw it. A matching script letter. Braakos. The Broken. "Why?"

"Because otherwise, you'd be dead, Orlana. You were minutes from death when I set you down outside the Marshes. Shadow spoke to me during that flight, and he said that the only way to save you was to bond myself to you so that you could feed on my power until I got you to a healer. He walked me through the process."

I closed my eyes and lay my head back. "It has to be a choice that a person makes, Darius. I couldn't say the words. I don't understand how it worked with me being unconscious."

Shadow spoke up then. "Because we already had a bond. My soul is tied to you, and I spoke the words for you. I couldn't lose you too, Orlana, and you'd already offered Darius a bond. I hope you're not too angry."

I'd thought that I understood mine and Darius's relationship. I'd thought that I had been a friend, but he'd done too many things that didn't work with that thought. He'd hurt his brother to save me, and now he'd bound himself to me.

That was when I remembered that I'd told him that I loved him, and my heart sunk.

"You fought Arturus," I said. "You chose me over him."

He sat up and grew serious at the mention of his brother. "Yes. I didn't kill him, but I fought him. In the process, I showed him my greatest secret."

"That you're just as much a warrior as your brothers?"

Darius sighed. "I had a single purpose for training after Yasmine died. To kill my father. Now my brother will have to report to him that I can fight, and he'll be prepared. It had to be done, though."

"Thank you," I whispered.

While my eyes were closed, scenes of our time together flashed through my mind. All the memories seemed brighter than they had been before we'd fought Azulus's troops. The bond was keeping our memories together alive and unclouded.

When I opened my eyes, Darius was staring at me. "Do you regret your choice?"

He shook his head. "No. You could have killed him, but you didn't. I know that your father will hate you for it, and I know that a part of you hates that you didn't exact your revenge, but I'm glad you didn't. Thank you for choosing my heart over your hatred."

I nodded to him, and the room quieted again. "I'll be glad when we can go swimming again," I said.

"Want to go after dinner? I hear that there's a waterfall nearby."

I smiled at him. "Yes, but only if you can find me a tunic and trousers."

"You're sure you wouldn't prefer a sela?" he asked with a grin.

I snarled at him. "I'll wear one if you wear one."

"I might just do it. Of course, I'd probably throw an illusion on as soon as we were around other people."

"Damned cheater," I said with a smirk.

Chapter 31

The breakfast table in Inoras was nothing like I was used to. It was the first time that I'd eaten breakfast where the food was the least important part of the whole thing. This was a group of the most important people in the world, and all of them were trying to get to know their new comrades in arms.

Marcellus and Talia sat at the head of the table, the leaders of the rebellion. Darius and I sat next to my father closest to them. On the other side, King Sundryl, the king of the elves, and several of the arden kings sat across from us. An elven woman and a very scruffy-looking human man sat next to him.

The rest of the fifty seats were filled with human kings, generals, and diplomats, and there was an air of excited tension that came with the knowledge that we hung on a precipice. In only a week's time, we would either be free of

King Azulus, or we would all be dead. There would be no more second chances.

Arden troops and supplies were still arriving, and in only a few days, only the most important generals and diplomats would be allowed at this table. Marcellus and King Sundryl had made sure that everyone showed up to meals together. We needed to work together, and that meant that we had to get to know each other.

"I feel a bit out of sorts sitting next to kings," the scruffy man said to Marcellus as he picked up a piece of sausage and took a bite.

"That's because you won't shave that damn beard, Teffin. I'm sure that your wife would appreciate it if she didn't have to taste yesterday's meal every time she kissed you." Marcellus replied. Marcellus's plate was full of strips of meat that looked nearly like travel rations.

The scruffy man turned to the elf next to him. She grinned and ran her hand over his beard. "Don't tell him to shave. I like it, and I'll have you know that not every woman likes a man without any hair."

Marcellus huffed, and the scruffy man said, "I might ought to trim it a bit if I'm going to have to sit next to all these fancy folks, though. Never imagined I'd be eating," he stopped talking for a moment as he picked up a fruit that I'd never seen before, "whatever this is next to the king of the elves. Might be time to clean myself up a bit."

"I'll trim your beard for you," the woman said. "That way no one cuts it too short."

Everyone laughed a little bit, and I just watched. I felt like the scruffy man this morning. I knew a few of the people, but mostly, I had no idea who most of them were. Especially the elves and humans, but even some of the ardens were from other kingdoms. Everyone was an outsider at this table, but they were all used to meeting and greeting other "fancy people" while I'd done my best to get out of doing that.

"How are you feeling this morning," Talia asked me. She was so soft compared to Marcellus who walked around like a disgruntled bear half the time. Her voice was quiet and almost frail while his was always gruff. Except when he was talking to Darius, and then it was like they were children again, playing and joking with each other.

"Much better." I turned to King Sundryl. "I can't believe what your healers managed. I was sure that I was dead. I can't believe that I feel almost normal."

This was a man who understood how to find happiness in anything. He'd weathered a thousand years of constant alertness. Despite that, he seemed like the most cheerful man at the table. "For someone who did so much, it was nothing. You and your people bring us ever closer to victory. The elves long for the chance to spend time in the human world. We have feared for our children for so many years."

He smiled at Talia who was listening to our conversation. "I was sure that I'd lost my granddaughter when Marcellus captured her, but the fates had other thoughts."

"Yes," Marcellus interjected. "You and Darius managed to break my father's most dangerous troops. Most especially, the ones that I couldn't fight. I thank you both. The fact that we now have time to welcome the ardens to the fight is an even greater victory. We may not have won the war yet, but we're many steps closer."

"What is the plan now?" I asked. "Azulus is coming, so do we just sit and make arrows?"

A hint of a smile crept across Marcellus's lips. "No. The first step will be to utilize the arden weaponry to create traps and obstacles to give our troops on the walls an even stronger advantage. Your father has been walking me through the various weapons available to us."

"After that, we need to decide on ways to react to my father's most obvious strategies. He has the gift of prophecy working for him, but much of the troops that he depended on for creative attacks are no longer an option."

"But what do I do?" I asked.

Marcellus raised his eyebrow in question. "What do you mean? You've done your part. You can join the war council, but since you have minimal experience in actual war, you may want to leave that to some of the rest of us. Is there something you'd prefer to do?"

I sat back. Everything had been so rushed and important before, but now it felt like I was insignificant again, like I didn't matter. I was surprised they even let me sit at this table with them. "I'd like to join the war councils," I said. I had to take a deep breath before I made a scene. I didn't do well when people dismissed me like this. "Remember that I've fought your father's soldiers and lived. How many of these humans or other ardens can say that?"

"I told you she wouldn't take well to sitting things out," Darius said with a laugh.

Marcellus was drawn to Darius's comment, but then he turned back to me. "Princess Orlana, please understand. What you did and what we're about to do are very different things. We welcome your skills in battle, and maybe you could even spend some time training the other ardens, but please don't try to pretend that your three attacks on my father's army were the same as full-scale siege warfare. This is going to be the largest battle the world has ever known."

My lips quivered as I tried to hold back my anger. Relegated to training ardens instead of making decisions. I could feel myself growing warm as I stared at Marcellus. Then Darius said, "He's right, and you know it. The best thing you can do is to train the other ardens to fight like you."

I turned on him, my anger turning to the person who I wasn't afraid of lashing out at, and he saw how angry I was, but he didn't flinch. "We have days. None of them will be ready to fight like me in years. Trying to train ardens to do more than they already can do is an exercise in futility."

I stood up as I tried to keep from making a bigger scene than I already had, and my father reached out, grabbing my wrist. "I taught you better than this, Orlana. You're not a child."

That was too much. My father had never understood that it was best to leave me be when the flames were this close to the surface. I stared down at him, and I couldn't stop myself.

"Damned right, I'm not a child, Father. *I* slaughtered the djinn. *I* trapped and killed the solen fae. *I* brought down two ifrits, killed thousands with them, and then gave you and the rest of the ardens the time you needed to get here. Maybe you shouldn't worry about my manners so much."

With that, I pulled my arm away from him. After what he'd done, I wanted nothing to do with him. How anyone could question my decisions after what Darius and I had done was beyond my understanding.

I glanced at Darius, who was staring at me. He'd taken Marcellus's side. We may be bound, but he still listened to his brother more than me. I hadn't been wrong when I had thought that things would be different now that we weren't alone together.

The brand that connected us may have brought our souls closer together, but I didn't *feel* closer. Our little adventure was over, and Darius was not mine any longer. We may be closer than friends, but he wasn't all mine as he had been when we'd been working together. His brothers had an older and stronger claim to him than I did.

I walked out of the room, and Shadow whispered to me. "Why are you angry?"

"They aren't giving me the respect that I've earned. They want me to train ardens instead of letting me do anything important. I bet they're even letting my father command troops."

"He's done it before. He fought in the last war with Azulus, and from what I understand, he did as well as could be expected against overwhelming odds."

I gritted my teeth. "You're supposed to be on my side, Shadow. Everyone else is turning against me. Why can't you support me?"

Shadow was quiet as I walked through the corridors made of white stone. I needed to find a place to think, a place where no one would find me.

"Orlana, you're acting like a spoiled princess," Shadow whispered. Immediately, I felt my muscles tighten up. He'd never said anything like that before.

"And you're being a terrible friend," I responded. I changed direction and went back to my room. I was nearly running as I moved through the corridors. I needed to be alone.

Shadow was quiet as I walked into my room. I set him down on the bed and said, "Stay out of my head. I want to think, and I don't want you involved. Talk to Darius if you get bored since he's your new best friend."

He didn't reply as I turned around and walked out the door.

Chapter 32

Vines crept along the pathway through the gardens. Their arrow-shaped leaves seemed to point the way through the twisting maze of blooming flowers behind the castle. I had to admit that Inoras was the most beautiful place I'd been to. Especially the castle. Everything else was so devoid of stone that I felt like a complete outsider, but here, next to the white stone walls of the castle, I could appreciate the beauty and still feel at home.

I wondered what the world had been like before Azulus had taken control of it. Had the arden fae thousands of years ago come to Inoras and helped to build it? Had the solen fae asked for their help to uncover the stone of the desert? Had we bonded with the djinn over the flames that filled us both?

I didn't know, and I doubted anyone did. Maybe some of the solen fae did. The ardens were so decimated in the last war that there was no one that remembered the time before Azulus. It was a terrible thing that we'd all been forced into our own little corners of the world to hide in the shadows.

The time of hiding was done, though. I would push our people together again if we survived this. It was wrong that we'd been so isolated for so long, and I wanted to know this other world.

Those thoughts only brought my fight with Marcellus and Darius back to mind, and as soon as I thought about it, I felt heat fill me. I knew that I was inexperienced in many respects. I knew I didn't have the knowledge to lead the defense. It wasn't that they had told me that I was out of my depth. It was the way they'd said it.

They'd treated me like a child, and that infuriated me more than anything. I would have understood if they'd treated me like someone who was inexperienced, but they'd offered me a worthless position to keep me out of their way.

I came to a bench made from the still-living branches of the hedges. They'd been shaped to create a seat, but they'd also been woven into intricate designs. We could create many things, but no arden could have grown this bench. For just a moment, I let the wonder break my thoughts. This was a work of art in a world of beauty.

I sat down and lay my head back as Darius did when he'd relaxed in the bath. I tried to let my tension and anger fade, but no meditation helped. This anger had deep roots, and until I understood why I was so angry, it wouldn't be leaving.

I could have taken the dismissal from Marcellus. He didn't know me. He was just a warrior who had no reason to trust me with anything. All he'd heard was that I was a good fighter. He didn't know what I'd done, and I was sure that he attributed nearly all the success to Darius. He trusted him.

When Darius had taken Marcellus's side, it had set me off. Darius had been with me from the beginning. He'd seen me do things he never could have. He'd seen me be a solid ally even when I'd been out of my depth. I hadn't killed a man before beginning the mission, but now I'd killed more men than most soldiers had.

That was what really bothered me. Darius had seen how quickly I'd grown to fit the needs of the mission, but he hadn't backed me up. We'd spent the past few weeks constantly living on a razor's edge, and we'd trusted each other, both of us sacrificing for the other's benefit.

But now that we were back in the real world, he'd abandoned me. There was no loyalty to me any longer. Instead, he'd gone back to his brother.

Then there was Shadow's betrayal. He had been my best friend for my entire life, sharing a bond with only me. Now, he'd bonded Darius as well.

I was alone, and that's what bothered me. That's what hurt me. I'd never been so alone.

I stared up at the sky and watched the clouds float by. I felt the anger fade now that I knew what had made me overreact. It was replaced by a terrible sadness. I'd been abandoned by everyone that I cared about.

I was truly alone for the first time.

"How are you doing? It's good to see you out of bed for once." a soft voice pulled me from my thoughts. Anger flashed through me at the interruption. I'd come here to be alone.

But when I looked up, the anger was washed away as I saw who had spoken to me. Ona. Dressed in a sela, she looked far more out of place than I did, and yet, she looked exactly as she should. Ona was probably the most beautiful woman I'd ever met, but it was more than her looks.

She was beautiful because of the kindness in her eyes. There was no doubt as to why Azulus had taken her as a wife, but even after all the years with him, there was so little darkness in her that she was like a fire in the night, pushing the shadows away.

"It's good to be out of bed. I'm glad that I didn't die before getting to see the famed elven kingdoms."

Ona grinned and said, "Truth be told, I'm not all that impressed. There's not enough sun or open space. I wasn't meant for the forest, but sometimes we all have to do what's best rather than what makes us happy. I'll do my best to enjoy my time in the forest, and then I'll do my best to never have to come back."

She sat down next to me and put her hand on my knee. "Now, tell me why the beautiful and famed arden princess is sitting all alone in the hidden gardens instead of telling all those men up there what they should do?"

I chuckled at her. Ona somehow knew how to cut right to the heart of a problem. "They don't want me up there, Ona. They asked me to train ardens rather than sit on war councils."

"Sounds like good luck to me. Have you ever sat in a war council? They're miserable, like chewing rice cooked without water. Everyone thinks they know best, so they'll argue for hours on the most minor things. Then, after everyone's bickered themselves blue in the face, Marcellus will make all the decisions. My husband was the same way. As my family used to say, the wind may blow in all directions, but the clouds only follow one. If you want to have input, have

Marcellus tell you his plan, and then ask questions that make him think."

What Ona said made sense. Why hadn't I thought of that? I couldn't convince an entire table of commanders that I was right, but I might convince Marcellus. And if I couldn't, he'd explain why I was wrong, and then I'd learn something.

I'd taken it as an insult instead of working around the suggestion. I could learn a thing or two from Ona.

"Thank you for the advice," I said. "I guess I overreacted a bit. I just don't like it when people treat me like a child."

Ona just grinned at me, not replying.

"What? What's so funny?"

"Oh, it's not that they were treating you like a child. They were treating you like a woman in a man's world. Do you see any Queens running around? How many warriors have you seen with tits?"

I was taken aback by how accurate that was. I'd grown up knowing that my mother had been a warrior. One of the strongest. I knew that solen fae women were warriors, though few had been bound to Azulus.

"What about Talia?" I asked.

"Talia was treated like a silly little girl until just recently. Disregarded repeatedly until she demanded that her mate take her opinions seriously. When you're the bedmate of the warrior prince, people tend to take you a bit more seriously. Then there's the whole prophecy thing. When you can see the future, it helps people to pay attention."

"Well, I'm not jumping into bed with Marcellus anytime soon."

"I bet Darius is happy for that," Ona said with a sly smile.

I bit my lip and tried to turn away, but Ona squeezed my

leg and scooted just a little closer. "Darius is a different kind of man, Orlana. You probably already know that, but you should realize that he's different now than before he met you. His eyes smile now, and they never did before."

"Strange way of showing it," I said. "If he showed interest in something, I'd back him. Especially in public. He did the exact opposite today when he took Marcellus's side."

Ona shrugged. "Men are stupid creatures. They think with their heads instead of their hearts. Trust me on this. I've been around some of the smartest men in the world, and Darius is one of them. He's still stupider than the most average of women when it comes to making other people happy. You're a Firebrand, Orlana. You're supposed to be quick to anger, but when it comes to Darius, maybe you could be just as quick to let go of that fire."

I nodded to Ona. There was something more though. Something that neither Ona nor Darius was saying, but I couldn't place it. I hadn't realized it until Ona had brushed over it by saying that about Darius. Darius understood women, and though I was sure he rarely cared if he pissed one off, he would know how to keep from doing it.

"Thank you for the advice, Ona. I tend to explode, especially when it's Darius who's frustrating me."

She gave me a knowing smile and said, "The people we care about the most are the ones who frustrate us the most. Now, I hear that Marcellus has a few minutes before he's supposed to inspect the defenses. Might be a good time to have a quick chat with him."

"I will, but first, I have to ask a question I've wondered since the day I met you in Assama. How did a woman like you end up marrying Azulus when you knew how horrible he was?"

Ona's face didn't lose the cheer in it as she said, "That's a long story that I might tell you another time, but simply said, when Azulus wants something, he gets it. I didn't want anyone to get hurt in that process. I may not carry a sword like you, and I may not cause chaos like Darius, but I know how to protect the people I care about. Orlana, try to remember that. Sometimes strength doesn't come from training with a sword or building muscles. Sometimes it comes from the heart."

"I've never witnessed it, but I'll trust you on it, Ona."

She grinned as I stood up. "Run along, Princess Orlana. There's a very stupid man with wings who desperately needs you to point at a map and yell loudly."

Chapter 33

"That's a good point," Marcellus said as he stared at the map. "Is there any way to set a timer on the thermal disruptors?"

"No, but they'll work until they've absorbed a certain amount of heat. They last months in the arden caves where no one is throwing fireballs. The only problem you'd run into is if someone tries to start a campfire or shoots a flaming arrow."

Marcellus nodded as he ran his hand over his cheek. "I doubt your father considered them weapons, though. I wonder how many he brought."

"They take very little time to make since they're not complicated at all. You could have the Binders here make them with plenty of time to spare."

"So that's how you dealt with the djinn? Darius tried to explain it to me, but he seemed unsure how they worked."

I nodded. "Now, I know you've already planned to set traps along the way, but do you really think that the charging infantry is what we need to worry about? We have sturdy walls, the best archers in the world, and we have enough Firebrands to cover the ground in flames."

"What would you suggest?" he asked, leaning back in the chair and looking up at me.

I stepped back, needing a bit of room around me. He was listening. Really listening. I could see the respect building in his eyes. "What if you launched them at the remaining solen fae?"

Marcellus shook his head. "No, you and Darius did a lot to eliminate that threat. At this point, the thing that we need to do is keep the walls safe. As you said, we have the greatest archers in the world. All of them will have a quiver full of steel arrows, so magical protections will be useless. No one except maybe me could survive a few barrages of steel arrows."

"It was a good idea, but the thing you need to remember is that soldiers are what win major battles. Irregular troops like solen fae and djinn are good at being that extra push to break through lines, but they can't win the battle like thousands of soldiers wearing steel armor can. We need to protect the walls because he has the numbers."

I nodded to Marcellus. That made sense. This was what I'd wanted. I didn't have to be right. I just needed to know that my ideas were being taken seriously.

"If you have any other thoughts, let me know. The thermal disruptors are brilliant. It will let the ardens focus on the oncoming troops rather than the fire heading to the walls."

"But I have to go take a look at the defenses. My father draws closer, and even with all the additional help, this castle was not nearly as fortified as I'd hoped it would be. Elves like pretty things, and pretty things will end up getting us all killed."

He stood up, and I swore he looked even larger than he had this morning. He made Darius look tiny.

"Thank you," I said. "I'm sorry for the way I acted this morning. It's been a long couple of months."

Marcellus chuckled. "If I were going to be upset at explosions at the breakfast table, I'd be furious with myself constantly. Ask Darius about how many times my family dining table had to be rebuilt."

I grinned and followed him out of the war room. Darius was leaning up against the wall with that mischievous grin on his face. "Couldn't stay out of it, could you?"

"Have you ever known me to trust someone with wings to make decisions? You're meant to be pretty and carry things for us. All those muscles don't leave a lot of room for thinking."

Marcellus laughed, "Thank the gods that I didn't have to spend two months with you. One of us would have died."

Darius chuckled and said, "Because Talia was so much easier?"

"Talia will be the death of me, but at least I'll enjoy it." He grinned at me and said, "I don't think I'd enjoy burning to death."

I shrugged, and Marcellus turned back to Darius. "I need you to come with me. You're the only other man with wings, so you need to see what we have to work with. I don't want to have any kind of aerial fights, but if Father comes up with something clever, I need you to understand the defenses if I'm not around."

Darius nodded to him. "I'll catch up with you in a few."

Marcellus turned and walked down the hall, his back stiff as a rail where Darius tended to almost slink around. They were so different, yet so similar.

"Will you let me take you flying this afternoon?" he asked.

"I should still be pissed at you," I responded. "You took Marcellus's side this morning."

Darius looked like he was about to say something he'd regret, but he bit his tongue. "I apologize, Orlana. I should have explained that you aren't as inexperienced as Marcellus believes. You obviously convinced him to change his plans, which is unusual."

"I accept your apology, and I'd love to go flying. If we're going to die in the next few days, I'd at least like to see some of the elven kingdoms before then."

He smiled at me, and for a moment it was like the world faded away. I wanted so badly to believe that I'd overreacted to everything this morning, and we could go back to the way things were before I'd been wounded. "Maybe we can play a game or two of Thief. I'd love to win a few of my own favors from you. Or maybe you can spend your last one."

Feeling his breath against my neck woke that part of me up that had begun to sleep since being injured. "Maybe I'll let you win if you promise to use your favors in fun ways."

Darius pulled away, and I saw the lights dancing in his eyes as he smiled at me. "*You* let me win? I let you win those few times so that you'd keep playing."

"Go look at the wall, Darius. And don't take all day, or I may have to find another person to play Thief with."

Chapter 34

The last light of the day fell over Inoras as I sat on the ramparts and looked towards the gate to the mortal world. Shadow lay across my lap as I waited. There was nothing else to do.

Darius had offered an evening flight, but then he hadn't shown up. He was still gone with Marcellus on their own flight out of the gate. He'd chosen Marcellus over me once again.

This afternoon, I'd hoped that things would go back to the way they had been. The hope had been unfounded, and Darius was proving once again that I didn't mean the same to him that he meant to me. I wouldn't be his first choice or worry.

But I wasn't angry. Not this time. I'd been right from the beginning, and I never should have thought anything had changed. Maybe I was more than a friend, but I wasn't family, and I almost certainly never would be.

"You said that he'd make a good husband," I whispered to Shadow. "This isn't what a good husband does."

"I've told you from the beginning. There is more to Darius the Silent than meets the eye. Do you really think that he abandoned you to go for a flight with his brother?"

I sighed. "That's what it looks like, doesn't it?"

"Nothing he does is what it looks like. Nothing. Trust me, Orlana. I know that you're still angry at me, but you've trusted me for a long time. Trust me now. He chose you over his Arturus, and he'd choose you over Marcellus as well."

I shook my head as the world went dark. "I don't think I can trust you on this, Shadow. I told him no more lies. No more masks. I can't imagine why he couldn't have just told me what he was doing. It's not like we were far away."

"I don't know," Shadow said, and he didn't seem sure of himself.

I stood up and slung Shadow's sheath over my shoulder as I made the walk down the stairs. I knew that this was a small thing. Nothing to explode about. But it had come while we were already on shaky ground.

As I walked under the arch that led into the castle, my fingers brushed against the stone of the doorway, and I wished I was back home. Back in the Emerald Caverns where everything made sense.

I'd been told that I was out of my depth since the beginning, and I'd coped each and every time. It hadn't been easy, but I'd done it. Go up against the greatest army in the world and sabotage the most powerful pieces of it? I'll do it. Get stuck working with someone I'd grown up cursing. I'll manage. Protect the heart of the man I loved over the mission, over my revenge. Yes, I can do that.

But I didn't think I could do this. I could manage being a soldier and doing terrible things, but loving someone who didn't love me back was too much. I was struggling to find the reason to keep going. There was nothing easy about that man. Nothing. He was a ball of lies and pain wrapped up in a pretty package.

But he was also kind and clever. I didn't care about the pretty part. I cared about the man behind the masks. He'd wanted me to be an arden uncaged, and I'd done it. For him. But could Darius the Silent ever live without the masks and complications? Could he ever be Darius the Simple?

Because right then, I needed a little simple. I needed a bit of earth to hold on to when the world felt like it was flying out of control. Darius wasn't being that rock to hold on to, and I knew he should be. I should be able to count on the man that I'd professed my love to.

And instead, I'd been abandoned again, left to flutter in the winds of madness.

"I'm sorry," Shadow whispered. "I didn't ask to bond Darius, and he didn't ask me to bond him. We made the decision to save you. It was the only way to bind the two of you together without you saying the words."

"It doesn't matter. I'm not mad at you anymore. I'm just... I'm just done. I think I need to step away from the madness of it all for a while. Marcellus already told me he didn't need me. No one *needs* me. Not anymore. I did the thing I had to do, and I'll stand on the front lines when Azulus comes, but until then, I think that maybe I just need to let myself fall apart a little."

I felt something strange from Shadow. An emotion that I'd never felt before. Sadness. No, it was more than that. It was anguish. Even more than when he was given to me.

I couldn't hold the weight of Shadow's emotions on my shoulders, though. I'd been strong for so long. I knew what it was to trust someone to hold me up now, and I yearned for it. Just a few moments without having to be strong.

But the one person who could have done it was the one man I couldn't ask it from. No, I couldn't be an uncaged arden any longer. But before I wrapped the bars back around me, I was going to give in to the grief. All of it.

Chapter 35

I walked down to the training yard. I knew that most women let their emotions go with a good cry, but that wasn't me. I hadn't grown up like that. I felt tears well up, and they would eventually fall, but not yet. No, first something was going to break.

I passed soldiers who were stripping off their armor. Humans, elves, and even a few arden fae. They'd been training, and I smiled at them regardless of the tears. This was as close to home as I would find. I'd never had an audience, but I didn't care. There was nothing to prove to anyone. This was about me, the only uncaged arden fae, and there was no one that could stop me.

The training yard was built of sand, and I wondered how much would be left when I was done. Practice dummies built of wood that had been covered in padded cloth ringed the yard. I didn't need them. I had something better.

With the most basic Stonewaking skill, I drew fifteen pillars from the ground. As the magic flowed through me into the ground to raise these pillars, I felt the first tears begin to fall.

Then I drew Shadow who quivered in my hands. He didn't know this side of me. No one did. Not even me. And he was afraid.

I closed my eyes and felt the Drums of Pain meditation race through me. Memories of Darius's voice filled me as I stepped up to the first pillar. I could feel the people watching me.

A steady rhythm of Darius's words ran through me. Each laugh. Each joke. Each whisper.

He'd chosen to abandon me, and I couldn't let myself be hurt again. I leaped into the air, flames propelling me to the top of the pillar, and I began an aerial dance that I'd never done before. I'd never felt like this before.

The pain of loss filled my body as I dove towards the next pillar. Shadow sliced through the stone as easily as if it had been flesh, and my other hand caught the top of the pillar. Heat flowed from my hand to the stone, and I threw the red-hot, hundred-pound piece of stone across the yard.

All of it was done in a single movement, and I heard the crash as I flew into the air, once again propelled by flames. An image of Darius holding his wrists as blood flowed to the ground after my first flight. I'd still hated him then. He'd been the enemy that was sure to betray me.

And maybe he had.

The tears fell as I moved across the field. As I crossed from one pillar to the next, I spun, and flames raced across the field to hit the opposite side pillar with an explosion.

I needed to break things. I needed to let the fire inside me out, or I was sure that I would explode. With each expenditure of flames, I didn't feel any better, even though I should have.

An image of Darius in the bath for the first time. That first time that I'd attacked him when he'd held me so close. When I'd looked into those golden eyes for the first time. Gods, it felt like someone was ripping my chest open.

If flames wouldn't help, maybe the sword would, and I dropped to the sand. Faster than the human eye could see, I cut the fourth pillar into pieces and kicked it square in the center, sending the pieces flying.

Another image flashed through my mind. The first time that Darius had kissed me. He'd held me down and forced that kiss on me, and no matter how badly I'd wanted to stab him, I'd known right then that he meant something to me.

Those golden eyes of his had burned into me, dragging me into what I'd thought was love. It had been another mask, another lie.

And the sword didn't help to release the emotions. The movements didn't help. The destruction didn't. Nothing did.

I fell to my knees and let go. As image after image flashed through my mind, flames rose from me, coating me in their warmth. I remembered how he'd pushed me to stop holding myself back. The way it had felt with him above me, the inferno doing its best to burn the world away.

And the fire around me rose high above me, a bonfire in the night. My tears hissed as they hit the twisting, writhing flames that coated my body, and I felt just the slightest bit better as the flames slowly grew around me.

Then I saw him above me, smiling as I lay dying in the Marshes of Sorrow. A terrible ache filled me as I looked into his eyes again, and the flames grew hotter and rose higher.

All that pain and longing rushed out of me in an explosion of light and heat as I knelt on the sands of the practice field. And then it was over. All the sorrow that I'd felt was gone.

I opened my eyes and looked around me. The sand had turned to glass, and the soldiers gawked at me as I slowly stood up. I didn't say anything as I walked across the field.

Marcellus and Darius stood by the stairs, their eyes wide, and I didn't even look at them. I just brushed past them and continued the climb. I didn't want to talk to them. I didn't want to see them or be around them. Not tonight. Tonight, I'd let hope and love die. Then they'd been burnt away in an inferno that nothing could have rivaled.

And in their place lay only ashes.

Chapter 36

I sat in the war council with a blank stare on my face. I may have had an emotional explosion last night, but that didn't change the fact that Azulus was coming. Plans still had to be made.

"Talia says that my father will encircle the castle immediately. He will send out troops to the towns outside our walls and raze them to draw us out onto the battlefield rather than fight behind the walls where we have the advantage. We can't take that bait, so we must get everyone and anything of value into the safety of the castles."

"Teffin," he said as he looked at the scruffy man from the breakfast, "I'll need you to work with some of King Sundryl's men to make sure that happens. I don't want a single person to stay anywhere outside of a place with walls. Everyone needs to be inside. Farms and homes can be rebuilt and replanted, but anyone that's outside of a place with high walls will end up dead."

"My father won't let his soldiers go far to keep from stretching his troops too thin. He needs every one of those soldiers when it comes time to assault the castle. They won't wait out a siege because feeding three hundred thousand men will be a more difficult task than simply taking the castle in his mind. He believes his army will decimate any resistance because it's never failed him before."

Marcellus looked regal even without a tunic on as he stood at the head of the table. Black wings that sparkled like arden scales drew the eye. His imposing and confident image would inspire fear or courage, depending on what side of the fight you were on.

Next to him, leaning against the wall, Darius was forgotten. But Darius didn't forget anyone in the room. His eyes scanned their faces, and I knew he was reading their emotions. He didn't have the power of a djinn, but he could read a man better than anyone I'd ever met. That was how he was so good at cards.

The warrior and the diplomat. Honest and brutal versus conniving and beautiful. Two sides of the same coin because, in the end, they both always got what they wanted. They just accomplished it in different ways.

"What does Princess Talia say that Azulus will do during the battle?" one of the elven commanders questioned.

"The possibilities change with each vision," Talia said as she stood up from her seat. "He hasn't decided what he'll do yet, so it's impossible to say. He knows that I'm here, and so he won't commit to a plan until the very last moment. He'll also see what we're doing and base his decision on that. Remember that he has some gift of prophecy as well, though I don't think it works the same way that mine does."

The commander nodded. "What kinds of approaches have you seen?" a human king asked.

"In one vision, he committed his entire army to the battle. This was before the ardens arrived, and we fell. In another, he used an arsenal of arden weaponry that he'd held onto since the previous war. We fell to that as well."

"How many visions have you had where we won?" This question was from my father.

I raised my eyebrow as Talia turned to Marcellus. He smiled at the table and said, "None."

Immediately, a raucous reaction consumed the table. I didn't join in. Instead, I watched Marcellus and Darius as Darius had taught me to do. They smiled at each other and then Darius nodded to Marcellus, who turned back to the table.

"This is a good thing," he said, his voice just a touch louder than it had been only moments before. "It means that my father will be overconfident. He'll have seen the same visions. There is a reason that we haven't decided on a plan yet."

The room went silent and then a different human king, in obvious disbelief, said, "You haven't come up with a plan?"

Marcellus smiled and said, "I have about a hundred plans. I have a system of arden communication tools to react to his assault. I've fought under my father since before your kingdom had a name, and if there's anyone that will be able to read him, it's me."

The way he looked, there was no one in the room that would argue against him. There wasn't a doubt in my mind that he would rule this war council with a steel fist, and I saw the expressions on everyone's faces as the realization struck the rest of them as well.

"I think that should conclude this morning's meeting. There was an incident on the training field. King Finneon, would you please have your ardens deal it?"

My father cocked an eyebrow at me before saying, "It will be done."

Then everyone began standing up and walking out of the room. I stood up and followed them. When I got into the hall, I felt a hand wrap around my arm, and I whirled around at the unfamiliar touch, only to see that it was Talia.

"Orlana," she said with the same kind of smile that Ona wore. The kind that could brighten a room. "What are you doing this afternoon?"

I frowned. What was this about? "I was thinking about going through the arden arsenal to find out what my father brought. I feel like I may help the war effort more with traps than with anything else."

Marcellus and Darius walked up then, and I glanced at Darius for only a moment before turning back to Talia as she began to talk. "I was just thinking that maybe it would be a good decision for us to all get out of here for a few hours. As Marcellus said, we can't make any decisions until Azulus gets here."

"That sounds like fun," Darius said, and I ignored him.

"I really should go through the arsenal. I don't trust anyone else to do it."

Marcellus chuckled. "I'll give you an inventory of everything that your father brought as soon as we get back. There's no need to look through it yourself when someone has already made the list."

I chewed my lip. I really didn't want to go anywhere with Darius. Not after he ignored our plans last night. Not after he chose Marcellus.

But I couldn't just say that. Everyone knew that we'd had something, and with a glance at Talia, I knew she had something to do with this. I didn't want the confrontation with either of them right then.

"Then I guess I'm free for the afternoon."

Talia smiled, and I saw a twinkle in her eye as she said, "Great. I know just the place."

* * *

Darius held me by the waist as we flew through the forests that filled the elven kingdoms. The world was beautiful even if it was too flat for my liking. Trees that couldn't be found anywhere else rose above the forest treetops, branching out into massive, building-sized tufts that overshadowed everything around them.

Everything was green even though I hadn't seen a drop of rain fall, and crystal-clear rivers ran throughout the forests. They made me think about the day that Darius and I had played in the river when I'd thrown the fish at him.

The day that I'd told him I'd be uncaged for him.

"What's going on with you?" he whispered in my ear as we flew.

"Nothing." I didn't have to answer him. If he was too stupid to understand what had upset me, then that was on him. I wasn't here to change him. I didn't have the energy to do that.

I wanted to be his number one, not his number three, and if that wasn't going to happen, I didn't need to waste the time

250

and thought on him.

"If it's about last night, I'm sorry. Marcellus wanted to show me some things he'd done outside of the elven kingdoms. It just took longer than I'd expected."

"That's fine," I replied tersely. I didn't want to talk to him, and I didn't want to hear his excuses. All I'd wanted was for him to let me know that he was canceling on me.

He was quiet for a while, but then he whispered, "What happened last night on the training field? I've never seen you do anything like that."

"I don't want to talk about it." The hints weren't working, so I would just have to be direct. He didn't say anything after that. In fact, he seemed to pull away as well.

The minutes ticked by as we flew, and I heard the soft sound of giggles from Talia up ahead. Darius shifted his grip just slightly and pulled me tighter against him. I was reminded of the times that he'd flown with me before. The way his warmth had flowed into me and helped to calm me.

The way we'd felt so close.

But now, even as he held me tight against his chest, we felt miles apart, and there was just the slightest piece of me that wished that things could be different. That maybe I shouldn't have given up on him so quickly.

I'd been happier with him than I'd been with anyone else. Ever. He'd made me smile and laugh, but more than that, he'd pushed me to be me. Not the princess I'd been born to be or the warrior that I'd been trained to be.

He'd pushed me to be whatever I wanted to be.

That's what had made it all feel so much worse. I'd never wanted anything as much as I'd wanted Darius. I'd thought that I'd wanted revenge. I'd lived my entire life wanting nothing more than revenge for my mother's death, but when given the chance, I'd chosen Darius over it.

And I still didn't regret that choice.

Even as I watched him pull away from me by choosing his brother over me, I didn't regret letting Arturus live. No matter what happened, I was glad that Arturus was still alive and there was still hope for Darius to come out of this without being broken.

Even if I wasn't sure if I would.

* * *

We landed in a shaded glade unlike any I'd ever seen before. Twinkling lights filled the air, blinking into existence and then disappearing. They were everywhere, but I couldn't figure out what was making the light.

"Teltha trees," Talia said with a grin. "They drop this twinkling dust when it's time for them to pollinate."

It was beautiful. Like nothing else in the world. Marcellus set down the pack of food that he'd brought. He pulled out bottles of wine and some cold pork, handing each of us a satchel of the meat.

"It's not much, but it'll do," he said. He sat down, his back up against one of the Teltha trees. "At least we're out of that damned castle. We haven't had a chance to talk much away from prying ears. And gods, I cannot stand the thought of one more king telling me how we should fight Father. If those idiots were in charge, we might as well just slit our own throats."

Darius chuckled and pulled the cork from his bottle of wine. He took a deep breath and exhaled. A puff of green smoke floated from his mouth to the ground and took the form of a massive frog. Its tongue flicked out, ending at a flickering light, and Talia laughed as she watched the illusion.

It was funny, but it wasn't Darius. He was performing for Talia, and it frustrated me to see him do it. I wondered if he even knew that he'd put the mask back on. The illusion vanished and Darius had a sip of the wine.

"So what was it like working with my brother?" Marcellus asked.

I glanced at Darius and smirked. "He's the biggest ass I've ever met, but I wouldn't have survived it without him." I wouldn't make up lies about him.

"Damn right I have a big ass," he said. "The women love it almost as much as my hair." He ran a hand through the sandstone-colored hair as he grinned.

Talia raised her eyebrow. "You mean the whores, don't you? The ones you pay to compliment you?" Darius glared at Talia, but I had to sit down as laughter overtook me. I had almost said the same thing.

"I see that you've experienced my younger brother's vice."

"We stayed at a brothel in Assama, and his frequent visits to them have been a topic of conversation many times."

Darius didn't look like it bothered him at all to be the butt of a joke, and I wondered if that was because of the mask or because he simply didn't care.

"I stayed at a brothel with Darius as well," Talia said. "After he rescued me from Azulus, I stayed there for a night, and I have to admit that it was eye-opening. I think everyone gets to know Darius at a brothel."

Talia had a way about her. Like Ona. It was easy to feel comfortable around her.

"What better place to learn about a woman than a whore-house? I'm sure an elf like you would have preferred long walks in the forest."

Marcellus jumped into the conversation then. "I think she enjoyed long flights more than long walks. I don't blame her there. Walking is slow."

"What purpose is there in being with a man with wings other than flying?" I quipped. "It's not like they help you rub our feet."

Marcellus grinned at Talia and said, "Maybe Darius just isn't using them right."

"I object to this kind of slander," he exclaimed. "It's one thing to poke jabs at my laziness or enjoyment of clothing-optional establishments, but let's not make up lies about my skills in the bedroom. Wouldn't want to ruin my reputation."

He raised a hand and a block of crystallized air formed under him as he sat down. He reached into a pocket and pulled out the deck of cards. "Since we have a bit of time, does anyone want to play?"

Talia grinned and said, "Playing cards with a prophet. You're about to ruin your own reputation."

Darius squinted at her for a moment and then slid the cards back into his pocket. "That's not fair. Seeing the future is obviously against the rules."

"So is putting an illusion on them," I countered.

Darius glared at me. "I never cheated you. Not even once."

I shrugged, and Marcellus chuckled. "I like you, Orlana. I haven't always been a fan of the women that my brother spent time with, but I like you."

I saw a glance between Marcellus and Darius, and every-thing got quiet again. I wondered what was shared in that glance. What kind of disagreement did they have, and what had Marcellus said that had bothered Darius?

I uncorked my wine bottle and took a sip. It was excellent wine. Much better than anything we'd drank elsewhere on our journey with a slight sweetness that wasn't found in any arden wines. "Elvish wine?" I asked.

Talia nodded, and then her eyes seemed to lose focus on the world for just a moment. When they refocused, she said, "Arturus has been healed. He can fly again."

Marcellus and Darius both nodded. "It's too bad," Marcellus said. "It'd have been better if he hadn't been able to fly. That'd have made the job of separating him from my father much easier."

"Why would you separate them?" I asked.

"So that we can fight my father while other people keep Arturus busy. Now that he can fly, he'll have to be wounded or trapped before we can manage it."

I blinked. "You're seriously going to try to keep Arturus alive through this battle?"

Darius and Marcellus both nodded. "It will be difficult, but it's necessary. As soon as Father is dead, he'll be able to command the army to fall back."

I just stared at them. Hundreds, maybe thousands of lives would be lost trying to keep Arturus at bay while Marcellus and Darius tried to kill their father.

"You disagree with this approach?" Marcellus asked.

I just shook my head. Convincing Darius might have been possible, but not both of them. They'd already made up their minds to save him, and I just stared at the ground.

Their loyalty only extended to each other. And maybe Talia. Marcellus might choose Talia over Arturus.

I glanced at Darius, and his expression had hardened slightly. He still wore the mask as always, but I could see the tightness in his neck and the hardness of his eyes. He knew what I was thinking.

"Let's go for a walk," Talia said as she stood up. "Let's enjoy ourselves and forget about all the death and destruction while we can. No more talk about the battle. Not for the next few hours."

"Yes, Lady," Marcellus said with a grin.

I expected Darius to make a comment, but he didn't. His eyes stayed on me as I stood up and followed Marcellus and Talia. This little trip into the woods was going to be just as difficult as I'd expected.

Chapter 37

Two days until Azulus arrived. That's all we had left, accord-ing to Talia and the scouts. My nerves were on edge, and I could feel flames hiding under my skin. All that anyone could talk about was what we needed to do, except that there was nothing to do. Nothing at all.

The defenses were as strong as they were going to be. Traps had been placed. There were no allies rushing to our rescue. Everyone was as trained as they were going to get.

And there was no definitive plan. Talia had seen us win in a vision, and that had brought many people hope, but then she'd seen five more where we lost and everyone inside the castle was killed.

We all knew that there was nothing else we could do, but we were all trying to do any little thing we could to make even the slightest bit of difference. And it was driving me crazy.

Darius walked out of the private study Marcellus had commandeered. His face was grim as Marcellus walked behind him. I needed a distraction. Anything to take my mind off the future, and there was no one else I could turn to.

I approached Darius, and the barest hint of a smile crossed his lips. "Afternoon, Orlana," he said.

"Darius, is there any way you could come with me? I need to think about something other than the war. I need to just forget about the world for a while."

He arched an eyebrow and turned to Marcellus for just a moment before saying, "I wish I could. Marcellus needs me to check on some things, though."

He turned to walk away, but I grabbed his arm. "I'm using my last favor, Darius. Help me to forget that we may die in two days."

His eyes got harder than I'd seen before as he stared at me. "You're using a favor now?"

I nodded to him. I had put it off for two days. I'd wandered the castle, talked to Talia and Ona, and I'd even done a bit of training with some ardens, but none of it helped. Everything and everyone was so focused on the war that I couldn't think of anything else while I was here. And I needed to. I needed to take a break from it all for a few hours so that I didn't feel like I was going to explode.

"Fine," he said. "Let me tell Marcellus. Then I'll help you to forget the world for a while."

When he walked away, Shadow spoke to me for the first time since I'd turned the sand to glass. I'd wondered why he'd been so silent, but I didn't have it in me to try to draw the reasoning out of him.

"I thought you were done with him."

"I don't have anyone else. I just need to get out of the castle. I was never nervous before we attacked Azulus because he'd helped me to relax."

"You don't know what you're doing, do you?" he whispered.

"What am I doing?" I asked.

Shadow sighed and said, "Your bond is pulling you to him. Even after doing your best to break away from him, you crave his presence. Your souls are closer than others because of the magic that binds you."

Then Darius was there, and he looked at me questioningly. He knew that I'd been talking to Shadow, but he didn't know about what. Shadow hadn't spoken to him this time.

"Let's go," he said, as his lip curled in a grin. "You can take off your clothes and get soaking wet." He gave me a wink and continued, "At the river while we're swimming."

Typical Darius.

* * *

Crystal-clear water ran through the enchanted elven forest. The wide river that seemed to meander aimlessly through the trees reminded me of the day that we went swimming outside Borlet. "This is what you wanted, isn't it?" he asked.

I nodded and watched him. For the first time since we'd met, he hesitated for just a moment, and then he pulled off his boots and trousers, leaving them on the riverbank.

I stripped down as well. I knew normal people would think that this was an intimate swim, but it was just the way we'd grown together. This was us, no physical walls between us. I got into the water, following him toward the center of the river.

He turned to look upstream and let the current carry the water past him. I stood next to him, and for the first time since we'd gotten to Inoras, I felt like there was something holding us together.

I glanced through the water and saw the brand on his hip. I wondered what it would have been like to be bound like this before we'd been forced to be around other people. People that didn't understand the two of us when we weren't who we'd trained ourselves to be for so long.

I followed his gaze, just watching the water flowing through the forest. "Do you ever wish that we'd stayed gone? Just done our job and never come to Inoras?"

Darius shook his head. "I'd have regretted it for the rest of my life. Especially if Marcellus had lost the war."

"That's true. I've spent my life training with a single purpose. I'd regret it too if they'd lost. I don't know if I'd regret ignoring it if they won though. Sometimes I wonder if any of it matters. Maybe we all would have been a lot happier if we'd just found someone and enjoyed the small things. That's all we were doing while we waited around for your father, wasn't it? Just being happy doing simple things like bathing together."

Darius sighed, and I knew he was just as unhappy here as I was. "It would have been nice to have had a bit more time together before coming here. I wasn't completely ready to be done with it just being the two of us."

We stared upriver and just enjoyed the way the water felt running across our bodies as the sun beat down on our naked skin. I reached my hand out and let my fingers find his. "We could die in a few days. I never considered that a possibility when we were attacking the army, but I can't stop thinking about it now. These could be our last days in this world."

He said, "It's been on my mind a lot lately too. And truthfully, I'm not sure if I care. I've had one purpose in my life all this time, and if we win, then that purpose is gone. If we lose, then I'll die, regardless. I just hope that I get to live long enough to see my father fall. If I get to see that, then I can die happy."

I turned to look at Darius. How could he not care if he died? I thought back to our conversation about what we'd do when this was all over, and I realized that I'd never really considered the fact that the one purpose in my life would be gone as well.

I'd grown up with the two-fold goal of killing King Azulus and freeing the arden fae. In two days, that would be done, and what would I do? The hate that had kept my fire burning all that time would be snuffed out. That was the problem with surviving on revenge. When your enemy was dead, what else was there? What else do you cling to for purpose in this world?

The thoughts ran through my mind as I looked at the one person who had understood me. He had worn that mask of arrogance and laziness for so long that it almost seemed strange to see him without it here. He looked like the blanket that had been used for too long. The one that always worried about the people that used it, and never received the attention it needed. But when the people were gone, when its purpose was gone, what did it matter if there were holes in it?

But I wasn't done with him, and I hoped he wasn't done with me either. I could cling to him, and maybe he could cling to me. Maybe together we could find a purpose beyond the hate and rage. Maybe we could find something that would fill that void that both of us had.

And I felt a warmth grow inside me. Where I'd thought only ash resided, I felt a smoldering heat, like the coals of a fire that had burned out. All it would take was the smallest bit of fuel, and that fire could burn again.

"What if your purpose was me, and mine was you? What if we held onto each other until we found that thing that everyone else seems to have?"

He turned to me then, finally breaking the spell of the river's current. He looked at me, and I saw the darkness of his eyes recede and that golden glow shined through. For a moment, I thought that maybe I'd given him hope where there'd been none before.

But then he shook his head and stepped back as he looked into the water at his waist. He said, "No. I'm too broken for you to be stuck with, Orlana. I couldn't do that to you."

I stared at him for a few seconds as the rejection hit me. Once again, I'd opened myself up to him and made myself vulnerable. Anger rose in me as I felt him put that wall up between us once again.

I snarled at him and turned to show him my shoulder. "I asked for this, Darius. I know your past. I know the reason you wear a mask around everyone, and I see the tears hiding in those eyes. I didn't turn away. I didn't push you away for being weak or broken."

My hands clenched into fists, and I felt my claws dig into my palm as the rage turned to words rather than the violence I craved. "Gods, we're all broken. I was seven when I vowed vengeance on your family. I learned to kill before I'd learned to read. You say you're broken, but I haven't ever cared, and I don't think you care that I'm broken too."

I put my hand on his chest and said, "I told you I loved you,

Darius, and I meant it. When I thought I was going to die, I had no regrets except that I hadn't told you that. I didn't tell you so that you'd say it back. I told you because you needed to hear it and because I needed to be honest with you."

I snarled again and took a step back as he argued with me. "You don't understand." His wings stretched out, and the wind raged around us as he began to lose control of his emotions. The mask dropped, and I saw a tear roll down his cheek.

"I can never love you, Orlana. I can't marry you or give you children. I can't be the man you deserve. No matter how badly I want to, I can't. You're the shining star in my life right now, but I know that no matter what I do, I can't have you. I can't force that on a woman as wonderful as you."

I felt the flames inside me rising to the surface, and I was sure that steam rose from the water around me. "I never asked you for anything. Not marriage or children or even love. I don't know how else to say it. I told you what I demanded that day we went to the river. I want you to drop the masks and the lies and the confusion. That's all I've ever asked."

I turned around, no longer able to look at the man who had fled from any kind of relationship with me beyond friendship. "But you won't ever do that. You don't know how to live without the lies. I'd hoped that I could trust you to stand by your oath, but you're no different from anyone else. You'll stand by your oaths until it becomes difficult. Then you'll forget about them. You'll forget why they were given. Stay away from me, Darius the Liar. I have enough problems as it is without having to deal with broken oaths."

I walked towards the shore. I needed to put my clothes back on and begin the run back to Inoras. The last thing I wanted was for Darius to carry me.

Then I felt his hand wrap around my shoulder as he whirled me around. The anger turned to rage, and I lashed out at him, my claws raking across his chest. He didn't flinch as the strips of crimson turned the water around his waist a soft pink.

Instead, he wrapped his hand around my neck. The winds whipped around us as I stared into his eyes. I saw the pain in them as the mask faded away. When he bent down to kiss me, he *tasted* different. He'd talked about tasting a kiss, and I hadn't understood it until now.

He pressed his lips against mine with a desperateness that he'd never shown before. Not the teasing way he'd started his games with me, and not the need-filled way he'd pushed me to escape my self-imposed control. No, this was entirely for him. He wasn't kissing me for me. He was kissing me because he couldn't stop himself.

And he tasted differently. Like he'd cried a thousand tears, and all that was left was that brittle saltiness after there were no more tears to shed. I didn't pull away. Not this time.

When he finally released me from the kiss, he whispered, "You're all I think about, but I can't keep you. You'll want something more. Someone that can love you."

"Then take me now while I only want you."

That was all it took, and the wind lifted us into the air.

Darius held my head in his hands as he crushed his lips against mine, fanning the flames inside me. Heat rose between us as his body called to me. Everything inside me had needed his touch for too long. My nails ran over his back, drawing the heat from him. There was no teasing now, and as he moved his lips to my neck, I knew he needed my touch just as much I'd needed his.

"Gods, Darius," I moaned as his teeth pressed against my

264

skin, and his nails raked across the scales of my shoulder blades. The air that swirled around us and lifted us out of the water teased every inch of my body.

The rest of the world seemed to disappear as I was lost in the sensations that coursed through me. I barely noticed as we turned so that we floated through the air horizontally.

"I've missed you," Darius whispered in my ear as he lay on top of me. "I've missed this." His hand moved between my legs, and I spread them for him.

The winds carried us through the air, suspending us in a vortex as though they had been made solid. "Me too," I said with a gasp. My body had been ready for him, and when he touched me, I pulsed in time with my heartbeat.

The only reason I knew that we'd arrived on the shore was that the cool ground pressed against my back. My complete attention was on Darius and the throbbing that filled my body.

I'd known it would be like this as soon as he'd kissed me. I'd imagined it a hundred times since I'd woken up in Inoras. Of all the men in the world, only he'd found his way into my dreams. Only he had found his way into my heart.

Darius slid down to between my legs. His lips left little bruises along my inner thigh as he teased my body into desperation. His fingers slid inside me, and another gasp escaped my lips as I closed my eyes. But I still saw him in my mind. His golden eyes and sharp cheekbones. The way a few strands of his sandy hair always fell in front of his face.

That smile that told me I should be a little worried.

His lips and tongue found my core, and I arched my back as the sensations wove their way through me. Gods, there wasn't a man in the world that could make me crave him like Darius. Everything in the world could be burning around us, and I wouldn't be able to convince myself to push him away. He hadn't lied when he'd said that he could play a woman's body.

I wound my hands in his hair, pulling him tighter to me as I began grinding against him. I'd never felt the need to control him like this, but the world was crumbling around us, and I was afraid that even this could be ruined.

His hands moved up my stomach, his nails digging into my soft skin, and the flames inside me rose to the surface. I needed more than kisses and licks now. I needed to feel him. I needed to feel his weight on me and his hands around me.

I needed to feel him inside me.

I pulled him away from me, and he smiled. That smile said that he knew exactly how he was making me feel. "I need you inside me," I whispered to him, and he didn't hesitate.

He crawled on top of me, but I wanted something different. I rolled both of us over so that I was on top of him, and I grinned as I sat up. His manhood was wedged between us, and I slowly ground against him.

"I thought you said you wanted me inside you," he asked as his hands ran over my breasts.

The winds swirled around us even faster, picking up leaves and dust, and I stared down at him as I positioned him to slip inside me. Everything before this had been just a teaser, and as I sank down on him, I knew that this was right.

Darius ran his hands under my body as flames began to flow from my skin into the wind that whirled around us. His nails dug into me as I slammed myself down on him.

"That feels so damned good," he moaned out as he began to thrust upward, matching my pace.

It felt wonderful, and everything inside me ached to find a

way to make it last forever, but my body wanted something different.

Once again, Darius seemed to know exactly what I wanted, and he sat up to where I was sitting on his lap. I pressed my lips to his because no words could describe the way I felt.

The world darkened as more debris filled the air, blocking out the light of the world, and Darius's eyes glowed with the fire that never seemed to go out. A beautiful light in the darkness of the world.

His hands held my bottom and forced me up and down on him faster than I ever could. When I finally pulled away, I felt my body nearing that explosive end, and no matter what I did, I wouldn't be able to stop it.

As I looked into his eyes, my hands running through his hair, I knew we were both thinking the same thing: this could be the last time.

And he kissed me again, his tongue dancing with mine. He moved faster, pushing the ecstasy coursing through my body to even higher highs. Even as I felt the waves of flames rush from my body into the swirling winds around us, I couldn't help but wish it weren't happening.

Because then it would have to end.

I screamed out as I was thrown into that final moment of bliss. A rush of perfection that felt like it lasted minutes. That moment where nothing mattered but the now.

As soon as the flames of passion stopped flowing from my body, I looked at Darius. He was illuminated against a wall of orange and red, and I kissed him. He still tasted of tears, but I didn't pull away from them. I would never pull away from his fallen tears. The pains of the past had built the man that I'd fallen in love with, and I would never let that push me away from him.

When he pulled away from me to moan out his own release, he closed his eyes. He was just as lost as I'd been, completely unburdened from the weight of the world as he used my body for his pleasure. Just a few moments of pure bliss where nothing mattered.

When he opened them, I knew it was done. The momentary bliss was over, and I let the flames fade from around us. Our escape from whatever kept us apart was over. Darius smiled at me, and the winds dissipated, dropping the dirt onto the ground in a circle around us.

He laid his head back on the ground with a smile on his lips. He didn't say anything, but I knew what I wanted to do. I crawled off him and curled up on his shoulder. This was our position, and as I ran my leg over his, I tried to forget the world for just a little longer as I watched him close his eyes. There was some bit of peace in him where only a short while ago, there'd been only anguish.

Darius's chest rose and fell slowly. Unlike the other times we'd been together, he hadn't done this for me. He'd needed it; he'd needed me. The world was crumbling around him just as much as it was crumbling around me, but for some reason, he couldn't tell me why it was all happening.

I looked at him and knew that no matter how good that had felt, it wasn't the same. We may lay exactly as we had in Stormcrest, but there was a wall between us, and it seemed impassable. We'd found that spark between us again, but as soon as we left this riverbank, that divide between us would starve it.

Love needs fuel just as much as a fire. We'd never be able to feed that fire in Inoras. And at this point, I wasn't sure we'd be able to find it anywhere.

But at least there were embers where there had once been only ash.

Chapter 38

"It's like no one's ever sat and watched the end of the world coming," Shadow whispered to me.

We were walking through the gardens as we tried to escape the panic that we felt everywhere. King Azulus's troops were within view from the ramparts. They were still on the other side of the gate, but they were close enough that we could see them.

"I doubt anyone has. How often does the end of the world happen, anyway?"

"More often than you'd think. I've seen it happen three times. The world doesn't actually end, you know? Yes, kingdoms are crushed. Society changes. People leave their old ways. Dragons disappear."

That stopped me. "Wait, you were there when the dragons were around?"

Shadow didn't respond for a few moments before saying, "Oops."

"Now hold on. We've been together for eight hundred years, and you've never mentioned dragons? They were real? Not just some story from before the Disciplines?"

"I'm not supposed to talk about things like that, Orlana. It's one of the rules I swore to the gods before I was given the chance to come back."

I pulled Shadow from his sheath and looked at the blade. I'd known he was old, but he didn't talk about his old lives very much. Just a comment every few years that made me question things.

"Were you a dragon?" I asked.

Shadow laughed so hard I had to hold him tightly so he didn't rattle out of my hands. "No, that's ridiculous. Dragons are far too pompous to allow themselves to be put into a sword. They'd consider it an insult to be wielded by anyone other than a god, and the gods don't want to deal with dragons."

This was the most I'd ever gotten out of Shadow about the old times. I'd asked about the gods before, and he'd gone quiet. I didn't want him to do that, but I wanted to know more. This was the best distraction I'd had in so long.

"Then what were you?"

"Which time? I've been born and died many times. Unlike the rest of you, I wasn't born into this sword, and so I remember all my lives. At the same time, I have to abide by some very strict rules. The consequences of ignoring them are not things I like to think about."

I chewed my lip. "Can you tell me anything about the old times?"

"I can't just sit and tell you stories of my past lives, if that's what you're asking. I can't give you the answers to questions that are lost to the past. I *can* tell you what I've learned in all of these lives. The rest of it doesn't matter. Dragons, the Night Realm, the Realm of Flame. These are interesting, no doubt. Especially to scholars. But they don't *matter*."

"The only thing that I've found that matters is that each life matters more than anyone can imagine, and at the same time, it doesn't matter in the least. What you do tomorrow decides the fate of so many people, but even if you lose, even if every person in this place dies a terrible death, they'll be reborn."

"The world won't crumble away. Eventually, Azulus will die because everything ends. Someone else will take his place. There will always be evil in the world, and there will always be good. In reality, what happens tomorrow doesn't matter at all."

"But, it matters because it matters to you. It can bring peace to your soul. It can give you the chance to experience something different, a life without the pain that weighs you down. A life without the chains that bind you to the oath you gave me at seven years old. It could let you find happiness."

I felt a tingle run through my body at his words. Somehow, it resonated in a way that nothing else had. "But how do I find happiness, Shadow?" I whispered to him.

"You don't find happiness, Orlana. You can't will it into existence with enough work. Happiness is knowing that nothing matters, yet every second matters more than anything else. The taste of a hot cup of ignas tea. The warmth of a fire after a long day in the snow. The way the wind blows before a storm. The kiss of a lover after you've missed them."

"These are happiness. They don't matter at all. They don't

help you achieve your goals or save lives, but they help you smile. They make life worth living."

I closed my eyes and remembered how Darius had made me feel yesterday on the riverbank. Our flames had both burned so low. Even his kiss hadn't made me feel the same thing. And when we'd come back to Inoras, we'd said nothing.

"I've enjoyed those little things, Shadow, but when I imagine them now, they don't make me feel happy. I could care less about a cup of ignas tea."

"That's because you've tasted ecstasy, and now you believe you'll never have it again. Nothing can compare to that. People talk about love, but they have their words wrong. Love is what you feel for your father. It's what Darius feels towards his brothers. It's a bond, no different than that symbol on your shoulder."

"What you had with Darius wasn't love. It was life-altering. It reshaped your very soul. It was ecstasy, the thing that the very gods are made of."

"No arden has made flames as you did on the training field. Never in the history of the arden race has anyone burned so hot that they turned sand to glass. You touched the realm of the gods when you were with Darius, and now you feel you'll never touch it again."

"You say you'll have no purpose when Azulus is dead, but what purpose could be greater than living in ecstasy?"

I felt tears well up in my eyes, but I wouldn't let them fall. Not now.

I began to walk again as I whispered to Shadow. "But he says that he'll only hurt me, that I'll want more than he can give."

"Why can't he give more?" Shadow whispered back as I

turned a corner and saw Darius and Ona sitting on a bench together.

Darius noticed me immediately and stood up, not saying a word as he walked in the opposite direction. I stared at him as he walked away and felt the tears press ever harder for release. I couldn't let them go or else I'd never stop crying. A thousand tears would fall until there were no more tears to shed.

Darius turned a corner in the maze, and Ona said, "Come here, Princess Orlana. I think it's time that we talked."

Chapter 39

I sat down on the bench next to Ona who wore a crimson sela. "Sweetheart, it's time that you understand Darius a little better."

I felt the first tear fall. Then another. And another. It was like each tear sputtered against those embers that were still just barely alive inside me, each one threatening to put the last bit of fire inside me out.

"What can you possibly say that will help me understand him better?" I whispered to her as I tried to control myself.

"My husband hurt Darius as a child. He tried to forge Darius as you would a sword. As he'd done to Arturus and Marcellus. By beating it until it changed. By putting it to the fire until it stopped resisting. Except Darius isn't a piece of steel. He's made of glass. The stoutest glass the world has ever seen, but glass doesn't bend. It cracks, and it melts, but there is no bending."

I nodded to her. I knew this about Darius. Where Marcellus was capable of bending, Darius was his own man, resolute to the end in his beliefs, and each strike of the hammer would only make him turn his anger on the man who held it.

"But that isn't what broke Darius. No, Azulus didn't do it. In fact, no one did. Except maybe the gods."

She sighed and took my hand in hers, and I had a hard time not letting the tears flow freely. Something about Ona made you want to feel more.

"Now, I heard this from Darius, so it's not word for word, but Azimre, Darius's mother, was a prophet. Not like Talia. Talia sees small things that can be changed, but Azimre was a reader of fate. What she saw was what would happen no matter what."

"She loved Darius more than anyone in the world. Where Arturus is his father's son, Darius was his mother's. She would never have set out to hurt Darius. Not in a million years. So when she told him of a vision that was terrible, he knew it was to save him heartache rather than cause it."

A vision had broken Darius? What could be so terrible about that?

"When Darius was young, maybe twenty years old, Azimre told him about a vision she'd had. In it, she spoke to the gods, and they told her he was destined to walk this world alone. If he ever fell in love with a woman, she would be struck down in front of him to prove that he would never be allowed to love."

Ona took my hand in hers and continued, "He believed her for a long time until he met Yasmine. He couldn't stop himself from loving her, and he broke his promise to his mother to never fall in love with a woman. The day that he told his father that he loved her, she died only moments later. From that point forward, he swore to himself to never let himself fall in love again."

I couldn't believe what she was saying. How could he be destined to be alone, and why would a curse like this be put on him?

"Azimre was always right. She saw this very moment. Every one of her visions has been proven correct. Darius knows that if he lets himself love you, he'll be condemning you to death as he did with Yasmine."

I closed my eyes as Ona continued to talk. "I don't know what to tell you, Orlana. Darius is terrified that what happened once before will happen again. He cares about you more than anyone. Maybe even more than his brothers, and he can't let you die."

I nodded to her, finally understanding why he'd pushed me away. I didn't trust this vision, but at least it all made sense now. Darius's actions his entire life had been solitary. He'd never let anyone in. Not until me.

And he was pushing me away as fast as he could, but he couldn't just leave me because the bond between us wouldn't let him stay away. He'd fallen for me, but he was trying to stop destiny from ruining it all.

"Thank you, Ona," I said. "Thank you for helping me to understand. I hate the words you've given me, but I'm thankful that I don't blame him any longer."

"You're the first that he's felt this way about, if that's any consolation. Even more than Yasmine, I think."

I stood up and opened my eyes. "I don't know if it helps, but thank you for letting me know. I think I need to be alone for a while, though."

Ona nodded, and I turned. I couldn't believe it. If Ona was right, then I couldn't push Darius because he wasn't being selfish. He was doing everything in his power to keep me safe.

That didn't make it hurt any less. In fact, it made it hurt even more.

Even Shadow didn't try to help me through my agony as I walked back towards my room. I couldn't see the sunshine. Not now. I needed the dark. I needed the stone.

I needed my cage.

Chapter 40

The walls of this cage were white stone, not the glimmering rainbow of colors in the Emerald Caverns, but they were enough. I'd closed the window coverings and sat in the darkness of my room. Not on the fluffy bed or in one of the wooden chairs.

On the cool stone floor.

I needed to feel the stone against my flesh as the tears finally fell unfettered. I didn't have the strength to hold them in any longer. How could I fight to keep Darius when all he was doing was trying to save me?

I couldn't. There was nothing in my power to change him. He was not steel. I couldn't fight him or argue with him until he bent for me. No, fighting and arguing would only shatter him more, and I couldn't do that to him.

This was how he'd felt when he'd been young. There was

no desire inside me to break things any longer. All I wanted was my cage so that no one could see me, so no one could try to break the emotions that ran rampant through me.

Somehow, that ember inside me had swelled, growing and feeding on the knowledge that Darius cared enough to sacrifice his own happiness.

"How is this possible?" I whispered to no one. Shadow lay across my lap as he had when I'd first received him, when I'd first heard that my mother was dead. I'd sat and cried like this then. It was the last time that I'd given into sadness.

I'd nearly died only a few days ago, but even that hadn't hurt as much as I did at that moment. I hadn't cried then. I'd regretted nothing when I closed my eyes, and I still didn't regret our time together.

No, I would never regret loving Darius. Not ever. I'd never forget him, and I'd never forget how he'd changed me. When we'd stood in the river together, we'd talked of death, but even talking about whether we wanted to survive had brought my flame back.

My anger had stoked the flame. My pain had stoked the flame. The only thing that had tried to dim it was when I'd thought he'd abandoned me. That he hadn't wanted me.

I put my head in my hands as the tears fell to the ground, creating little rivulets that would eventually become salt trails when my tears had run out.

"We are each tested in our own way," Shadow whispered. His voice was sad. Like when he'd thought I would die. "But it is up to each of us how we face these tests. I can bring you no hope this time, Orlana. It's up to you how you handle this test."

"I know, Shadow. You can't fix things for me. Thank you

Chapter 41

I woke frantically searching for Darius, but he was gone. Darius had held me all through the night after I'd cried myself to sleep. But now he was gone, and he'd never hold me again. Not like that.

The light of dawn had only just begun to shine through the window, and as I stood up, the door to my room opened. I jumped up, hoping it was Darius, but it wasn't him and my heart sunk.

Instead, it was Talia who was smiling from ear to ear. Behind her, Marcellus stood looking just as brutish as ever. Talia didn't say anything, and I questioned how anyone could smile like that right now. She had to have known what had happened between Darius and me. Then there was the battle that loomed. No, this morning was not one for smiling.

She said nothing as she strode through the room in an

elegant ruby-covered dress. With her hair done up in a complicated braid, she looked like a queen at a banquet rather than the mate of a warrior on the morning of a battle.

She stopped in front of me and said, "Orlana, please trust me. I would prefer it if you kept those claws away from me."

"What are you talking about?" I asked with more than a little confusion as I tried to wipe the sleep out of my eyes.

"Just stand there and don't hurt her, Orlana," Marcellus said from the doorway.

"Alright?" I said, and Talia put her hands on my cheeks. She didn't hesitate as she moved her face towards mine. Then, when her lips were half an inch away from mine, I tried to pull back. It was too late, though.

She breathed out, and as I began to pull away, everything changed. The bedroom disappeared, and I was somewhere else. Talia and I were looking at a solen fae woman dressed in an emerald sela on her knees in front of a bed. The room was something from the sands. In the bed, a young solen male lay with sandy blonde hair. He turned, and I caught a glimpse of black feathers.

This was Darius.

Three women stood on the other side of the bed dressed in clothing I'd never seen before. Made of fabrics and in styles that I'd never even heard of. They looked to be older, but not ancient. Gray mixed with the brown, blonde, and black of their hair.

This female solen was Azimre.

Talia took my hand and said, "This was Azimre's vision. I've tried to find it many times since you and Darius came here after I heard his curse. Fate is a tricky thing, Orlana. Watch carefully."

How was this possible? Everyone knew prophets had visions, but no one could whisk someone away into one. There was no record of this ever being a power. And if this was Azimre's vision, those women were gods.

"I beg to know the fate of my youngest son," Azimre asked without looking at the women.

"Why do you beg this boon?" the one on the left asked. The blonde woman with eyes that were as black as pitch. She stared down at Azimre as though she hated her.

"He is soft, and my husband treats him poorly. I doubt that he'll survive to become a man."

The three women turned to each other, and they all nodded. "Your boon is granted," the one on the left said.

"The child will survive his father and live to see his death," the second continued.

"But only if he is fed the flame of a hard life to temper him, to purge the impurities."

The third took over, speaking in a rhythm that seemed to echo my heartbeat. "The true test will not be with sword, spear, nor ax. This child's heart will be tested instead. Over and over again, he will be tempted by love, for he will find none from his father. Alone he will be in the world."

The first's voice came in with a higher pitch but kept the same rhythm. "And though he will yearn for love, it will cause only heartache. His love will be the death of any woman. For, when the boy loves a woman more than he loves himself, the woman he looks to will be struck down, and he will find her dying at his feet."

The second woman's voice was deeper, and the rhythm picked up. I felt my heart mimicking the rhythm. "There will never be a healer near enough, and the crimson river that flows from her will remind him that only pain will come from love. No woman will be immune to this, and he will be destined to walk this world alone."

Azimre began to cry over her youngest son. She loved all her children, but Darius was her favorite because he was just like her, and now she saw he would be forced to follow her own path of a loveless life. She begged through her sobs, "Is there nothing he can do to find love?"

The third, whose eyes seemed to glow with white light, said, "A sea of tears will be his home. The only way to prevent a sea of crimson is to burn away the need for love. Women will call to him, as men called to you, but he must never look for the bonds of love."

"When there is nothing left for him to cling to, when there is no hope left in him, he will find a way. He will find the answer that he thought impossible."

The vision disappeared, leaving Talia and me in a black nothingness with only the stars overhead. She laughed and said, "Don't you see? They gave you the answer!"

I felt my own tears drying on my cheek. What could she mean, and how could she be laughing after hearing that? I'd just had confirmation of what Ona had told me.

"Oh Orlana, this is a good thing. We all talk about Azulus being so clever, but no one gives Azimre the respect she deserves. She told Darius exactly what he needed to hear, just as she did with Azulus when she told him about me. She told Darius that anyone he loved would lie at his feet dying. She told him that there would never be a healer close enough. The tricky thing is that she left out the last part because if she'd told him that, he'd have continued to have hope."

I held out my hands. I was so far out of my element here.

with Prince Darius."

"She was more than friends with Prince Arturus," he said. "I heard what you saw in the Marshes of Sorrow. She knew Prince Arturus before we knew each other, and though she knew that she could never marry into that family, she might have if it had been possible."

He took a deep breath and let it out slowly. "I miss her, and everything about this war with Azulus reminds me of her. I want you to know that I love you, Orlana. Your mother would be proud of how fiercely you burn for everything. You've truly become your mother's daughter even if you never really knew her."

He heaved the heavy burlap sack across the floor and said, "This was her armor. Wear it with pride as you kill Azulus. I'm proud of you. Prouder than I ever imagined."

I saw a tear roll down his cheek, and I pulled him to me. "I love you, Father. You brought the ardens here. You fought the fight you knew you could win, and we wouldn't have a chance without you. Thank you."

I pulled away and he said, "Be safe, Orlana. Watch the shadows, and give no quarter for they'll give you none. May your spark forever find tinder."

"And may your flame forever burn," I replied.

I put my hand on his shoulder, and he mimicked the motion. Both of us pressed our nails against the soft skin under our collar bones. The Gesture of Faith. I smiled at him as I pulled away.

"Burn them to ash," my father said as he turned and walked out of the room.

That was exactly what I planned to do.

* * *

I'd never worn arden armor. The creation of it had been lost in the previous war with Azulus, and I wondered how many wonders of the arden people would be lost this time around.

It moved like nothing I'd ever worn before, almost as though it had been made of air that was as hard as steel. My flames flowed through it without a problem, but other magic would dissipate harmlessly against it.

Only by slipping through the cracks had Arturus been able to kill my mother with magic. I wouldn't make that mistake.

I looked over the ramparts at the army that seemed to go on forever. Hundreds of thousands of soldiers still waited just beyond magic and arrow range. We'd done the best we could to wound Azulus's army, but seeing the men and women assembled below us was eye-opening.

Then there were the siege towers, catapults, and battering rams. Hundreds of them all built just outside the gate in a day. Three hundred thousand soldiers and hundreds of sorcerers had built them all in nearly the same time as it had it taken them to move them here.

He had at least ten times as many soldiers as we did, and they were all trained in battle. There was no doubt in my mind that this was going to be terrible. Hundreds of thousands would die today, their flames extinguished because of one man's desire to live forever.

Behind the soldiers was a single tent made of gold and black. A similarly decorated flag had been raised high into the air. Azulus's tent. The one man who could stop this all, but he wouldn't. He was too close to the one thing he'd always wanted. Immortality.

I took a deep breath, and Shadow whispered, "War is a terrible thing, but maybe this time, it's necessary. Hundreds of thousands may die today, but it will free their children. It will give so many a chance at a better life. One where they don't grow up clinging to hate."

I nodded. That's why I was fighting today. So that no one else had to grow up the way I had. No one else would have to carry the burden of revenge for eight hundred years.

"It's terrifying, isn't it?" Darius's voice said from behind me. I turned to look at him. I hadn't had a chance to talk to him since Talia had shown me the vision.

"Darius, have you spoken to Talia?" I asked. Somehow, it was difficult to speak about the thing that had broken him for so long. I should have been shouting from the rooftops, but it had been his deepest, darkest secret for so long. It didn't feel right to speak of it in the open air, but I had to tell him now.

He shook his head, and I took his hand. "Darius, you don't have to be afraid of loving me. The curse has run its course."

His eyes hardened as he looked down at me. "What do you mean?" he asked.

This was it. Somehow, I had to convince him that the thing he'd believed for so long was over. That if he loved me, I wouldn't die.

"The curse was that the moment you truly loved someone, they would be struck down and lay at your feet dying. Talia found your mother's vision and showed it to me. Your mother didn't tell you the last line."

I could feel Darius's hand begin to shake in mine, and I continued on, knowing that I was rocking him to the core.

"When there is no hope left in him, he will find a way. He will find the answer that he thought impossible."

"That's what one of the gods told your mother in her vision. You've never felt more hopeless than you do now, and Talia found the way. You chose me over your brother, and you could only do that if you loved me truly. Then I fell and lay dying at your feet."

"If you hadn't bonded me, I would have died, but I didn't." I smiled up at him. "You don't have to worry any longer. Your love won't kill me."

His breathing quickened, and he asked, "And Talia is sure of it?"

I nodded to him. "I asked the same thing. She's sure."

It took Darius a few moments to process what I was saying, but then he bent down to kiss me, and every ounce of desperate longing flowed from him to me. A lifetime of hopelessness evaporated in an instant. It was like time stopped for that moment, and I forgot the army, forgot the stakes of today, forgot everything except the man that I'd fallen in love with.

When he pulled away, he said, "I love you, Princess. I want to live for you. I want to be the thing in your life that replaces the hate. I've spent my entire life thinking I could never have someone like you, and I never want to live another day without you. When this is all done, marry me."

I'd never felt so much joy in my entire life. I'd thought that I'd been left with nothing, that I'd be all alone forever because the one man who would ever understand me couldn't love me. The ember inside me caught fire, flooded with all the love I felt.

I said the only thing I could. "Yes, Darius. I'd love to marry you."

Then the horns blew, and both of us whirled to look at what

was happening. The engines of war began to roll. Massive siege towers and catapults. The soldiers began the march towards the gate. Protected by magic from solen fae and sorcerers, the wooden arrows would be useless. The soldiers would be safe until they were within range of the heavier steel arrows.

The men on the ramparts began to shift. Humans who'd known the horrors of minor wars stared at an enemy that seemed to go on forever. They didn't understand the magic that would help us win this fight. Elves that had never been in battle but had imagined it daily for nearly a thousand years knew the stakes and the very strong possibility we'd die. The arden fae knew firsthand how terrible Azulus's army could be.

All of us shook at least a little bit.

Boulders flew from the dozens of catapults. Stones larger than a man that could only be moved with magic filled the air, and humans cowered while elves prepared. They had a weaker control over the wind, not enough to crystallize the air, but enough to make the winds whip around.

Boulders shuddered in their trajectory as the magical winds buffeted them. Some were stopped, but a few made it through, crashing into the walls with horrific booms. Men screamed as they were crushed and knocked off the ramparts. Theirs would be the first, but they certainly wouldn't be the last.

Darius's eyes glowed gold as he stared out at Azulus's soldiers in steel plate with huge tower shields. "Gods, I wish I could go down there and start killing," he said.

And then I saw the shimmer of black wings in the air over the gate. Marcellus the Black hovered above it, and for just a second, a visible hesitation ran through the soldiers as they marched. They all knew what that single solen fae could do to a regular human army.

Golems, the elvish attempt at creating ifrits, stood at the bottom of the walls. Their stone bodies would be difficult to fight for soldiers, but the sorcerers would destroy them quickly.

Stonewakers and Firewakers raised stone and flame, giving them life as Daphon had while we'd trained. They'd be short-lived, but there would be many men who would die to the ardens' creations.

Through a Binder's sphere in my pocket, Marcellus's voice called out to all the commanders, "Steady men. Repel the catapults and wait. Ardens, burn the siege towers when they get closer. I'll deal with the gate. Archers, knock steel arrows. Load the catapults with pitch and set them on fire."

As the troops continued to march, their fear of Marcellus was overcome by the fear of their commanders, an explosion rang out. Someone had stepped on one of the explosives. Men flew into the air, but the rest of the soldiers continued to march, unfazed by the new knowledge that the field they crossed had been trapped.

Marcellus looked down at Darius, and he rose into the air. "Don't get yourself killed," I said to him as he flew to meet his brother.

"I could say the same to you, Princess." I watched him move and for a moment, I was afraid of dying. Not because I was afraid of death, but because I couldn't fathom how badly it would hurt Darius.

I took a breath and let it out slowly. Every fire burns out eventually. It is enough to have enjoyed the warmth that it provided.

Thousands of steel arrows ripped through the air towards the marching soldiers, but few found their mark. The soldiers were too well armored and too well trained to fall to simple arrows. A few screams rang out, but not enough. Archers would not be the answer to this battle. It would come down to the sword and magic.

A group of ten figures rose above the army at the same time that the catapults launched pitch-covered boulders at the lines of soldiers. They exploded in flames as soon as they left the catapults. Men died as the boulders crushed them. More explosions began to ring out as the arden traps were triggered.

It wasn't enough, though. Not nearly enough. Azulus's catapults fired continuously, and the elves struggled to push the boulders back. Several of the boulders hit the ramparts, and the battle began in earnest.

Arrows fired without any real rhythm as the archers became frantic. Marcellus dove into the lines of the enemy, his two swords cutting swathes in the troops. I watched in horror as the bodies began to pile up around him. I had never seen anyone move like that. Now I understood why the world feared Marcellus the Black.

The siege towers got close enough to let down their gates, but the ardens sent flames to burn them to the ground. Azulus's sorcerers set the wind to gusting around them, carrying the flames to the river, much as Darius had done with my flames.

Several of them caught fire, but not enough. The draw-bridges snapped down, and soldiers ran onto the ramparts. Binding spheres were thrown, exploding at several of the siege tower gates, causing the entire towers to crumble.

Stonewakers, Flamewakers, and the few Firebrands set about attacking the siege towers, and many of them fell. Still, it wasn't enough, and as the drawbridges passed over the ramparts, men began to create footholds. The ramparts weren't large enough to overwhelm them with numbers.

I ran to the nearest of the siege towers and drew Shadow. "Burn them all, Orlana," he whispered.

I jumped into the air, flames carrying me to the side of the wooden structure. I caught myself on one of the poles and immediately pressed my hand to the side. Fire coated it as I hauled myself to the top of the tower.

As it burned, the soldiers inside rushed to get out, but I dropped onto the drawbridge, Shadow in hand. They tried to fight me, but they were just normal men. Flames would be useless against their armor, but I was more than capable of stopping a few humans with Shadow.

I moved among them, Shadow a blur, as I found the chinks in their armor. A few spear thrusts found my armor, but none found a gap. As smoke filled the tower, I retreated across the drawbridge, cutting through the heavy wood as I did.

Elves with spears formed around me as several of Azulus's soldiers tried to leap across. The spears found their marks each time, and then one of the primary supports on the tower was weakened enough, and the entire thing collapsed.

A cloud of dust and smoke rose into the air as I moved to the next tower. The sound of screams and clang of steel on steel was all that I heard now. The wind was gusting everywhere, and flames flashed as smoke began to fill the ramparts with a haze.

I couldn't take down every siege engine, but I could help. As I jumped into the air a second time, I felt the air rush out of my lungs as a solen fae struck me from behind, slamming me into the side of the siege tower. His sword crashed against my armor, and I felt the tip of the blade poke through, jabbing into my side.

I gritted my teeth against the pain as I clamped my hand on a wooden support. I let the flames that sat just under my skin rush outward, wreathing me in red and orange. The solen fae that held me screamed, and I smelled burnt feathers. Clinging to the support with one hand, I looked down and saw his broken body twenty feet below me.

That was when I felt the siege tower shake. The top was already burning, and before I'd had time to climb back to the wall, the entire thing collapsed.

Chapter 43

I fell through the air, trying to right myself as I fell. I'd been in the air enough times that my body didn't panic immediately. I needed to get my feet under me so that I could slow my fall with flames.

I'd never tried to maneuver in the air, though, and my feet seemed pushed upward. I twisted in the air, and I looked down at the ground as it rushed to meet me. My heart caught in my chest, and I knew that this was when I finally died. I might survive the fall, my arden body and armor protecting me just enough from the thirty-foot drop. The soldiers on the ground wouldn't let me live, though.

And then I felt powerful hands grip me, but when I turned to look, there was no one there.

Darius.

"Gods, woman. Did you forget you don't have wings?"

defenses and punched through them with a single strike.

And each time a sorcerer approached, he was killed instantly by Darius. Gods, they were invincible when put together. Two brothers who had been built to work in tandem, their skills complementing the other perfectly.

Though these two were decimating their section of the battlefield, other parts weren't fairing as well. Another catapult fell to the ground as the solen fae fought on the ramparts, giving cover to the siege towers.

Explosions still filled the air as new traps were sprung. I heard elves screaming as they died on the ramparts. The smell of death was everywhere, and still, the enemy soldiers continued to march. We were nowhere near finished with the battle. Another wave of siege towers rolled towards the walls.

Enemy catapults hit the walls even more often now, their boulders clearing out entire sections of defenders.

I'd thought that magic and the arden Bindings would even the odds, but seeing the waves of soldiers continue to roll across the ground, I wasn't so sure. Marcellus and Darius could only do so much. I could only do so much.

I ran to Marcellus. We had to end this. We had to kill Azulus.

As I approached, he turned to me as he cut a man's throat. We didn't have time to slaughter enemy soldiers. We had to focus on the true goal. As Darius had said, if we could kill Azulus, Arturus would stop the slaughter.

And gods, there had been enough slaughter already.

"You can't kill them all, Marcellus," I yelled. I focused on my powers and a ring of flames rose from the ground around us. Rising taller than even Marcellus, there was no way that anyone could see through them enough to come through. Or to shoot through.

"I can try," he said with a grin. Darius appeared next to him and arched his eyebrow. They were both covered in sweat, but I wondered how long they could have kept this up.

"I don't know if we'll win like this," I said. "The siege engines are doing their job, and soon enough, there will be enough towers in place that they'll gain a foothold. You can't leave the gate, or they'll get through there."

Marcellus looked around and saw the next two dozen siege towers rolling into place on the walls. They lined up next to the ones that were still in place, and more enemy soldiers flooded the walls. The battle raging on the walls was fierce. That was the one that mattered.

Marcellus sighed. "I can't be everywhere."

"You can be in the one place that matters though," I said, and I turned to look at the black and gold flag that rose high into the air.

"We won't win that fight," he said. "Maybe you can fight my father with that armor on, but Darius and I won't survive it."

"And don't forget that my father has more experience in battle than anyone I've ever met."

I took a deep breath and said, "These men are all going to die. Hundreds of thousands. Even if we win, we'll be slaughtering more humans than there are fae in the entire world."

Marcellus took a deep breath and nodded. Darius nodded as well. "Arturus isn't with Father, to my knowledge," he said.

"We'll wound him if he comes," Marcellus said. "You hit his wings as you did in the Marshes of Sorrow, and then we'll just have Father to deal with. Orlana, you'll have to keep his attention. If he turns on Darius or me, we'll die."

I nodded, and Marcellus spoke into his Binding sphere. "Stonewakers and Firewakers, focus on defending the gate. Teffin, gather some of the exhausted troops and set them just inside the gate in case it falls."

There was no answer, but I saw men of stone and flames make their way to the gate. We wouldn't have much time, but we would have some. Darius scooped me into his arms, and we took to the air. Looking down at the army below us, I was still in awe at the numbers. I'd had no idea what a solid mass of humans could do against magic and superior skills. Humans and steel armor were a force to be reckoned with.

"Be careful," Darius whispered to me as the wind rushed around us. We'd never moved this fast before. Not even when we'd run from Arturus.

Marcellus was lagging, and as we got closer, Darius slowed. Then I saw the man that I'd vowed to kill all those years ago. Unlike Arturus, he was no man's sword. King Azulus, the man that was responsible for so much suffering that even his sons hated him.

With skin as dark as the night sky and white lines that crisscrossed over his whole body, there was no doubt who he was. He stood without armor on, unafraid of magical battle. He watched as the three of us approached.

There was no guard here. He didn't need it, and I was sure that if there had been, he wouldn't have allowed them to interfere. We were the three people that he would want to kill more than anyone else.

Darius set me down far enough away that I wasn't afraid of him using magic against me. Marcellus landed next to us, and I saw his eyes had turned as black as night.

"My rebel sons have come," he sneered as he took a step out

of his tent. "Come to give your surrender?"

"We're here to end this once and for all," Marcellus said as he crouched, preparing himself for battle. He held his swords in front of him. Marcellus was a master of swordplay, but he was barely a fae when it came to magic. Steel was his greatest ally when it came to battle with magic.

Darius smiled grimly at his father. "You came here for eternal life, but there's no good ending to this day for you. Either you die, or two of your sons die. Tell your soldiers to go back to Kharn, and none of us will be placed on a pyre tonight."

"There will be no pyres for you. You're both blood-traitors, and you'll be left for the scavengers. Darius, I'm surprised at your gall. How many times did I put you in the sand without even holding a weapon? And Marcellus, have you not learned from the beatings I gave you? You'll never be a match against a real fae."

He turned to me and said, "And you brought an arden to battle? A woman at that. Is she here to throw rocks at me while you die?"

I drew Shadow from his sheath and said, "I'm here for revenge. You're the reason that my mother died. You're the reason that my people were forced into caves for eight hundred years."

Azulus shrugged. "I'm also the reason that wind blows and the rain falls. I'm the cause of many things, little arden. If you'd like to join your mother, then step forward. Otherwise, go fight with the rest of the children while I show my sons what being a traitor means."

"He has every power in the world except the corrupted ones," Shadow whispered to me. "You know how to fight them. Get close and let me do the work."

I ran, and the surrounding plants reached up to grasp at me, but flames had already encircled my boots, burning them away. Azulus raised his hand, and a thousand crystal shards flew through the air at me. I raise Shadow to cover my faceplate, and they shattered harmlessly against my armor.

As soon as I moved Shadow away from my face, I saw flames erupt from Azulus's hands, and I didn't try to block them. Instead, as soon as it was close to me, I turned it, forcing it back towards him. He may have had the power of an arden, but he hadn't spent his life training in the Disciplines. He was a child compared to me in the Firebrand Discipline.

The flames evaporated as he released them, and he smiled at me. He pulled a sword from a sheath on his waist, and he waited. As I neared him, he put his hand to the side, and a shout rose from the air. Marcellus appeared in the air, locked in crystalline bondage.

"You'll never be as quiet as your brother," Azulus muttered. Stone rose around me, creating a box ten feet tall. I snarled and began to cut through it with Shadow. Gods, if I'd only studied a little harder in the Stonewaking Discipline, I could have used this against him.

I heard shouts, and the clash of steel filled the air. Where were Darius and Marcellus. Please let them both be alive. I pressed my hand against the stone and willed it to crumble. It wasn't clean or efficient, and I was exhausted as a small doorway of stone crumbled and turned to sand.

I ran through it and saw that Darius danced with his father, their blades flashing through the air. Darius wielded two daggers made of steel that I'd never seen. Marcellus was still hanging in the air as he watched his brother fight his father.

But he wasn't struggling, wasn't fighting his bondage. This was a trick. Somehow, he was hiding something. I didn't have time to think about it as I rushed to Darius's side.

Azulus raised his hand, but I leaped, flames pushing me higher. As the stone walls rose into the air, I used them as a springboard to move even faster towards Azulus. Finally within striking distance, I let Shadow do his work. Using safe, quick strikes, I drew Azulus's attention away from Darius, though Darius's strikes still missed his father.

He moved faster than I'd ever thought possible, and even as I used fire and steel to attack him, he dodged and danced out of the way. Wind swirled around him, a shield against the flames.

And then he cried out as Darius appeared on his side. He'd appeared from the air, and the other Darius disappeared as he pulled his dagger out of Azulus's stomach. He'd tricked his father, who had expected him to miss every strike.

As he went for another stab, Azulus spun, and his sword found its mark, cutting across his chest in a terribly deep wound. Darius stepped back, and I saw the wound for what it was. Death.

I felt a burning in my shoulder where my brand was. He was draining me. He would survive as long as I did.

He fell to the ground, and blood poured from the grievous wound. He didn't even try to get up. I attacked with renewed vigor, pushing Azulus towards Marcellus. Whatever he was planning, Marcellus would have an easier time of it if Azulus was closer to him.

Azulus continued to dance as though he didn't have blood pouring from his side. The winds buffeting my sword were worse than I could have imagined, and I set the ground around him on fire. It rose around him in a swirling vortex, never actually touching him.

And then Marcellus moved. In a flash, he was free and swinging his swords at his father. I'd always heard that he had no magic, but control of the air was the only way that he could have escaped that bondage. The winds didn't push his blades away as though he were stopping them with his own powers, and he managed to leave two thin strips of crimson across his father's back.

Azulus didn't cry out, and he continued to dance between the two of us. Three serious wounds should have slowed him down at least, but he looked to be unfazed by the pain or the blood loss.

But then Marcellus stopped again, a snarl rising from the back of his throat. Shadows clung to his ankles, holding him in place, and when the shadow fell over us, I knew who I would see. Arturus the Hunter hit the ground in cloud of dirt, and he immediately attacked Marcellus. With a thought, I burned the shadows around his ankles away in a sputter of flame.

Marcellus danced with his brother, and I sent waves of fire at both Azulus and Arturus, doing my best to keep them both busy so that Marcellus could do his work. I couldn't stop looking at Darius, who lay unconscious on the ground. I prayed the bond would work as well as the stories had told.

Even if the bond was between an arden and a solen.

Marcellus struck Arturus across the shoulder, but then he stumbled as a shadow pierced his ankle, cutting through his Achilles tendon. He groaned as he hit the ground, and I stopped doing anything logical. We were done if I continued to fight like men were supposed to fight.

I leaped at Azulus, and surprise lit up in his face, but he danced out of the way, his sword coming down and hitting me in the back. My armor stopped most of it, but my momentum was thrown off. As I passed him, I put my hand out, and my fingers brushed his robes. They burst into flames, and he snarled as he snuffed them out. Burns covered anywhere that the robe had pressed against his skin.

I hit the ground poorly, and instead of the roll I'd planned, I hit face first. Arturus's massive sword came down across my back. I knew that it was the end as soon as I heard the crunch. My armor protected me from the edge of his sword, but it hadn't been strong enough to stop the force. I didn't need to check to see if I could move my legs.

Icy fear flooded me as I realized that we'd failed. Marcellus was trying to stand, but Azulus or Arturus would kill him in moments now that he was unable to move like he normally could. I was paralyzed. Darius was dying.

We had lost.

Arturus kicked me, flipping me onto my back, and I groaned as pain shot through me. "Darius's arden," he breathed. "She fought well."

"They all did," Azulus said. Blood ran from his wounds, and large pockets of skin had bubbled up where I'd burned him. If Arturus hadn't stopped him, Marcellus would have killed his father. Once again, I questioned if I'd made the right decision by letting him live that night in the Marshes of Sorrow.

"Today mattered," I whispered to Shadow.

"Yes, it did. You did what you were supposed to do, what you were made to do."

I smiled up at Arturus and said, "I'm glad I didn't kill you that night in the Marsh. I'm glad that I chose his heart over my vengeance."

"Sorchna's daughter," he whispered. "Your eyes burn the same way that hers did. I'd know that flame anywhere. You fought well, Princess. Your mother would have been proud."

"I'll see you in the next life, Orlana of the Emerald Caverns," Shadow said. "You found something that was worth living for, and that's all that anyone can hope for."

I glanced at Darius and smiled. We would leave this world together. That was a kindness I hadn't expected. I hadn't ever been afraid of death. Not really. After learning what I had this morning, I'd feared it for him. I couldn't let him go through life thinking that he'd lost the one person who he could love.

But now? Now we'd leave together, and that wasn't such a bad thing. We were broken. Maybe it was better to begin all over again. Maybe it would be better to grow up in a world where we could know love without all the pain, and then when we found each other, no one could stop us from uniting our souls.

"I understand why Mother took her life, Father," Marcellus said as his wings lifted him a foot off the ground. "It was so she wouldn't have to see this day. The day that you chose yourself over your family."

Azulus raised his hand, and dozens of crystal shards flew towards him. He tried to block them with his swords, but many of them broke through his defenses, striking his shoulders and his chest.

He tried to hold on to his swords, but I knew what those shards could do. His shoulders would have shattered. His muscles would be ripped to pieces. He coughed, and blood ran from his lips. He was going to die.

We were all going to die.

He fell to the ground, and Arturus whispered, "She didn't kill herself because of Father." I didn't know if it was loud enough for Marcellus to hear, but I didn't think he was talking to Marcellus.

As the breeze blew in the relative silence, Azulus said, "Finish them and be done with it. We need to join the fight at Inoras." He turned around to go back to his tent.

"I'm sorry," he said as he looked down at me. "I was wrong. All those years ago with your mother, I was wrong."

"Father," he said without turning around.

"What do you want, Arturus? Have you become soft again? Does your solen fae side need to be taught again how a man acts? There are thousands of men we could take as captives for you to execute."

I glanced at Azulus and saw a shadow snaking its way up from the ground behind him. The one power Azulus didn't have and had no sense of.

"I'm sorry, Father. Mother was right. You're the monster she always claimed you were."

"Darius could have killed me, but he didn't. This arden could have killed me. She didn't. They did this because they cared about me. They love me. Yet, you'd have me kill them, and I can't do it. Not my brothers. I cannot destroy the only people in the world that still care about me."

"You'll regret that," Azulus snarled, and then he gasped. A wickedly sharp shadow was sticking from his breast. It had pierced his heart, and not even King Azulus was able to survive that. Then it was gone, and he collapsed to the ground without another word.

Arturus blinked away tears, and I smiled up at him. "You're as good a man as Darius always said."

Chapter 44

I felt exhausted, and I had no idea how Darius and Marcellus had flown all the way back to Inoras. As soon as we were there, I saw the lines of Azulus's troops retreating. Marcellus was calling out orders from the Binding sphere he held, but all I could do was look at the death and destruction that covered the castle that had been so beautiful only this morning.

Gaping holes in the walls had formed from the boulders that had crashed into it. Houses had been crushed and burned. The streets had been painted in crimson.

But more than anything, the bodies made me sick. So many dead and wounded from both sides. There were fewer than the hundreds of thousands that we'd expected, but it was still a soul-crushing number. The bodies had fallen from the ramparts in such great numbers that they lay in piles. Dozens on top of each other.

I wondered how many of them I knew. How many ardens from the Emerald Caverns had perished in this war to end all wars? I wasn't ready to hear the body counts or read the list of who had died.

Marcellus and Darius stood next to me on the ramparts. Marcellus had given all of his orders through the Binding sphere in his pocket, and he could see nearly everything from here.

Marcellus turned to me and said, "I'm impressed with your skills, Princess Orlana. I didn't have time to tell you earlier, but I had serious doubts about whether you could back up what people said about your skill with a sword. I was wrong, and I wanted to apologize for it. I've met very few people, and I don't just mean women, who could have stood toe to toe with my father and live for even a few moments."

He smiled at me and patted my shoulder. "If you're ever interested in becoming better with the sword, let me know, and I'll personally train you. There are maybe ten people in the world that can match you without magic right now, and I don't know if there's anyone that could stand toe-to-toe with you if you were using magic now that my father's dead."

That was probably the best compliment I could have received from the best warrior in the world. Maybe all those years of training had been worth it. "Thank you, Marcellus. I'll consider it and let you know. I think I need a little break from fighting for a while though."

He nodded to me and said, "That's an open offer. Now I need to leave you to see to the aftermath of this atrocity." He took to the air and left Darius and me to ourselves.

I looked out at the destruction again, and it nearly turned my stomach. The broken bodies that littered everything were a nightmare.

Darius put his hand on my armored shoulder and whispered, "So many. It didn't feel like there were this many when we were fighting."

"We were on the ground. We never saw the line fighting." I pulled Darius to me, and he grunted and pulled away.

"Sorry, Orlana. Your armor has a few sharp points, and I'm still just barely put back together."

I looked down and saw a bit of blood coming to the surface of his waist. "What happens next?" I asked. As I'd been told so many times already, I'd never been in something like this.

"We mourn, and we celebrate. There will be a funeral, and then there will be a feast. If I know Arturus, he'll hold his own funeral for his men." Darius paused for a second and then said, "I think that Marcellus and I will let King Sundryl and your father be in charge of the celebration. We have something else to attend to."

I looked up at him and could see the sadness in his eyes. "Your father?"

He nodded. "I hated the man, and I'm glad we'll burn him tonight, but that doesn't change that he was my father. He was terrible, and I'd never wish my childhood on anyone, but the three of us wouldn't be who we were without him. He deserves a funeral, but there will be no celebration in his honor."

"I'd like to join you if that's acceptable. If your father hadn't lived, I wouldn't have been forced to put up with you for so long that I grew to like you."

"You mean I wouldn't have had time to woo you. A woman like you needs a bit of fire in her man. You needed to see that I wouldn't bow and scrape to Your Highness."

Men were stupid creatures. He may have been right, but he shouldn't be *telling* me. "I think it was a mutual realization that we wouldn't throw ourselves at each other. The women I've seen around you go all moon eyes."

"That's possible. I truly hate moon eyes."

He looked up, and I followed his eyes. My father. The robes were gone, and in their place were a tunic and trousers. They were covered in blood, and a thin cut across his face showed that he'd been in the midst of the fighting without armor and without the training that I'd had.

He limped to me, and I saw he had another cut in his trousers right above the knee. He hadn't shied away from the battle. I was proud of him for fighting.

"Orlana," he whispered. "The gods have been good. I thought for sure that you were dead when I saw you flying with Darius."

I embraced him, careful not to press too hard. He seemed like he was just as weary as the two of us. "I almost did, but a miracle happened."

When he pulled away, he asked, "What miracle?"

I gave him a broken smile. "A man realized that love was more important than fear."

* * *

Two sets of funeral pyres burned that night. Thousands upon thousands of souls were sent to the heavens on rivers of smoke as the flames consumed their bodies. I'd been right. There would be many orphans because of today. Too many.

But at least it would be the last for the time being. All the kings who had come for this battle had signed a treaty that

316

there would be no war between them for the rest of their lives. In the case of the humans, that would be a short time, but it would give the world time to heal from this.

Shadow Soul had been right. War was a tragedy. There was no victor when so many people were taken from you. So many people. People I'd grown up with and people I'd met once I'd come to Inoras.

"This meant something," I whispered to no one in particular.

"It did. Their souls will grow from it. They'll be stronger, and even if they don't remember the choice they made when they came here, their souls will." Shadow seemed to mourn them just as much as I did, but he had a different perspective. He'd seen more death than I ever could. Or maybe I had seen just as much, but I didn't remember it.

"You say that happiness is what we should all strive for," I said as I watched the pyres burning, "but how did this help anyone to be happy?"

"Sometimes it's not your own happiness that you should strive for. Sometimes it's your children, your husband, your wife, or even your neighbor. Sometimes, that's enough to be worth the sacrifice."

I nodded. I'd been willing to sacrifice for Darius and for the ardens. Even after I'd found happiness in the arms of Darius.

"I'm glad I don't have to sacrifice anymore," I said. I'd seen enough death for a very long time. My heart hung heavy in my chest even though I'd had the best news I could imagine this morning.

"I'm glad that Darius isn't on that pyre," I said.

"I'm glad you're not on the pyre. I couldn't stand the thought of being Darius's sword. He's an ass."

As I chuckled, I felt a hand on my back. When I turned to

look, I saw it was Darius with a serious expression on his face. "It's time," he whispered.

I nodded to him and followed as we left the crowd of people bearing witness to the sacrifice of all these men and women. The people who had come together to end the tyranny of a single man and free all the peoples of the world. Those men and women on the pyres would be remembered as heroes, but that didn't change the fact that they wouldn't get to see a world without Azulus in it.

And that was a terrible thing.

Darius wrapped his arm around my waist and lifted me into the air. "Just so you know, I'm glad you're not on the pyre. I couldn't imagine having to lug that sword around with me all the time. Shadow's an ass."

I grinned in the darkness. So he could still hear the conversations between us at least some of the time. That was fine with me. I had nothing to hide anymore. Darius had let down his walls, and I would put none up.

"I think that you two would be a perfect fit. You both like to tell me I'm wrong as much as possible."

I could feel Darius pull me closer to him. He needed my warmth this time. A single pyre with a single body on it had been placed in between the two funerals.

Arturus had built his father's pyre. He'd prepared his body and whispered the prayers. Being his father's eldest son, it was his right, and no one judged him for claiming the right.

Darius landed, and I saw Marcellus had brought Talia. That was fitting as well. The funeral behind us wasn't for her. She didn't have a people, at least not like I did. She'd grown up in a human village, a life of simplicity, and none of those farmers were here.

318

But Azulus mattered to her just as much as he mattered to me. He'd been the reason that we'd been brought into this world and met the men who mattered most to us. He'd built these men into the wonderful men that they were, even though they'd all nearly broken because of it.

"Our father was a man who understood and lived by a single rule. Being powerful was the only way to be safe," Arturus said in a gravelly but soft voice. "He was not a kind man, and he loved only Mother, but he did care about us. Otherise, wouldn't have pushed us as hard. He may not have loved us, but he cared."

"I wish that I'd grown up with another father," he continued as he stared into the bonfire in front of us. "But I'm thankful that he made me as strong as I am. I'm thankful that I'll never fear another man as much as I feared him, and I'm thankful that the worst part of my life is over."

Marcellus nodded to him, and I could see that Talia wrapped her arms around Marcellus's waist as he stared at his father as he burned. "He wasn't always as cruel as he was after Mother died. There were times that I saw pride in his eyes. When he taught us swordplay as children, he smiled. The day that I took a castle on my own, he laughed and congratulated me."

"You're right. He wasn't a kind man, and the world is better for his passing, but I thank him for teaching us to be strong, to be capable of doing whatever it took to get what we wanted. I think that even as he watches us now, that he's proud of us. We did what no one else could do. We beat him. The three of us. Together."

There was silence, and the crackling flames of the pyre echoed the Flames of Peace meditation, but then Darius spoke up. "I never saw him be kind. I never saw him have pride in his children." His eyes sparkled with a bright intensity. "He was the cruelest man I have ever met, and the only thing I am thankful he gave us was each other."

"No one should have had to go through life as we did. Each of us, in our own way, fought our own battles. We trained ourselves and taught ourselves to become the best at what we do. He may have helped you to wield a sword for the first time, but he didn't teach you to be a swordsman."

"The only thing he ever did right was to be our enemy. He didn't train us. He didn't teach us. He was simply the enemy that we could never conquer, the rock that we couldn't budge. Until now."

"I'm glad to see him burn. I finally feel like I can be a man instead of a child fearing his wrath. I will never be thankful for anything from him."

"I am thankful for Mother for surviving long enough to show me that there is good in the world. I'm thankful that a part of her is in each of us. She was there to hold us as we were healed from the wounds that he inflicted."

"I know why he was banished from the Night Realm. I know why his own people, why his own father pushed him away. Even they knew that inside him, there was only evil."

"Thank the gods that none of us lost that piece of Mother. Even you, Arturus, held onto her. No matter how many times Father punished you, you still held onto the good."

He turned around, and I glanced at his brothers, who didn't say a word as they continued to watch the flames consume their father. I went to Darius, who was walking across the field towards Inoras.

"I'm so sorry, Darius," I said.

"Don't be. You didn't do anything wrong. That monster is

burning, and I couldn't be happier."

"No," I said as I reached out and touched his hand. "I'm sorry that you had to live through having him as a father."

He turned around and looked at me. "You don't understand, Orlana. I'm not sorry that I had to live through it. I just give no credit to him for making me into the man I am. He didn't do it. He didn't teach me or help me. He was simply the enemy. You don't thank the battle for making a sword strong when it doesn't break. You thank the smith who gave himself to make sure it didn't."

"My mother is who I credit with all of it. She taught me to resist the darkness of my father. No matter how many times he hurt her, she never let down her walls, and she never let the darkness win. Her death wasn't her giving up. It was her way to make sure that the darkness of my father never claimed her."

"I'm not sad about my life. Arturus may wish he had a different father. I don't. I regret nothing, but I refuse to give that monster an ounce of credit."

I wrapped my arms around Darius and said, "I love you, and I wish you hadn't been forced to fight that battle for all those years. I don't love you because you didn't break or because you're the sharpest sword I've ever met. I love you because of the goodness in you."

Darius was quiet for a few minutes, and he ran his hands through my hair. "I love you too, Orlana. You just keep fighting for whatever you want. For me, for those orphans around the world, and even so that no one will call you princess. You're as stubborn as they get, and I love that about you."

"Thank you," I whispered to him.

"Let's go back to Inoras," he said. "We have a wedding to plan."

I wore the dress that fit me, the first dress in a very long time. It was a dress like no other.

I'd had to talk to Daphon to make the frame. He'd done something that no other Stonewaker could have done. He'd created a dress made of black stone so thin that it was almost like wearing a second set of scales. They were too flimsy for anything functional, but they fit me.

I'd had a Binder wrap those black scales with an enchantment that let them flicker with flames. Not enough to burn anything. Just the occasional flash of fire, like in Marcellus's wings.

It was pointless, and I knew that, but if I was going to wear a dress, it was going to be mine. This was my wedding, and I could think of nothing that would fit me better.

I wasn't the typical bride today, but I was sure that Darius wasn't the typical groom, either. That was fine with me. The people would get their beautiful princess in Talia, and they would get their gossip in me. It wouldn't be the first time that I surprised people.

"You're up first," I said. "Go show the world that your big strong solen fae is all yours."

Talia chuckled. "I think that they'll be a lot more worried about yours being off the market."

"Probably true. Marcellus didn't have the same flock of women following him. I'm going to have to get very good at carrying a stick to beat them off with."

Talia glanced at Shadow, who was on my back. That was the other reason I didn't quite look like the princess that everyone was expecting. "I think you're already covered," she said.

I grinned at her and gave her a hug. "I'm glad that you'll be my sister, Talia. I never thought I'd want a sister, but you've changed my mind."

"I always wanted a sister," she said, "but I never expected her to wear armor to her wedding. It's fitting, though."

She pulled away and gave me one last smile before walking out of our dressing room. I watched as she walked away, leaving me alone in the room.

But I wasn't alone anymore. Never again.

"I'm so proud of you, Orlana," Shadow whispered. "And thank you for letting me be a part of your wedding. I never expected to see another one, and they were kind of my thing."

"Are you going to tell me what you mean by that? Do I hear a story coming?"

"No! I can't break any more rules just to entertain you. I do love your dress. The first of its kind, to my knowledge. Very typical of you to be the anti-princess."

I grinned as he continued, "Though, you could have chosen a little lighter stone coloring. A pretty blue or green, maybe. Weddings are supposed to be joyous, not so morose."

"They match my scales."

"You chose that coloring because of Darius's wings, didn't you? Sly girl. Even when you try to shrug your heritage, you can't do it, can you?"

"So what if I'm still a little bit of a princess now and then?"

"I'm not judging you. I think it's cute. My little Princess Orlana finally embracing what she was born to do. In her own way, of course. Wouldn't want your father to be too proud of you."

I laughed at that, and I noticed that somehow my laugh had changed. Not in a huge way, but it seemed just a little lighter, a little less gruff. The weight of my oaths was gone.

"Thank you, Shadow. For all the help over the years. There

isn't another person who could have been as understanding as you've been."

"I'm glad you've noticed," he said a little too smugly. "Some days were more trying than others. You have no idea how difficult it is to guide a young arden fae when all she wants to do is blow things up."

I thought back to my childhood of causing mischief. Trouble-making had been my only real entertainment back then. "So, are you going to toast me in your speech?" he asked.

"I can't toast my sword at my wedding, Shadow. None of the people here even know about you."

He sighed. "Fine. Well, congratulations Orlana. I wish you a long and happy life with your big strong solen fae since you'll be too busy talking to everyone else tonight."

* * *

Unsurprisingly, there was a marriage hall in Inoras because why not? Unlike the caves that the ardens lived in, there was no lack of space in the elven kingdoms. And today, I was very glad that I was in Inoras instead of the Emerald Caverns.

It was beautiful in that very elven way. Vines curled around everything, a stark contrast between the vibrant green and white stone that everything was built with. As I looked down from the balcony overlooking the hall, I couldn't help but notice the arden touches that my father must have insisted on.

The vines sparkled with tiny seed emeralds. Why he'd brought seed emeralds from the Emerald Caverns was beyond me, but I was thankful for them. They turned the otherwise elven wedding ceremony into something uniquely all-encompassing. I didn't feel at home, but I also didn't feel like a stranger.

The only thing that would have made it better would have been a roaring fire beyond the platform where we'd bind ourselves together. That, and a little less sunlight.

Then I saw Darius, and I could barely believe it. His long, sandy blonde hair was bound in a tight braid that ran to the middle of his back between his wings. He wasn't wearing something ridiculous as I'd imagined. Instead, he wore a beautiful crimson tunic made of silk that covered his entire torso, including his arms.

He flashed me a smile, and I began to walk down the stairs. I could feel the audience watching me silently, and I tried to walk slowly, like a bride was supposed to. It was a struggle because all I really wanted to do was to run towards Darius.

I heard murmurs as I walked, and that brought an even wider smile to my face. I looked at Darius again when I'd made it down the stairs, and I could already see that there was no mask on his face. The smile that he wore was just as real as the one I wore.

We'd been through so much that I doubted that anyone would have known as quickly as I did. I'd wondered what it would be like to walk through the crowd with everyone looking at me. I'd never been the center of attention in front of so many people, but at that point, I didn't even notice them.

It was like the rest of the world faded away, and as I walked, my steps sped up. By the time that I'd gotten to the stairs up to the pedestal, I took them two at a time.

The priest gave me a disapproving look, and I ignored him as Darius grinned at me. I'd ignored enough of my father's disapproving looks that no priest would make me feel self-conscious.

"When men and women are born, they are but half of what they could be," the priest began. "Their other half is waiting for them to find each other so that they can finally be whole."

"A marriage is more than promising to love one another for the rest of two people's lives. It is a binding, a unification of two halves into a whole. Whether prince or pauper, this binding is forever."

I could see that sparkle in Darius's eyes as he looked at me. There was no confusion and no doubt whether we were right for each other. Not anymore. This was what he'd wanted forever, and what I'd never known I'd been missing.

"These two, Princess Orlana of the Emerald Caverns and Prince Darius of Kharn, have decided that they have found their soulmate, their other halves. Today, we witness as they bind their souls together."

Both of us held out our arms, and the priest pulled a small knife at his side. Darius and I pulled our sleeves up, and the priest held my wrist.

I didn't look at the blade as the sharp edge bit into my wrist. My eyes were on Darius the entire time. The pain was nothing because I'd have gone through any amount of pain to bind myself to Darius like this.

A thin stream of blood ran from my wrist, and the priest said, "Press your wrists together and become one. Let your blood bring your souls together, never to be parted."

I looked down at the matching wounds on our wrists, and I placed the cut across mine on top of the cut across Darius's. A green silk ribbon was wound around our wrists and tied, keeping our blood flowing into each other's bodies.

I took a deep breath, and before the priest could say another word, Darius bent down and pressed his lips against mine. There were no walls, no questions, and no masks between us. Today, and forever more, we were one.

We would never be alone again.

He pulled away from me, and a whisper on the wind said, "Thank you for being too stubborn to die."

My lip curled in a smile. "Thank you for wearing a tunic," I whispered as I pressed my hand against his chest. And felt bare flesh.

An illusion.

Both of us laughed as the crowd clapped, none of them understanding our laughter.

We turned and continued to laugh as we walked through the crowd. There was no reason not to. For the first time since we'd met, there was nothing left to worry about. There were no trials and tribulations or oaths to be fulfilled. No hate and no cage.

We were free.

We'd found the thing that we would continue living for now that our purpose was complete. We would live for each other. To show the other a better sunrise than the last. To find new things to make them laugh.

Because in the end, nothing matters, yet everything does. And we were going to experience the everything. Together.

About the Author

Olivia Hart is a fantasy romance author who is in love with all things out of this world. She writes about the darker side of fantasy romance with sassy heroines and flawed heroes.

You can connect with me on:

🌐 https://www.amazon.com/Olivia-Hart/e/B08WWLLTFH

🐦 https://twitter.com/AuthorOHart

📘 https://www.facebook.com/AuthorOHart

Made in United States
North Haven, CT
14 August 2023

40278171R00186